06/03

	DATE DUE		

THE FELINE
FRIENDSHIP

THE FELINE FRIENDSHIP

Michael Allen Dymmoch

Thomas Dunne Books
St. Martin's Minotaur ≈ New York

THOMAS DUNNE BOOKS.
An imprint of St. Martin's Press.

www.minotaurbooks.com

Excerpt from "Days" on page 142 from *Collected Poems* by Philip Larkin. Copyright © 1988, 1989 by the Estate of Philip Larkin. Reprinted by permission of Farrar, Straus and Giroux, LLC (USA) and Faber and Faber Ltd. (elsewhere).

Excerpt from "The Nine Sentiments" on page 181 from *Handwriting* by Michael Ondaatje. Copyright © 1998 by Michael Ondaatje. Used by permission of Alfred A. Knopf, a division of Random House, Inc. (USA). Reprinted by permission of Ellen Levine Literary Agency, Inc. (Canada).

Library of Congress Cataloging-in-Publication Data

Dymmoch, Michael Allen.
   The feline friendship / Michael Allen Dymmoch.—1st ed.
      p.   cm.
   ISBN 0-312-31016-1
   1. Thinnes, John (Fictitious character)—Fiction.   2. Caleb, Jack (Fictitious character)—Fiction.   3. Police—Illinois—Chicago—Fiction. 4. Police psychiatrists—Fiction.   5. Chicago (Ill.)—Fiction.   I. Title.

PS3554.Y6F45 2003
813'.54—dc21

2002037198

First Edition: May 2003

10   9   8   7   6   5   4   3   2   1

For
HUGH HOLTON
and
THE MEN AND WOMEN
of
THE CHICAGO POLICE DEPARTMENT

ACKNOWLEDGMENTS

The author wishes to thank the following for answers to various technical questions: Commander Hugh Holton (deceased) and Detective Jack Stewart (retired) of the Chicago Police Department; Allen Matthews, LCPC, Stephanie Patterson, LCSW, and Carol Fitzsimmons, MSW, ACSW; Craig Luttig, CPA; and James G. Schaefer. I have taken liberties with the information given me. Any errors are my own.

Thanks also to my editor, Ruth Cavin, and cover artist, Alexander Barsky, at St. Martin's Press; my agent, Jane Jordan Browne; the reference librarians at the Northbrook Public Library, Northbrook, Illinois; Judy Duhl of Scotland Yard Books, Winnetka, Illinois; Janis Irvine and her staff at the Book Bin, Northbrook, Illinois; Barbara and Teresita at the U.S. Post Office, Northbrook, Illinois; and the Red Herrings of Scotland Yard Books. All of you helped me to bring Thinnes and Caleb to life.

THE FELINE
FRIENDSHIP

ONE

I was on my way home. It was about one A.M., but I lived in a good neighborhood—I thought, a safe neighborhood . . ."

The woman sat erect, her hands in her lap, squeezing her keys until her fingers whitened. She was sallow without makeup, and her hair was pulled tightly back. Her suit was expensive but stark. With her height and her thin figure, she looked as severe and homely as the proverbial old-maid librarian. It was odd, because with a minimum of makeup and a flattering hairstyle, she would've been quite attractive.

The interview had thus far yielded Caleb no clue as to why she needed a psychiatrist. Her childhood had been uneventful, her adolescence relatively serene. Her present circumstances seemed enviable.

"There was only one other person on the street—a man. He was coming toward me, walking on the street side of the sidewalk with his hands in his pockets. He was wearing a trench coat and a hat. And he had his head down as he approached me. He didn't seem to notice me as we passed. And he was so ordinary, I didn't really pay attention.

"Then I was going past the alley behind my apartment. The man had gone out of mind, you know, the way things do as soon as they go out of view, things you scarcely noticed in the first place?"

Caleb nodded.

"Suddenly he was right behind. He grabbed me." Her voice was without affect; she might have been repeating the time. "He put a hand over my mouth and told me not to scream." She glanced up at Caleb. He kept his expression neutral. "I hadn't thought to scream before he said that. But then I tried.

"He dragged me in the alley and raped me."

She looked at the keys in her hands. The key holder was a black plastic cylinder, about the size of a cigar, with five parallel indentations incised around its shaft. It was some sort of martial arts device—Caleb couldn't remember the name.

"He was so strong . . . I tried to fight him. He kept saying, 'Don't scream!' I was trying to plead with him to stop, not to hurt me. But he was like a machine. Like the mechanism in the back of a garbage truck that just keeps coming down on whatever's been thrown in. He just kept on—as if he couldn't hear me, or didn't have any more feelings for me than the truck has for the garbage."

An interesting analogy, Caleb thought.

"I couldn't believe it was happening, like a nightmare where you're in danger and helpless and can't wake up."

The moment of realization, Caleb thought, in the stretched-out time scale of panic, where you're moving in slow mo, and your attacker is like the fast guy in the comics.

Keeping her gaze on her lap, the woman shrugged. "I lost my innocence. Do you know what that means?" She glanced at him, then down again. "Not just my virginity. I lost the certainty that the universe is a good place. I lost God—He never helped me when that—I can't think of a word strong enough to describe that *monster*—when he was raping me. I prayed. *God! Help me!* Only He never did.

"He took my dignity but he didn't take everything. He left me with rage. If my anger was electricity, I could electrocute the bastard. If it were actual heat, I could incinerate—no—vaporize him! It's so hideously ugly it makes me hate myself. It terrifies me—what if I lose control and go postal?

"And there's no cure—it's like herpes. It's forever. I can go for days without thinking about it, but then I read in the paper or hear on the news that some woman's been raped, and it all comes back."

Caleb stifled a shudder. He'd never been raped, but he'd been a victim of his own out-of-control rage. He understood her anger with the clarity of a fellow sufferer. He forced himself to say calmly, neutrally, "How long ago did it happen?"

"Fifteen years."

"What made you decide to see someone now?"

"I've been thinking about it for a long time."

"But what was the emergency today?"

"Did you hear the news this morning?"

"No."

"A woman was raped. She's the second in two weeks."

"What did you hope to get from therapy?"

"I don't know. Relief? If I could get a—what would you call it?—a synapsectomy? You know, have the part of my brain that makes the connections cut out, I would. In a minute! I want to get it in control. I'd like to have it fade away like the memories of what happened to me in kindergarten."

"What happened to you in kindergarten?"

"I don't remember." She laughed for the first time. "That's the point. Probably nothing." She glanced up again. "I mean, couldn't you put my head in a CAT scan and find out where that memory is stored and just zap it with a laser or something?" She looked back down at her hands.

"I'm afraid it's not that simple."

"Of course."

"I could see you at this time every week."

"Fine."

He took a prescription blank from the center drawer of his desk. "Do you have insurance?"

"Yes, but I'd rather pay you myself. My insurance doesn't cover enough of your fee to make it worth the loss of privacy."

He nodded. "But I want you to have a complete physical."

"With all due respect, Doctor. There's nothing wrong with me physically."

3

"That's very likely true, but I'd like to be positive. And therapy can be quite stressful. Think of it as a physical prior to initiating a rigorous exercise program." He started writing out the tests he wanted done.

"I find physicals very stressful."

He looked up. Her body language was completely congruent with her words.

"But you've managed to undergo them."

She squeezed her mouth into a tight line and nodded.

"It's a condition of my accepting you as a patient. If you need something to alleviate your anxiety . . ."

She shook her head.

Caleb put the prescription on the center of his desk.

Her face twitched as she stared at it. Finally, she took it. She said, "Next week, then. I'll have my doctor call with the results."

She stood up.

Caleb stood and offered his hand. She hesitated before she shook it and seemed to let go as quickly as she could. She turned toward the door but paused with her hand on the knob.

"They never caught the bastard."

TWO

Things had been going pretty well for Thinnes the last few months. Homicides were down citywide, and most of the numbers that were piling up were on the South and West Sides. All the cases he'd caught recently were no-brainers—done by idiots who left witnesses or fingerprints or bloody trails with road signs. And the Bulls had just nailed Seattle on their home turf. Thinnes was feeling okay.

When he got to the Nineteenth District entrance, there was a female nicotine addict pacing in front of the doors while she had her fix. She was only about five-two, but built. Her hair was short—a shade darker than her chocolate brown suit—and it framed a face shaped to just fit a man's two hands. Her dramatically dark brows overhung eyes like those waifs' in the starving artists' paintings. She had a straight, prominent nose, and a mouth that might have been inviting if it hadn't been fixed in a scowl.

He didn't recall ever having seen her before. Her suit was too expensive for a public defender's, her skirt too short for a state's attorney's. Probably Ms. CEO waiting to report a stolen Lexus.

If she was built to get a man's attention, her body language was a HAZMAT sign. She had her arms crossed. She was gripping the biceps of her right arm as she sucked in smoke from the cigarette. She seemed to be distilling enough nicotine to last a long time.

She noticed him staring and glared.

Keeping his expression neutral, he nodded before pushing into the lobby.

When he got upstairs, he noticed Evanger's door was closed, and that old variation of Murphy's law came to mind: *When everything seems to be going well, look out!*

Viernes, who was typing a report, paused to give Thinnes an index finger salute. Viernes looked like an FBI agent this morning, Bureau-issue suit and shirt, conservative tie. Thinnes wondered if he had court later.

Thinnes pointed at Evanger's office, and said, "Who's in the hot seat?" The closed door generally meant someone was getting his ass chewed.

Viernes shook his head. "All of us." Thinnes waited. "Evanger got sent to some seminar," Viernes explained, "and they're lettin' Rossi run things meanwhile."

Thinnes groaned. "I think I'll go home and call in sick."

The office door opened. Viernes said, "Too late. He's seen you."

Rossi came out with two pieces of paper. He looked around the room and walked up to stand over Viernes. He handed him one of the papers. Thinnes could see it had an address on it, on Western.

"Little turf dispute among the bangers," Rossi told Viernes. "See the beat coppers."

Viernes took the paper and took off. No doubt before Rossi could elaborate. Rossi turned to Thinnes.

"Who you workin' with?"

"Carl Oster."

"Oster? He's been on the medical a year!"

"So?"

"I got a new dick startin' here today. You're just the guy to show him the ropes."

Thinnes started to protest, decided it would just make Rossi's day, and shrugged instead. "What's his name?"

"Don Franchi. Coming over from Area One." Fifty-first and Wentworth.

6

Thinnes wondered what Franchi had done to get transferred to Area Three, but he knew better than to ask. If he couldn't get the new guy to talk, he had sources . . .

Rossi handed Thinnes the second piece of paper. "A woman just got raped. Round up your new partner and get over there."

Thinnes specialized in homicide. He hated working rapes. Rape was more like a drive-by shooting than anything else because it was often a matter of the victim being in the wrong place at the wrong time. But drive-bys usually happened in the killer's neighborhood and were perpetrated against known enemies or at least innocent neighbors. The bangers didn't often try very hard to hide their identities and even helped the cops out sometimes by bragging about their involvement. Clearing the case was a matter of digging until you found someone willing to talk. When you nailed the mope, the family was happy.

With rape it was different. Rape hurt the victim when it went down, and again when the cops investigated—no matter how careful they were. The offender usually preyed on strangers and went to great lengths to conceal his identity. When he was caught, it hurt his victims even more. Thinnes hated the whole thing.

"I haven't worked Sex in five years," he told Rossi. "I wouldn't know where to start with one. How 'bout I trade with Viernes?"

"Last time I looked, Thinnes, sexual assault was still considered a violent crime. You want to stay in this division, get going."

THREE

There weren't any new faces in the squad room by the time Thinnes had inspected the plumbing and checked out a car and radio. He was debating whether to ask Rossi where Franchi was when the lieutenant stuck his head out of the office, and said, "What're you doing still here?"

"Nothing." Nothing Rossi would accept, anyway. When he said, "jump," all he wanted to hear was "How high?," or "In which direction?"

Rossi disappeared, and Thinnes went to find the sergeant. "When this new guy, Franchi, shows up, send him out to the scene, will you?"

Dense fog had condensed around the city sometime last month and hung on. Today Thinnes had yet to see above the first floor of the buildings. The crime scene was in Lincoln Park, an upscale area of two- and three-flats—post–Chicago Fire solid brick construction—as well as large single-family homes. Not the sort of neighborhood where you expect a nasty rape. Apparently the victim hadn't.

The beat cars blocking the street were the only sign of something going down. The car the evidence tech had come in was parked near the mouth of the alley where—according to Thinnes's information—the woman had been beaten, raped, and dumped. She'd been removed to Illinois Masonic's trauma department, but yellow police-line tape still stretched across the alley and the sidewalk on either side of the alley mouth to keep the curious at bay.

Thinnes ducked under the tape and walked over to a beat copper who was watching the evidence tech do his thing. Thinnes nodded at the copper, and asked, "What's the story?"

The cop was young and confident, built like a linebacker. He had latex gloves sticking out from under his leather gloves. He shrugged and pointed to one of the beat cars; there was a passenger in the backseat. "Citizen—he lives behind that garage—" He pointed to one on the left with a half-open door. "Found the victim when he almost backed over her, on his way to work. He dialed nine-one-one and held her hand until we got here. He's pretty close to being in shock, himself. You'd better—" Something behind Thinnes derailed his train of thought, and he pointed back toward the mouth of the alley. "Uh-oh."

The woman Thinnes had seen at Western and Belmont, the one with the brown suit and sour expression, had arrived and ducked under the perimeter tape. She was studying the alley as if committing it to memory.

She must be press, Thinnes decided, since there wasn't a minicam van in sight. He wondered why she was so dressed up.

"Stay back behind the tape, Ms.," he told her.

He loved *Ms.* You could use it to mean *miss* or *ma'am*, depending on how you said it, and if your tone was just right, no one could make a beef about it stick. "This is a police scene."

Her pissed-off expression got more so. She reached into the briefcase-sized purse hanging from a shoulder strap and pulled out a detective's star. "I *am* the police. You must be Thinnes."

"Yeah."

"Thanks for waiting for me!"

He stifled the urge to say, *You're welcome.* Instead, he said, "You my new CO?"

"I'm Don Franchi." Her tone matched her make-my-day body English. "I was told to work with you."

After twenty-one years on the force, Thinnes wasn't easily surprised, but he hadn't a clue what to say to that. Instead he ignored her, and asked the beat cop, "Where's your partner?"

"She went to the hospital with the victim."

"In the ambulance?"

"Yeah."

Thinnes turned to Franchi. "How'd you get here?"

"I had to hitch a ride with a tac cop." One of the District's tactical officers.

Which explained her ongoing grudge. Well, piss on her! He wasn't a taxi service either. He turned back to the beat cop. "Why don't you drive Detective Franchi to the hospital and pick up your partner. Then check with your dispatcher about whether to come back here or go back to work."

"Sure thing."

Thinnes turned to Franchi. "Got that?"

"Got *what*?"

"You go to the hospital with him"—Thinnes hitched a thumb at the copper—"and get whatever you can from his partner. Then hang with the victim 'til she can give you a statement or 'til someone relieves you."

She formed an O with her lips, as if she was about to ask *who put you in charge?*, but no sound came out.

"Anybody asks you anything," Thinnes added, "Just say, *No comment*."

"*Got* it!"

As Franchi and the beat cop took off, Thinnes called the Area to ask for someone to help canvass the neighborhood. He was told Ryan and Swann would be along.

He saw a patrol sergeant—a white female, five-four, probably 140 pounds, short black hair salted with white—talking to the evidence tech over the perimeter tape. Thinnes joined them.

"What've you got?" the sergeant was asking.

"Not a whole lot," the tech said. "Looks like a blitz attack. Sommabitch either didn't take long enough to leave much or he's done this before and knew not to leave anything. You'll have to check the victim, but there's no evidence here of semen, so I'd guess he couldn't get it off or he used a condom. He did rape

10

her with a bottle he maybe got out of that trash can." He pointed to one of a dozen rat-proof polyethylene carts flanking the alley. It was the only one open. "Then it looks like he took off back this way. I got one fair footwear impression—looks like a Nike. It's pretty common, cause it's popular with the homeys, but if you find the shoe, we should be able to match it. That's about it. There's a lot of blood, but I'd bet it's all the victim's. After he did her, he broke the bottle and cut her with it. And with this fog, you probably aren't gonna find any witnesses."

"What else do we need, Detective?" the sergeant asked Thinnes.

Thinnes pointed back at the street. "Someone should record the descriptions and tag numbers of all the cars parked within a two-block radius."

She nodded.

"Get information on anyone out and about, especially what they're doing in the neighborhood."

Dead-ended against the back of a commercial building to the south, the alley was flanked by well-maintained garages and backyard fences. There was no graffiti or any of the litter or tossed-out furniture or abandoned cars that made alleys impassable in other areas. *This* alley was paved with bricks, which were missing only in a few spots marking sewer work. The pavement was clammy with condensation from the cold mist that hung in the utility wires and upper branches of the backyard trees. The fog carried odors of decay and lilacs, and a wood fire someone had going. It amplified sounds and distorted the locations of their sources.

The evidence technician was almost done. Numbered cards had been placed around the scene next to items of evidence, and the tech was recording their positions with a Nikon. Pictures of the undisturbed scene would already be on a numbered roll in the evidence tote.

The cool air was so thick with moisture that Thinnes imagined he could hear the camera's strobe flashes striking the condensation. He didn't imagine the odor of blood. As he got closer to ground zero, the smell got stronger. In front of a garage door marked with gory handprints, blood had pooled around a manhole cover, filling the hollows between its raised lettering and the cracks between the surrounding bricks.

Thinnes was very careful where he put his feet.

FOUR

One of the ironies of law enforcement is that the "witness" who reports a crime is often the one who did it. A glance at the man in the back of the squad car told Thinnes that probably wasn't so in this case. Hispanic, black hair and brown eyes, medium complexion, medium build, probably medium height, though it was hard to tell with him sitting down. He was wearing a business suit.

Thinnes watched for a minute. The man was staring straight ahead and from time to time, he'd shudder slightly, as if recalling something really bad. He looked like he was holding himself together by a thread as fine as spider's web. Being shut into the car for what must've seemed like forever couldn't have helped much either.

Thinnes opened the car door and startled him out of his trance. "Sorry," he said. "Mr. Santos?"

Santos nodded.

"I'm Detective Thinnes. I'd like you to tell me what happened, but maybe it'd be better if we went inside?"

Santos looked past Thinnes and sighed. "Right now I feel like nothing will ever be better." He had a Chicago accent. Must be second generation. Maybe third.

Santos looked down at his suit, spotted with the victim's blood. "Is it all right if I change first? I suppose I'll have to tell this to my wife."

Thinnes ignored the illogical change of subject. "I'd like you to tell *me* what happened before you tell your wife. But if you'd be more comfortable changing first, that's fine."

Santos nodded, and Thinnes backed away from the car.

Santos ended up changing in his kitchen, where his family kept the laundry equipment. He invited Thinnes to have a seat at the table facing the apartment's rear windows while he checked the dryer—around the bend in the L-shaped room—for something to put on. Thinnes heard the dryer door open, then Santos said, "I'm in luck." Then the dryer door slammed.

While he waited, Thinnes looked around. The Santoses lived on the first floor of the kind of three-flat common in the city. Instead of the usual narrow kitchen with a tiny adjoining back room, there was a single room the width of the building with a view of the small backyard. Beyond that was a two-car garage butting up against the alley. Thinnes couldn't help but notice how little was visible—between Santos's garage and the neighbors', their backyard fence and the wood fences surrounding neighboring yards.

Santos reappeared, dressed in gray sweatshirt and sweatpants, with crew socks on his feet. He'd pulled himself together, and he had the bloody suit wadded in a tight bundle that he started to cram into a garbage can near the back door.

"Mind if I take that, Mr. Santos?"

Santos looked startled. "Why?"

"There may be some trace evidence you picked up that could help us catch the offender."

Santos shoved the bundle at him. "Take it, by all means. But let me get you something to wrap it in." He dug a plastic bag out of a box under the sink and held it while Thinnes put the suit in. It wasn't an ideal evidence container, but it would do temporarily.

"I don't want it back," Santos said.

"No problem." Thinnes knotted the top of the bag, then put it on the floor near the door.

Santos pulled a chair out from the table and offered Thinnes a seat across from it. When they were settled he said, "There's not much to tell. I opened my garage door, and it was foggy enough that I couldn't see the garage across the alley from mine. I started my car, and when I looked at the rearview before backing out, I could just make out something in the alley. It looked like a pile of trash or old clothes. I got out to move it—I know better than to back over things—but when I got up to it— My, God!"

Thinnes waited, let silence draw out the rest of the story.

"When I realized it was a person— I thought she'd been run over. I ran to my car and called the cops on my cell phone. Then I went back for another look. She started whimpering and trying to get up. I was afraid to touch her—with all the blood. But when she started thrashing around, I had to do something. I took her hand and told her to hang on, that an ambulance was coming. It seemed to help. She seemed a lot calmer. I just held her hand until the police arrived. Like I told the officer."

"Do you know her?"

"I don't know. The shape she was in— I'm not sure I'd recognize my own sister."

"Have you noticed any strangers around lately?"

Santos shrugged. "Not while— I'm gone pretty much all day. Not that I know of."

Thinnes nodded. "Anything unusual happen lately?"

"What do you mean 'unusual'?"

"Out of the ordinary?"

"I don't know. You'd have to ask my wife."

Mrs. Santos was a young, old-fashioned woman, a homemaker, also Hispanic. He judged her to be her husband's age—give or take a year. She was predictably disturbed about the rape, the more so because she must've been walking out the front door to take her children to school as the rapist was attacking the woman out back in the alley. With the fog, she hadn't seen anything at all.

To the best of her knowledge, there hadn't been any suspicious strangers in the area lately—no door-to-door salesmen, no Seventh Day Adventists, not even a telephone-book deliveryman. And yes, she would phone the police immediately if she heard that one of her neighbors was missing.

Thinnes thanked her for her help and promised to have her husband back in time to walk the children home from school.

FIVE

By the time he'd sent Santos off with a patrol officer, Thinnes felt like the fog had seeped into his head. Though it had receded to a flat gray ceiling above the building tops, the air below it seemed thick enough to hold you back when you walked.

Reinforcements arrived in a ratty unmarked Caprice—Kate Ryan and Len Swann. Thank heaven for small favors.

"Not to minimize your support," Thinnes told them, "but where's the rest of the team?"

"You're looking at it," Ryan said. She was a natural redhead, with green eyes and pale blond lashes. The sharp pantsuit she was wearing made Thinnes think of Franchi and wonder why she'd arrived at the Area without fanfare and *with* an attitude. Nothing seemed to put Ryan out of sorts.

"Where're we at?" Swann asked. He was black, Thinnes's age but heavier, and with his grizzled hair and easy smile, he could have doubled for the late Mayor Washington.

Thinnes started filling them in but was interrupted by the clatter and whine of a Streets & San truck in the alley a block north. "Dammit!" he said. "Patrol was supposed to keep everybody out until we've gone through all those cans."

"You don't really think this guy would leave anything around that we could use?"

"No, but if we ever get him, I don't want some smart mouthpiece getting him off because we didn't cover all the bases."

Swann got back in his car, and said, "I'll head off the truck; you deal with patrol."

"Yeah, okay."

"What do you want me to do, Thinnes?" Ryan asked.

"Start canvassing the houses west of the alley. I'll talk to patrol, then start on the houses to the east. Swann can start here, on the street. You know the drill."

"Sure," Ryan said. "We just ask if anyone spotted Jack the Ripper slinking off in the fog."

"How do I know you're really a cop?" The speaker was a tiny, white-haired woman who peered around a door secured with a chain *and* a slide. And on the edge of the door he could see the retracted tongue of a healthy dead bolt. Guess you could never have too much security.

Thinnes held his star up in front of her face. She snatched it from his hand and retreated into the room to study it. Her upper body was bent at right angles from age, and any hope he'd had that she might have seen anything was killed when she held the badge almost to her nose to look it over. Then she closed the door and he could hear her fumbling with the chain and the slide before she opened it.

"Do come in." She was even more frail-looking up close. As he entered, she handed back his star, and said, "I misplaced my reading glasses." She closed the door behind him and turned the dead bolt, and he noticed she wore a wedding ring.

The old woman indicated the sofa, and said, "Sit down, Detective."

The room had a real fireplace, tall windows, and oak baseboards and crown molding as well as window and door frames. The walls were a gallery of framed photographs, from antique tintypes to eight-by-ten color portraits. A lot of the color shots were pictures of the same couple against different foreign backdrops. The interior space was filled with old-fashioned furniture that was well matched, new, and expensive. Every flat surface was covered with knickknacks that looked like souvenirs from foreign places.

As he sat down, the woman added, "I always wanted to say that."

Thinnes could feel his surprise showing. She either picked up on it or was just so wound up she didn't need prompting. "I watch *Homicide* every week, and *Law & Order*. I used to watch *NYPD Blue*, but it's gotten to be such a soap opera."

"Yes, ma'am," he said. He felt like Joe Friday—*Just the facts, ma'am.* Please! "Did you happen to notice anything unusual this morning, Mrs. . . . ?"

"Henderson. Lily Henderson. I can't say that I did. Except the fog. Though it's been foggy so long it's hardly unusual. But what do you mean? Has something happened?"

"I was hoping you could tell me."

She nodded and her whole upper body swayed. "I see. You don't want to lead the witness. I suppose you mean like a shot or a scream." Thinnes waited. "Well, the garbage hasn't been picked up yet. They usually come during the last half of *Oprah* and make it impossible to concentrate. But not this morning."

"Anything else?"

"Nothing unusual. But would it help to tell you what wasn't out of the ordinary?"

"It might."

"Mrs. Santos—next door—took her children to school at their regular time—seven-forty-five, and Mr. Lennox—he's on the other side—left for work late. As usual. I always can tell when he comes and goes, even in a pea-souper, because he slams his door. That was at eight-thirty this morning.

"I once fancied myself Miss Marple, you know—I'm quite observant. But I'm too imaginative. I always favor the more fanciful explanation, Occam's razor notwithstanding."

He wrote down 'OCKAM'S RAZOR' and nodded. He'd look it up later. For the next twenty minutes, Mrs. Henderson filled him in on the neighborhood news.

On the west side of the street, there was no answer at the four houses south of Mrs. Henderson's. At the south end of the block, a corner commercial building housed a real-estate agency. Next to that, and across the street, were a hairdresser's, a cleaner's, a travel agency, and a storefront promising "Psychic readings by appointment." All but the cleaner's would have been closed when the woman was attacked. He'd send Ryan and Swann around to interview their employees later. Meanwhile he worked his way back north on the street's east side.

A work-at-home secretary lived in the house across the alley from the commercial buildings. She'd been delivering her kids to school around the time of the attack. Her husband was out of town on business.

Thinnes had to pound on the ground-floor door of the next building, a three-flat. It was three or four minutes before anyone opened it. Thinnes flashed his star at the man, a white male in his late twenties or early thirties, wearing a T-shirt and jeans. Five-eleven, brown hair and eyes, 180 pounds or so.

The man said, "Yeah?" He didn't offer to let Thinnes in.

"Mind telling me your name?"

"Yeah, as a matter of fact." Thinnes waited. Finally, he said, "You gonna arrest me?"

"For obstructing a police investigation if you don't cooperate."

"What investigation?"

"First things first. What's your name?"

"Erik Last."

"See some ID?"

Last shrugged and backed into his apartment, leaving the door open. Thinnes followed. The room was off-white and sparsely furnished with chrome-and-black-leather furniture. There was a cell phone, a photography magazine, and the remains of a Domino's pizza in its box on the glass-topped coffee table. The walls were hung with black-and-white photos, some framed, most stuck in place with pushpins. Thinnes wasn't an expert, but they looked like the work of pros. Mrs. Henderson hadn't mentioned that she and her neighbor had so much in common; he wondered if she knew.

Last dug a photo-Visa card from the pocket of a jacket on the back of a chair and handed it to Thinnes. The likeness was better than most driver's license pictures.

Thinnes noted the account number before handing it back. "You got a driver's license, Mr. Last?"

"No."

It was going to be a long day if every interview was like this. "State ID?" Last shook his head.

"What's your date of birth?"

"August 23, 1968." Thinnes's guess about his age was good.

"What's your social security number?"

"You're not the IRS. I don't have to tell you."

That was true, but it didn't mean Thinnes wouldn't find out. He shrugged. "You live alone, Mr. Last?"

"No."

"You live with your mother?"

Last scowled. "I live with my girlfriend."

"She home?"

"No. She's downtown on a shoot. She's a model."

Thinnes thought he heard pride diluting the attitude just a little. "She have a name?"

"You kidding?" Last walked over and grabbed a magazine off the coffee table and flipped it open to the picture of a young woman. Her large, dark eyes and pouty expression reminded Thinnes of Franchi. Last jiggled the picture up and down in front of Thinnes's face. "Everyone in the Midwest with a camera wants her!"

"What's her *name*, Mr. Last?"

Last's face reddened, and he said, "Oh. Iris." He pronounced it 'eer-iss.' "I-R-I-S."

Thinnes knew enough Spanish to recognize the word for rainbow. "That her surname or her given name?"

"That's her whole name. You know, like Cher."

Thinnes nodded. "What time do you expect her home?"

"Not 'til tonight, after ten. What's this all about?"

"A woman was attacked this morning."

For a fraction of a second, the man looked startled, as if that was the last thing he'd expected to hear. Then his expression returned to surly. "I didn't attack her." Thinnes waited to see if he'd add to that. Finally, he said, "You got any other questions?"

"Yeah. Lots . . ."

SIX

Franchi was pacing like a caged coyote when Thinnes got to the hospital. If her expression was an indicator, the wait hadn't improved her earlier mood. "Well?" she said.

"*Nada*," Thinnes told her. "The only witness we have is the guy who found her."

"Do we know who she is yet?"

"No. The scumbag must've taken her purse, and the witness didn't recognize her."

"The shape she's in, her mother wouldn't recognize her."

"They still working on her?"

"She just came out of surgery. They wouldn't let me in the recovery room."

"What did the doctor say?"

"The guy who treated her's been in the ER since they sent her up to surgery. This's been a waste of my time. We could've had a beat cop sitting here."

In short, the burned-out resident told them, after raping the woman in every conceivable orifice, the bastard had made a determined effort to beat her to death, then sliced and diced her with a broken bottle. She hadn't lain in the alley long, the doctor added, or she'd have bled out before her neighbor found her. "If she's lucky, she won't remember it."

"You do a rape kit?"

"Yes. Your evidence technician took it."

As well as rolls of pictures.

"When can we talk to her?"

The doctor shrugged. "As I told Detective Franchi, she'll be out for hours. She has a concussion and a broken jaw, her eyes are swollen shut, and her hands are smashed, so when she regains consciousness, I don't know how you're going to communicate with her. Even if she remembers what happened."

When she regains consciousness, Thinnes thought. Not *if.* "Well, we're gonna try, Doctor. We have to get this asshole."

SEVEN

It took a while to arrange and deploy a guard. When Thinnes went out to his car for the drive back to the Area, Franchi followed him. He'd forgotten how she got there. As they came up to the Caprice, she said, "I'll drive."

He unlocked the passenger door and held it open for her. "Get in."

She looked like she was going to argue, but must've changed her mind because she did as she was told. By the time he walked around to his side, she'd unlocked and opened his door and put her seat belt on.

With the doors and windows closed, he could smell cigarettes on her, worse than the stench when he and his wife had spent an evening at a bar. He started the car and rolled down his window.

"What now?" she asked. "We go back and canvass?"

"Nah. We're done with the preliminary. Maybe we'll go back this afternoon and get the people who weren't home."

Even without looking directly, he could see the muscles of her jaw lock. Well if she didn't like it, she could put in for another transfer.

"When we get back," he said, "you can start checking on who with a similar MO just got out of stir."

"What're you going to be doing?" The resentment in her voice was an implication that she thought whatever it was would be more interesting.

He missed Oster. His old partner had been willing to do most of the scut work—running arrest reports, checking with BCI and NCIC, dropping things off at the lab. In return, Thinnes had done the greater share of the paperwork and gone to most of the autopsies. Oster'd accepted the deal because—in spite of his age—he was the junior dick. And he'd been smart enough to see the work as a team effort, to trust Thinnes not to grab all the glory. The other detectives in Violent Crimes had almost as much time in as Thinnes and weren't any happier to be stuck with the routine stuff than he was. So up to now he'd been working solo.

In answer to her question, he said, "All the fun stuff."

Ryan and Ferris were the only Violent Crimes dicks in the squad room when Thinnes entered. Franchi was right behind him, but she stopped just inside the room, and said, "I'll be back." She let the door swing shut behind her.

"Who's the lady?" Ferris asked. The short Irish Southsider was auburn-haired and paunchy, also mean-spirited and lazy. Thinnes had always figured he had something major on someone connected, or he'd have been gone long ago.

"No lady," Thinnes told him. "My new partner—at least for today." He immediately wished he hadn't said it. One of the things he hated about Ferris was the way everyone, himself included, seemed to sink to Ferris's level.

"Three partners in four years, Thinnes?" Ferris said. "That's some record. Somebody ought to warn the poor bit—" He shot a look at Ryan. "Broad."

Thinnes winked at Ryan, and said, "Yeah. I should've paired up with you, Ferris, we'd be rid of you by now."

"No, Thinnes," Ryan said. "You might've gotten rid of Ferris, but you'd be gone, too. You'd have gone postal and shot him."

"She-it!" Ferris said.

Thinnes dropped his stuff on the table he usually used as a desk and got himself coffee. "What's happening?" he asked Ryan.

"The rape's been reported on News Radio, and it looks like it's gonna be a heater. And Rossi's been running around giving orders like the captain of a sinking ship."

Ferris said, "Fitting." Just then Franchi came back in the room, and Ferris whistled as she got closer.

Thinnes watched her jaw muscles tighten, and she frowned almost imperceptibly before asking Thinnes, "You have a mynah bird in here?"

Thinnes just shook his head.

Ryan laughed. "Ferris is more like a parakeet." She walked toward Franchi as she said it, and shoved a hand at her. "I'm Kate Ryan. That's Ferris. He's a sexist pig, but harmless. Just ignore him."

EIGHT

There was a message waiting on Caleb's answering machine—a colleague he hadn't heard from in six months. "Jack, you gotta help me out. I got a court referral that I have to take or place. But I'm just leaving on the first vacation I've had in years. Can I contract the job to you? He's a sex offender, but relatively nonviolent, not a child molester."

As he dialed to return the call, Caleb considered the irony of being asked to counsel both a rapist and a rape victim in the same week.

"I'm seeing someone right now," he told the colleague, "a victim. It would be awkward if this man turned out to be the one who raped her."

"How old is she? And how long ago did it happen?"

"She's in her late thirties, raped fifteen years ago."

"Not likely, then. This guy's just twenty-three. First offense—or first time he got caught."

The man sitting across the desk from Caleb, slouching on his coccyx with his ankle resting on his knee was wearing black, black loafers over black socks, a black leather jacket, and charcoal gray slacks. Between glances at Caleb, his gaze swept the room, and he kept up a steady rhythm of fingertips on the chair arms.

Terry Deacon also chewed his fingernails.

From time to time he ran his fingers through his short brown hair. Between his nervousness, his youthful face, and his neat attire, he could have been mistaken for a college kid. But Caleb had read his file.

He asked him the usual things: Describe your family. At what age did you have your first sexual encounter? Do you date a lot? Ever had sex with a man?

"Christ, no!"

"Ever had a man make a pass at you?"

"No, but if one ever did, he'd regret it."

"Ever have sex with an animal?"

"Well, some of the women I dated were dogs. That count?"

"No."

"Then no, of course not. What kind of questions are these?"

"Routine. So all women are cock-teasers?" Caleb asked after a pause.

"No, of course not."

Caleb waited.

"My ma, for instance—she's practically a saint. But—I mean— They pretty much fall into one category or another."

"Tell me about the woman you raped."

"Allegedly raped."

"Didn't you plead guilty?"

"I pled guilty to abuse. That doesn't mean I raped her."

Caleb's silence eventually got to him.

"Christ! I was facing felony charges as opposed to a misdemeanor. I couldn't take the chance some jury wouldn't believe me. Look what happened to Mike Tyson."

"Tell me about the woman you *abused*."

"I just *said* I did to get off the hook."

"Why did you beat her?"

"She pissed me off. I mean, it's not enough I lay out a fortune takin' her out to eat, she expects me to spend on booze, too, and get nothin' in return. Huh!"

"You took her out for dinner?"

"Yeah." Long silence. "And afterwards, I ask her to come to my place for a drink."

"Just a drink?"

"That's what *she* said. 'Yeah,' I says, just a drink.' " Caleb waited. "Well, Christ! You think there's a broad on the planet doesn't know what that means?"

"What does it mean?"

Deacon looked at him as if he thought Caleb was trying to be funny. "You some kind of fag? Everybody knows a broad doesn't go to a man's place alone unless she's lookin' to get laid."

"Continue, Mr. Deacon."

"Well, she comes up and we have a drink. Then she says, 'It's late. I'd better go.' An' I realize she's not gonna put out. But I gotta have something to show for my time and money, so I say 'how 'bout a good night kiss.' She doesn't say no, so I start to kiss her. And suddenly she's pushing me away. Like I'm so repulsive, she won't even kiss me. It made me mad. So I grab her and give her a kiss—you know, French her a bit. The bitch tries to give me a knee in the balls. That's when I lost it."

When it became apparent Deacon wasn't going to elaborate, Caleb said, "Please be more specific."

"I gave her a little crack on the head, just to let her know I don't appreciate that. Then I shoved her onto the couch and fucked her. Only I was tired of lookin' at the bitch's face, so I did her doggy style."

A masterpiece of omission, Caleb thought. He'd seen the police report. According to the victim, Deacon had twisted her arm behind her back and threatened to break it if she didn't shut up. He'd slammed her face against the coffee table hard enough to blacken both eyes and give her a concussion. And he'd sodomized her before effecting vaginal penetration.

"When we finished, I go to take a leak, and when I come out of the can, she's gone. Next thing I know, the cops are banging on my door, charging me with aggravated sexual assault. Do you think I'd be dumb enough to bring a broad to my own apartment if I was going to rape her? And *then* do her without using a rubber?"

Caleb did think so. Deacon had freely admitted to the detectives that he'd had intercourse with the victim and had "maybe been a little rough," though he'd sworn it was consensual.

"I spent two days in County waiting to bond out because of that stupid slut, and I talked to guys that broke into women's apartments and strangled 'em half to death before doin' 'em, then hosed 'em out after with bleach or poured drain cleaner into 'em. Or guys who grab some broad off the street and beat 'em to a pulp and stick a knife in their snatch. *Those* are rapists. Not me. You know it's probably a good thing there's some of them out there—to keep the broads from totally takin' over everything. But I'd never be one."

"How *would* you describe yourself, Mr. Deacon?"

"Me? I'm just a— inconsiderate lover."

NINE

What've you got so far?" Rossi demanded.

Thinnes was helping himself to coffee from the pot in the squad room. "Vicious attack," he said. "Looks like a disorganized offender. No word, yet, on anything we can use to get DNA, but he definitely raped her with a bottle."

"You know who she is?"

"Not yet. Too soon for her to be in missing persons. I got word out to Neighborhood Relations to have the beat cops circulate her description. And I was thinking we could give it to the media, too."

"Check with the chief on that first." The Area Three Detective Commander. "What are you gonna do next?"

"SOP. Check for a matching MO and find out if there's been anything similar anywhere in the city. I'll check NCIC, too."

Rossi nodded. "Get on with it."

Franchi came back from a smoke break as he started to walk away. She stood just inside the squad-room doorway looking pissed off, but otherwise like a professional model. "Who the hell is *that*?" Rossi demanded.

"Franchi."

"The new dick?"

"So she says."

"They didn't tell me she was a merit appointment."

Merit appointees—a weasel word if ever there was one—got their jobs through political connections and often made up to 20 percent of the detectives in some Areas. It was common knowledge they didn't know shit from Shinola, which meant extra work for those who did.

"Crap," Rossi added. "They didn't even tell me she was a broad."

Franchi spotted them and stalked over. Thinnes made introductions. He hid his amusement that, for once, Rossi was all but speechless, muttering "Welcome aboard," before he hurried off.

"What's his problem?" Franchi asked.

Rossi, Thinnes could've said, but she'd figure it out if she lasted long enough. He shrugged instead. "Must've gotten up on the wrong side of the bed." He handed her a paper with Erik Last's DOB and Visa card number. "This guy wouldn't give me his sosh." His social security number. "And he claims he doesn't have a driver's license. Also claims he's never been arrested. Check him out for me, will you?"

"Where . . . ?"

He'd forgotten that she'd just arrived. "Come on. You may as well have the tour."

After pointing out the features of the squad room with its adjoining offices and interview rooms, Thinnes showed her Juvenile Division, and the closet-sized offices of felony review on the second floor. They took the elevator downstairs—and circled the Nineteenth District: interview rooms, front desk, tactical office, the administrative offices, and Neighborhood Relations. Along the way he introduced Franchi as the new detective to everyone she really needed to know. He didn't bother showing her around the lower level because there wasn't anything down there to interest a detective but the weapons and radio rooms. The workout room, candy and Coke machines he figured she could find on her own. He left her in the District lobby, heading outside for a smoke, and went back upstairs to read the canvass reports.

❧

Two hours later, Thinnes had made up a list of names and addresses to recanvass: individuals whose neighbors thought them suspicious; and everywhere—including the two other apartments in Santos's building—where nobody had answered the door. He didn't give Franchi another thought until she dropped a pile of papers in front of him—report forms and computer printouts.

"Erik Last," she said, "has no driver's license because it was suspended when he refused a breathalyzer three years ago. Apparently, he never had it reinstated. At the same time, he was arrested for disorderly conduct—it didn't stick. Otherwise, he's clean. Also. The Visa card he showed you is a corporate card— He's incorporated. He also has Discover, MasterCard, and American Express—high limits, good credit. And he has his own Web page." She dropped another paper on the table. "Here's a printout. One of the guys in Major Crimes told me he's hot in the fashion photography business."

"Good," Thinnes said. "What about the other stuff?"

"Neither LEADS nor NCIC has anything recent matching our victim or offender's MO."

"What about the graduation list?"

"There are fifteen sex offenders in the vicinity who've done their time and are free or on parole." Franchi handed him another pile of printouts and stood over him while he paged through it. It made him uncomfortable, but he didn't let it show.

He divided the names geographically, by last known address, and gave half the names to Franchi. "Check with these guys POs. See if you can find out if they've moved, where to. If they're employed, where they work."

"You want me to follow through if any look good?"

"Take it one step at a time. If you can find out where they work, let's see what hours they keep and if they were working when the rape went down. No sense warning our suspects we're looking at them 'til we have to."

She nodded and took her share of the names back to the phone she'd been using. Thinnes gave the rest of the printouts and the same instructions to Swann and Ryan.

TEN

Thinnes made a point to confirm when Evanger would be back and almost groaned out loud at what the sergeant told him. A week looked like a stretch in Cook County Jail.

He got himself coffee and started rereading the results of the canvass. A yellow Post-it note written on a report Swann had filed said, *Thinnes, you might want to interview this guy yourself. I didn't talk to him, but the neighbors think he's pretty weird.*

There was a name, Dr. Ice, and an address two doors down from the alley where they found the victim. Thinnes got up and walked to the table where Swann sat with a phone cradled against his ear. Swann must've been on hold because he asked Thinnes, "What can I do you for?"

Thinnes held up the note. "Weird like maybe he did it, or just strange?"

"Upstairs neighbor said at least nine on the weirdness Richter."

"Okay."

"By the way, Rossi's looking for you."

"Know what for?"

Swann opened his mouth to answer, but whoever he was waiting for must have come back on the line because he closed his mouth and pointed to the phone, then shrugged.

Thinnes said, "Thanks."

Rossi's door was closed, which didn't mean much. Unlike Evanger, who only closed his door to ream someone out in private, Rossi kept his shut most of the time. So he could nap undisturbed, according to rumor.

Thinnes knocked.

Rossi said, "Come in."

Thinnes did. "Lieutenant?"

"Where's your new partner?"

"Out having a smoke."

Rossi pointed to a stack of file folders on the corner of his desk. The rest of its surface looked like the mixed-paper dump at a recycling center—another contrast to Evanger.

Thinnes said, "What is it?"

"All our open rapes. I'm reassigning them to you so you can check for similarities with your case."

Thinnes didn't give him the satisfaction of protesting. He picked up the files, and said, "Anything else?"

Rossi shook his head. "Have fun."

"Thinnes," the sergeant said, "they got someone down in the lobby Missing Persons thought you might want to talk to."

Thinnes went downstairs.

The woman standing at the Nineteenth District desk was blond and thin and looked as comfortable as a cat at a dog show. When the desk sergeant pointed Thinnes out to her, she hurried across the lobby to meet him. Simultaneously, Franchi came in from her smoke break and came over to see what was up.

"Detective?" the blond woman said.

"Thinnes."

"Detective Thinnes, that officer—" She pointed at the sergeant. "Said you could help me." Thinnes waited. "My roommate's missing."

"Let's go upstairs, shall we?" She didn't reply, so Thinnes waved toward the stairs, and said, "Follow Detective Franchi."

Franchi took the cue and led the way without a fuss. When they got into the squad room, Franchi said, "Where to?"

Thinnes pointed across the squad room. "Let's see if the conference room's free."

She nodded and went to look.

Thinnes said, "What's your name, miss?"

"Joy Abbot."

"Would you like something to drink? Coffee or pop?"

"No, thank you. I just want to find my roommate. She—"

Franchi interrupted her by signaling for them to come.

Thinnes pointed toward Franchi, and said, "Let's go in there and talk."

The woman followed Franchi in and sat down in the chair Franchi pulled out for her. Thinness stepped around and sat across from her. He pointed at Franchi, then pantomimed taking notes on his palm with an invisible pen. She frowned but sat at right angles to them and dug a notebook and pen from her purse.

"Okay, Ms. Abbot," Thinnes said, "tell us about your room-mate."

"Katherine. Katherine Lake.

"My sister just had a baby, and I took a week off to stay with her. Katherine was supposed to meet me at O'Hare, to pick me up—she has a car. She didn't have to. I told her I could just get a cab, but she said we could stop and grab a bite on the way home, and I could show her my pictures."

Abbot put her forearms together on the table, wrist to elbow, and leaned forward. Thinnes put his hands on the table and leaned toward her.

"Only she never showed up," Abbot said. "It's not like her. You can usually set your watch by her. And she'd never forget!

"But just to be sure, I called. I got the answering machine. Then I thought maybe the Kennedy was gridlocked or she got a flat or something, so I waited."

She sat back. Thinnes mirrored her action. He noticed that Franchi was watching both of them, taking notes without looking at her notebook. He wondered what she was seeing.

"I waited over an hour," Abbot said, "then I took a cab home. There was no sign of her. Her car was parked in front—where it was when I left, so I don't even know if it was moved while I was gone—we can walk to work. So sometimes Katherine doesn't use her car for days at a time.

"Anyway, there wasn't any sign of her in the apartment. And from the messages piled up on the machine—she didn't show up for work on Friday. They called about six times. It was obvious something happened to her. I called a bunch of our mutual friends to see if anyone knew anything—Nothing. Finally, I called the police. They said I should check everywhere she might be first, and if I didn't find her, to call nine-one-one for a beat officer to come take a report or to come in to the police station. I spent all night and most of this morning calling everyone in her address book—her parents even. Now I've got them worried. Needless to say, I couldn't find her."

Thinnes nodded, he hoped sympathetically. "Can you get us a picture?"

"I brought one. I thought you might need it."

She opened her purse and took out a four-by-six glossy print of a gorgeous, smiling, brown-eyed brunette. Thinnes had to work to keep his reaction from showing. He didn't recognize the woman, but her dress was definitely the same color and model they'd taken off their rape victim. He held the photo out to Franchi, who half stood to reach for it. He saw the surprise on her face when she looked at it only because he was watching for her reaction—just the slightest widening of her eyes as she recognized the dress. Then she put the picture on the table and went back to taking notes.

"Does Ms. Lake have any distinguishing physical characteristics—scars or birthmarks or tattoos?"

"No." Abbot's eyes widened. "Didn't you say you were Violent Crimes detectives?"

ELEVEN

Illinois Masonic Medical Center—subdued lighting and polished floors, bright green monitors and olive drab oxygen cylinders. The surgical ICU. One of the nurses escorted the three of them into the room and stood by the door. Flanked by Thinnes and Franchi, Joy Abbot approached the bed with wide eyes and a hand pressed over her mouth.

The victim was still comatose. Her face was puffy and blotched with bruises, her eyes so swollen that Thinnes wondered if she *could* open them. Her broken nose had been set and taped, and a breathing tube stuck out of her mouth. But the most disturbing thing—more than the tubes, or the bandages covering her broken hands—was the line of stitches stretching like a zipper down the left side of her face and across her throat. The rest of the damage was hidden under covers. And inside her skull.

Witness Santos's comment that he wouldn't have recognized his own sister in her condition was right on. At least her roommate didn't. She said, "That can't be Katherine. My God! What happened?"

As Thinnes tried to think of a gentle way to break the news, Franchi said, "She was raped, beaten, and cut."

"Oh, God! Is she going to live?"

Live, Thinnes thought, not recover. It had to be almost impossible to recover from something like that.

Franchi said, "They think so."

Abbot crept closer to the bed and reached for the victim's bandaged hand, then stopped before touching it. She wrapped her fingers gently around the injured woman's relatively unda-maged forearm. "Katherine?"

There was no response, no change in the march of green squiggles across the EKG monitor.

Abbot looked at the nurse. "Is she unconscious or some-thing?"

"In a coma," the nurse said.

There wasn't anything else they could do at the hospital, so they took Abbot back to Area Three, where Thinnes had Franchi take her statement. He went to work, meanwhile, on getting a warrant to search Lake's room in their apartment. Abbot had made it clear they were welcome to toss the place if it would help, but Thinnes wanted an Assistant State's Attorney involved in any search.

It actually took several hours to establish that the woman in the ICU was, in fact, Katherine Lake. They had to get her dental records and take them to Illinois Masonic for comparison with the skull series the hospital shot. Thinnes delegated the job while he and Franchi reinterviewed Abbot in the Area Three conference room.

They asked her all the usual things: Did Katherine have a boyfriend? An angry ex? A stalker? Trouble with anyone at work?

All negative. Katherine Lake was a good worker, well liked by bosses and coworkers. She didn't drink much or frequent tav-erns in search of Mr. Goodbar. Abbot couldn't recall a single recent disagreement she'd had with anyone.

Eventually, Franchi excused herself for a nicotine fix, and Thinnes was left alone with Abbot. He asked her about her own life—any problems with boyfriends, neighbors, or coworkers? Any unusual encounters on the street; hang-up calls or wrong numbers; door-to-door salesmen or survey takers?

None that she recalled. She'd filled Thinnes in on their back-grounds—to date their lives had been pleasant and uneventful—

when Swann tapped on the door and poked his head in. "Phone for you, Thinnes."

He excused himself and went out to the squad room to take the call. He picked up and said, "Thinnes."

"Shiparelli. We're done vetting your search warrant. If you hurry, you can get Judge Judy to sign it between calls."

"Thanks." He put down the phone and looked up to find Franchi scowling at him.

She said, "I'm gonna have that bastard's balls when we get him!"

He wasn't sure if she was just blowing off steam. He wished he were working with Oster. When he'd made a statement like that, Thinnes knew just what he meant, and exactly how far he'd go. To be safe, Thinnes said, "No, Franchi. When we get him, we're not going to fuck anything up by putting a scratch on him."

She gave him a disgusted look, and said, "Teach your grandmother to suck eggs!" Then she stalked back into the conference room.

The apartment was in the Eighteenth District, on a street of well-kept brick houses and rehabbed two-flats, just south of DePaul University. Although neither of the women was associated with the school, the suggestion of a rapist working within blocks of all those coeds was a cop's worst nightmare.

The case wasn't a homicide, so Thinnes asked for the same Nineteenth District evidence tech who'd worked the alley Lake was found in. Thinnes curbed the car by a hydrant in front. The tech double-parked across the street as Franchi got out and opened the car door for Abbot.

When they got on the porch, Thinnes noted the names ABBOT and LAKE next to the buzzer for 1A. 2A was JEFFREYS and WELLS.

Abbot took her keys out of her coat pocket. Thinnes held his hand out for them. "Whoever attacked Katherine undoubtedly took her keys."

Abbot seemed to get paler, if that were possible. She handed over the keys as if they were too hot to hold.

Their entry was an anticlimax. Leaving Abbot on the porch with the tech, Thinnes and Franchi checked for intruders, alternately covering one another and advancing under cover. Franchi obviously knew the drill—thank God for basic training.

After they'd holstered their weapons, they called in the evidence tech, who walked Abbot through the place with her hands in her pockets so she could tell them if anything was missing or out of place. She wasn't much help—too angry or afraid.

The technician ran off a roll of film—reference shots, then lifted a few prints. Then he told Thinnes and Franchi to have at it.

"Hang around a few minutes," Thinnes told him.

He said, "I'll be on the porch."

The apartment was clean, furnished with white-painted wicker furniture and lots of wrought iron and glass.

"Pier One?" Franchi asked.

Abbot nodded.

There was little of interest in the living room, bathroom, or kitchen, so they went into Lake's room. Abbot stood in the doorway, watching, with her hands tucked into her armpits.

There were subtle signs that it had been searched—one of the drawer fronts not quite flush with the others, one of the bifold closet doors slightly ajar, the edge of the bedspread draped in a way it wouldn't hang if the bed had just been made.

"Is Miss Lake a stickler for order?" Thinnes asked, as Franchi opened the closet and started going through the clothes, pulling each thing out to look at it front and back and check the pockets.

"Oh, yes." Abbot pointed at the closet. "She must've been in a real hurry to leave that door open. She had the landlord in here three times, when we moved in, to get it to close all the way and stay shut."

Thinnes turned to the dresser. A sheet of plate-glass on its top protected a collage made of photos, greeting card inscriptions, hand-lettered slogans and poems, newspaper headlines, and magazine ad captions. Some of the items overlapped in a way that suggested the glass had been lifted and replaced carelessly. On top of the glass, an older couple smiled out of one framed photo, a fat, white Persian cat stared from another. Abbot confirmed that the people were Lake's parents, the cat a late, beloved pet. Flanking the frames were decorative perfume bottles, a jewelry box, and a designer tissue dispenser.

There were no fingerprints on the glass, not even smudges to attract the fingerprint powder. Thinnes called the tech back in and had him dust the underside of the glass, the photos, and the closet doors. Nothing. Not even the usual grunge that prevents prints from attaching but attracts fingerprint powder like a white shirt attracts coffee stains.

TWELVE

They sent Ferris to Subway to get lunch and ate at their desks. Afterward, Thinnes found Rossi in the Major Case Crimes office, reading an account of the rape in the *Sun-Times* Metro section. Rossi didn't look up as Thinnes reported the latest nondevelopments. "Keep me posted," he said, still without looking up, and waved Thinnes through the door. Thinnes waited for him to notice he was still there.

"What?" Rossi demanded.

"I'd like to request Franchi be assigned to someone else."

"Why? You think you're too good to work with a female?"

"I've got no problem working with women."

"What then?"

"I got a partner."

"Yeah? Who?"

"Carl Oster."

"He's on permanent disability."

"He's my partner until *he* says different."

"Don't bother to tell me about it, Thinnes, 'cause I don't want to hear. You don't have a partner. Franchi needs a partner—it's a match made in heaven. If you don't like it, you can put in for a transfer. I understand they're shorthanded in patrol over at the 'deuce.' " Second District. One of the armpits of the city.

Thinnes went out without closing the door.

In the squad room, Ferris was going head to head with the Assistant State's Attorney. "You get me some evidence," Columbo was saying, "and I'll get you a warrant."

Thinnes walked over to a spot ten feet from the coffee setup with a good view of the show, and put down the rape case files.

"You had that raincoat since college, Columbo," Ferris told the ASA. "I'd think they pay you enough to buy a new one every decade or so."

"What're you, the fashion police? You better stick to violent crimes."

At that point, Franchi came in from a smoke break and went back to the table where her paperwork was spread out.

Columbo spotted her and said, "And this lovely lady is?"

Ferris said. "No lady. Thinnes's new partner."

Thinnes got up to get coffee, and said, "Don't throw bouquets at her, Columbo. She's liable to hit 'em back and knock you cold."

Without even looking up, Franchi said, "Fuck you, Thinnes."

"No thanks."

"Look out, Thinnes," Ferris said. "She'll file a grievance."

"Naw, too busy filing her teeth." As soon as he said it, Thinnes felt dirty and small, the way he had the first and last time he'd ever hit a smaller kid—in second grade. It made him furious that Franchi could bring that out in him. He didn't feel bad enough to apologize, though. No point. He'd no doubt do it again.

"Thinnes," Columbo said, "you got a sudden death wish? You're asking for a harassment beef."

"That's how Detective Franchi got here, Columbo," Thinnes said. "And we got a pool going on how long before she files another."

Columbo shook his head, then walked over to shove a hand at Franchi. "Assistant State's Attorney Anthony Shiparelli, Detective Franchi."

She took it and shook. "Don."

"It's no wonder these guys can't come up with evidence," Columbo said. "They're too busy thinking up insults."

"Don't sweat it, Shiparelli," Franchi said. "This is a test. You know how adolescents are—always testing."

. . .

When he got to the bottom of his "To call" list, Thinnes stood, stretched, and put his jacket on. By the time he got to the squad-room door, Franchi—who'd never taken her jacket off—was on his heels.

"Where to now?" If she was still pissed about the harassment, earlier, she didn't show it, but obviously she didn't trust him not to go off without her again.

Thinnes decided to try acting as if they'd just been assigned to work together. He handed her Swann's note with "weird" underlined three times.

"This warrants a look."

She nodded and handed it back and followed him down to the car.

There was no bell near the door belonging to the address Swann had given him. The door knocker was an ornate brass eyeball with a thick fringe of lashes on the upper lid. With Franchi crowding behind him on the small porch, Thinnes grabbed the lashes and raised and lowered the eyelid twice. They waited.

The guy who opened the door the width of a security chain creeped him out. The tall, yellow-skinned Caucasian had black hair and eyes that bulged like Peter Lorre's. "Yes?"

Thinnes held his star up for inspection. "You live here?"

The man waited; Thinnes outwaited him. Finally, he said, "Yes."

"You're Dr. Ice?"

"No. Eyes. E-Y-E-S."

That explained the door ornament. Sort of. "First Name?"

"Doctor. D-O-C-T-O-R."

"See some ID?"

"Just a minute."

He went inside and closed the door, and didn't immediately reopen it.

"Should I cover the back?" Franchi asked.

Thinnes said, "Hold on a minute." He counted to ten, then knocked again.

Eyes's voice came through the heavy wood. "I'm coming."

"Mind opening the door?"

The door reopened.

Thinnes said, "Can we come in?"

Eyes stood blinking for ten or fifteen seconds before he shrugged and stepped backward into the room. Thinnes took it as an invitation and went in; Franchi followed.

The front room looked like a bizarro biology lab, its walls covered with shelves holding ranks of jars and bottles, and assorted anatomical models—all eyes. What made it even weirder was that all the containers, large and small, seemed to hold once-living eyeballs. And between the shelves there were posters featuring eyes, even an eye chart.

"Are you some kind of eye specialist?" Franchi asked.

Eyes nodded. "An amateur."

Thinnes said, "Are any of these human?"

The question seemed to startle him. "That's not what you came here to ask me. Did one of my neighbors complain?"

"Do they have something to complain about?"

"Certainly not! There's no law against collecting things."

Some things.

"What then?" Eyes demanded. "What did you come for?" He didn't invite them to sit, though to be fair that might have been due to a scarcity of seating. The futon in the center of the room, the end tables, chairs, breakfront, even the TV were piled with books and papers, most of the titles involving eyes.

"We need to know about anything unusual that may have happened this morning."

Something would probably have to be pretty weird for the guy to think it was unusual.

"Unusual in what way?"

"Any way at all," Franchi said. "Were you home?"

"Yes."

She and Thinnes both waited. After a moment, Eyes said, "Give me a clue."

Franchi blinked. "About what?"

"Whatever it is I'm supposed to have seen or heard."

Franchi looked at Thinnes and rolled her eyes, then said, "What *did* you see and hear this morning?"

"A very interesting report on the Discovery Channel about some new, artificial eyes they're developing to help blind people see. Well, not eyes, exactly, but . . ."

"That's it?"

"Then there was a special on Channel 20 about perception. That's a bit far from eyes, but it goes with seeing."

"Did you go out of the house?"

"Oh, no. Never. I have agoraphobia. I haven't been out of the house in years . . ."

THIRTEEN

By late afternoon, Swann, Ryan, and the beat coppers had rounded up some of the usual suspects, but they'd waited to interview them until Thinnes was free. "We got another guy coming in later," Swann told him. "Name of Deacon. A date rapist."

The first guy, pacing the Area interview room, was in uniform. Swann took off and left Thinnes and Ryan watching him through the two-way mirror.

"What's his story?" Thinnes asked.

"Denny Eames," Ryan told him. "Guy's a security guard."

"With his record? How'd he do that?"

"Lie?"

"Let's ask him."

Thinnes went in and held his hand out. "Mr. Eames? I'm Detective Thinnes. Thanks for coming in."

Eames seemed surprised but nodded and returned the handshake with a firm grip. Thinnes took the only chair and offered him a seat on the bench against the wall. Eames perched in the middle, on the edge. Thinnes leaned into his personal space, and the security guard squirmed.

"What's this about?"

"You work security, Mr. Eames?"

"No, I just get off on uniforms." Thinnes waited. Eames finally said, "It's a job."

"Some would say a smorgasbord of opportunity for an ex-con."

The muscles of Eames's jaw tightened, and he shifted on the

bench. "Some of us just wanna be employed. How 'bout you get to the point. I've got to get back to work."

Thinnes leaned back in the chair. "Okay. You aware of anything unusual in your neighborhood this morning?" Eames lived three blocks from the victim.

"No. What happened?"

"Were you home this morning?"

"What time?"

"Did you leave your house this morning?"

"I went to work."

"What time did you leave your house?"

"Six-thirty."

"What time did you get there?"

"Seven-fifteen."

"You punch a clock?"

Eames nodded.

Thinnes asked him about his standard day—what time he got home. The usual. Eames got more and more anxious, finally blurting out, "What's this about? Tell me, or I'm outta here!"

Thinnes took out Katherine Lake's picture. "You know this woman?"

Eames seemed to relax as he studied the photo.

"No." He handed it back. "She say I do?"

"You got anybody to vouch for your whereabouts this morning?"

"My wife—before I went to work. People who work in my building might remember seeing me. Why? What's this about?" His frustration sounded real enough.

Thinnes fanned the air with the picture. "This woman was raped."

"Oh! And you thought 'cause I got a record . . . No way! I got sent up for *statutory* rape. 'Cause my girlfriend was underage, and her old man's an asshole! It wasn't rape! She married me as soon as I got out. Now the asshole's got a felon in his family." Eames got to his feet. "You can pin this on somebody else."

Thinnes stood up.

Eames said, "You check." He stepped around Thinnes, to the door.

"Just one more question, Eames."

Eames paused.

"Your boss know about your record?"

"Ask *him*!"

After the squad-room door had closed behind Eames, Thinnes turned to Ryan, and said, "Well?"

Before she answered Ryan took a sip of her coffee, and combed her red hair off her face with her fingers. "I'd say, too pissed off to be lying."

"Me too. But check his story anyway, would you?"

"Sure, boss."

Thinnes gave her a look; she walked away laughing.

When the sergeant called from the Nineteenth District front desk to say Terence Deacon had arrived, Thinnes went downstairs to get him. Deacon was white, five-eleven, midtwenties, brown hair, hazel eyes. Shifty eyes. His rap sheet made him out to be a violent date rapist. He was watching the free show that passed for business as usual in the lobby. A tactical team had been doing a sting with Vice to rid a stretch of Western Avenue of johns trolling for prostitutes.

One of the tac cops was a bleached blonde with a killer body and a *very* short skirt. When she crossed the lobby with her partner, she wasn't wearing her ID—contrary to regulations—so she might easily have been mistaken for the working girl she was got up as.

Deacon's eyes followed her. "What a tramp," he told Thinnes. "They're nice to look at. They're nice to talk to. But they got disease written all over 'em. Keep 'em away from me."

Upstairs, Thinnes started with questions for which Deacon's rap sheet had answers—date of birth, occupation, education.

Then they got into the dicier stuff—the rape Deacon had been arrested for, the plea bargain that had kept him from doing the hard time he deserved, and his attitudes about women. Thinnes didn't contradict his version—that the woman had been willing until she'd gotten him aroused, then changed her mind. Then what could he do? If they'd had any kind of case, they'd have never let him plead abuse. It wasn't rape. It was a bum rap.

Thinnes kept his 'Yeah, right!' to himself and tried to find one thing he could like about the guy.

"Bunch of effin' bitches, all of 'em," Deacon insisted. "All they're lookin' for is a meal ticket and a chance to screw a guy."

"You had any *recent* experience with that?"

"Whadda ya mean?"

"You had any trouble with a woman the last few days?"

"Been stayin' away from 'em."

"That must be hard—young guy like you. I'd think they'd be all over you."

"Well . . . A little, maybe. In bars. But I'm real careful to let them make all the moves."

"So what kind of moves have they been making?"

Deacon squirmed.

Thinnes handed Katherine Lake's picture to Deacon. "So why would someone say they'd seen you with this woman?"

Deacon took it reluctantly, glanced at it quickly, and without hesitation said, "They got the wrong guy. I never date brunettes."

"Maybe she wasn't a brunette last time you saw her. Take a closer look."

Deacon shrugged and looked. He didn't hesitate at all before he said, "Nah. Gotta be somebody else. I never saw this broad before. And anyone says I did is a liar. What's this about?"

"Where were you this morning around seven?"

"With a friend. Which I take it I better be able to prove." Thinnes waited. "I was waitin' outside an apartment on Honore for the guy who lived there to come home. He owed a buddy money, and I was trying to help him collect."

"Did you?"

"Nah. The asshole never showed. But we were there half the night—'til eight this morning. Then I had to go to work.

"Oh, and you'll like this. A couple of uniform cops stopped their car around five to ask us what we were doing." Deacon laughed. "Never thought the fuzz'd bail me out. You ask 'em."

"Did you get their names or car number?"

"Nah, but one was a black broad with a big butt. The other was a skinny white guy." Deacon gave Thinnes his buddy's name and contact information, and the address of the guy they'd been after.

Slimy and smarmy as he was, he seemed to be telling the truth. Thinnes made a note to follow up on it, but finally cut him loose.

When he came back from escorting Deacon to the lobby, Rossi had left. Thinnes put the reports he'd finished in Rossi's in-box and told Franchi to call it a day.

"What time tomorrow?" she asked.

"Roll call's usually at eight, but I want to get out and recanvass before Lake's neighbors go to work. I'll be here at six."

She nodded, and said, "Good night."

Thinnes said, "See you," and watched her walk out of the room.

FOURTEEN

The light was on in the kitchen when Thinnes got home, and it was fifteen whole seconds before Toby showed up to greet him. Rhonda was home. The dog worshipped her and never let her out of his sight. Thinnes didn't blame him. He adored Rhonda, too. "Ronnie?" he called as he took off his jacket and threw it over the newel post at the foot of the stairs.

"Don't come in here, John."

He did, though. The kitchen smelled like the morgue, like meat and bleach. Rhonda was standing at the counter between the stove and sink, autopsying an eighteen-inch skirt steak, trying to trim out the fat. She had the water running; the sink was half-full of suds and bleach that she'd added to kill any bacteria. The chlorine burned Thinnes's eyes and throat, and he wondered how the dog could stand it. Toby had taken a position next to the stove and lay with his head on his paws, his eyes on Rhonda. Thinnes stepped behind her and circled her waist with his arms. He shook his head.

"I warned you." She knew how he felt about the smell. When he'd first started going to autopsies, he hadn't been able to eat beef or chicken.

He kissed the nape of her neck and reached up to turn on the stove fan. "You're gonna cook your lungs."

"Better than getting salmonella or e-coli."

He slipped his hands beneath her blouse, exploring under the satiny bra with his index fingers. "What's for dinner?" he asked as suggestively as possible.

"Filet of Rhonda's fingers if you keep that up."

He dropped his hands. "Sorry."

"Turn off the water, would you please?"

"Sure." He pushed down on the faucet and the water stopped. "What're you building here?"

"Stir fry."

"Hmmm."

"Why don't you take Toby for a walk, then get ready for dinner?"

"Where's Rob?"

"He had a game to tape."

Rob had talked his way into a job in the AV department at school. Thinnes was proud of the kid, but he didn't see much of him lately as a result. And poor Toby was starved for attention.

"Okay." He kissed her again, then turned away and snapped his fingers to get Toby to follow. As he took the leash off the closet doorknob, he wondered if he could talk Rhonda into dessert before dinner.

They were getting ready for bed, slowly undressing each other, when Thinnes had a flashback—Katherine Lake's battered face. Lincoln Park was supposed to be a safe neighborhood. Not unlike this one.

No one's safe. Nowhere. Never!

He could feel Rhonda react before she said, "What is it, John?" He could see the worry in her face.

"It's this fucking case I'm working!"

She didn't like him swearing, though she didn't complain. She waited. His trick. He knew how it worked, but he still felt compelled to talk. "A rape case." He didn't have to elaborate. Rhonda knew how he felt about working rape.

"Is Evanger mad at you?"

"Not Evanger, Rossi. Evanger's away."

"Oh." She sighed and rested her cheek against his back.

"And he stuck me with a new hire who's got an attitude."

"A detective?"

"Yeah. Don Franchi, a *meritorious* appointment." Thinnes purposely avoided mentioning Franchi was a woman. With any luck, he'd ditch her before it became an issue.

Rhonda turned him around and leaned her head against his chest. "You'll be all right." She wrapped her arms around him. "Ray wasn't a *real* detective when they assigned him to work with you." Ray Crowne, Thinnes's partner before Oster, had gotten on the job because he had a relative with clout. "I'm sure you'll work things out with Don."

"Hmmm."

"There's something else."

"I don't like you taking chances—with a rapist out there."

"It's a big city." She slid her hands down Thinnes's back and over his buttocks.

Thinnes let himself be distracted.

FIFTEEN

It was foggy the next morning—less than a block visibility—and on the way to work, Thinnes had the feeling he'd strayed into the Twilight Zone. At Western and Belmont, Franchi was standing outside, smoking in the same place she'd been the first time he saw her. Her suit was gray today, the skirt maybe a half inch longer.

She spotted him and dropped the cigarette, putting it out very deliberately with her foot. Neither of them said "good morning," Franchi fell in behind as he entered the Nineteenth District lobby and followed him up to the Area squad room. She helped herself to coffee after he did, then trailed him downstairs and sipped her brew while he checked out a radio and car.

In the parking lot, she walked to the passenger's side and waited for him to unlock her door. They still hadn't spoken as he pulled the Caprice onto Clybourn. Franchi drank her coffee and stared out at the fog. It was kind of weird, but at least they hadn't had any *nasty* words. Thinnes didn't hurry to break the silence.

The alley where the rape had gone down wasn't much different than the day before—fog-shrouded, eerie. Today, though, there was no crime-scene tape, no cops or cars with flashing lights. Thinnes parked and pulled the list of addresses to recanvass from his pile of notes. "We might as well split up," he said. "We'll get done twice as fast. You got a cell phone with you?" She nodded. He split the list in two and held both halves up for her to choose one.

She did.

He scribbled his cell-phone number on one of his business cards. "You come across anybody even a little off, call for backup."

She took it, glanced at the number, and slipped the card in her jacket pocket. "Got it."

"Call when you're done. We'll meet back here."

She nodded. She got out of the car and lit a cigarette, then started off into the fog.

Thinnes locked the car and headed the other way.

The sign on the mailbox said NEIL O'ROURKE. Thinnes wasn't sure if that was a given name and a surname or two surnames. He rang the door bell.

It was answered by a woman who filled the doorway. She wore a kelly green T-shirt that said KISS ME, I'M IRISH, and baggy gray sweatpants. She was flanked by a pair of identical toddlers.

"Were you here between 6 and 8 A.M. yesterday morning?"

"That was when that woman was raped."

He nodded.

One of the toddlers pulled the slack in her mother's pants leg across her face, then coyly peeked at Thinnes. Her twin hung on the woman's other leg like a drunk on a light pole. She stuck a thumb in her mouth and stared wide-eyed. Thinnes looked at their mother.

"Were you home?"

"Yeah," she said. "Like I could take five kids to breakfast at McDonald's without taking out a second mortgage."

How old is your oldest?"

"Eight and a half. These two are twins," she said as if it were necessary.

"Any other adults live here?"

"Just me and my husband."

"Neil?"

She nodded. "He wasn't here yesterday morning. He had to work OT."

Thinnes raised his eyebrows.

The woman lifted the kid playing peekaboo onto her hip and said, "He works the eleven to seven shift—usually gets home between eight and eight-thirty. If he gets home on time, he takes the kids to school. If not, I take 'em—the whole crew. Yesterday he had to work late, so I bundled them all up and we walked in the fog."

"What does your husband do?"

"He's a cop like you. Only he works at Fifty-first and Wentworth."

"Could I see some ID?"

She sighed. "I suppose so. Just a minute." She backed into the room, dragging the floor-bound child along. She kicked the door shut.

While he waited, Thinnes wondered how a couple with five kids could afford to live in Lincoln Park. On a cop's wages. Well, if O'Rourke wasn't robbing and raping young women, it was none of his business.

Mrs. O'Rourke reappeared a minute later without the kids. She handed him a driver's license. Thinnes noted the particulars—her name was Loreli—and handed it back. She gave him her phone number reluctantly and only after he promised to keep it out of any public reports.

"One last question, Mrs. O'Rourke. Do you know if your upstairs neighbors were home yesterday morning?"

She laughed. "They've been on vacation for two weeks. Italy. My husband's been taking care of their cats. They should be home Sunday if you need to talk to them."

As he walked to the next location, a sixties song guided him through the fog. The bass anyway. He couldn't remember the title or hear the words, but the tune was one of those things that gets in your head and parks for hours. He leaned on the bell; eventually the music stopped.

Lily Henderson's next-door neighbor was exactly as she had described him—very nondescript. Caucasian, medium height, weight, and complexion, with medium brown hair. The only thing notable about him was his eyes—big, sad, brown eyes. He said, "Yes?"

Thinnes flashed his star. "Walter Lennox?"

Lennox nodded.

"I need to ask you a few questions."

"Ah. Yeah. Sure. Why don't you come in?" When he backed up to let Thinnes past, he tripped over a pair of loafers left just inside the entry. He caught himself by grabbing the edge of the door. He waved an arm in the direction of the front room and closed the door behind Thinnes.

The room was cluttered but not dirty, with drapes and a couch like the one Thinnes's mother had when he was small. And he would've bet the tan rug was original equipment with the apartment. An empty beer can—MGD—and a plate with a half-eaten hot dog sat on a recliner facing the TV.

Lennox scrambled to gather the newspapers and magazines that were piled on the couch.

"Sit down. Please."

As Thinnes sat, Lennox dropped everything on the floor and added the can and plate to the pile. He sat on the edge of the recliner.

"Can I see some ID, Mr. Lennox?"

"Oh, yeah. Sure." Lennox got up and went to a closet behind the door. He dug a leather checkbook organizer from the right inside pocket of a suit jacket that matched the slacks he was wearing. There was a brown-and-yellow tie hanging from the left side pocket.

As he handed Thinnes an Illinois State ID card with his left hand, Lennox said, "What's this about? Someone get burglarized?"

"Not exactly. Could you tell me what you were doing yesterday morning?"

Lennox waited as if expecting him to explain, then said, "Ah . . . Yes. I got up—I overslept—and I— So I didn't have time for breakfast. So I just dressed and shaved—That is, I shaved first, then dressed. And I went to work."

"How?"

"The usual way." Thinnes waited. "Oh. I see. You mean, how do I get to work? The Red Line. I walk to the Armitage station and take it to Jackson. Then I walk from there to my office."

"Where do you work?"

"Lawrey and Heinz. I'm Mr. Lawrey's assistant."

"What time did you get there?"

He had to think about that, unfocusing his cocker spaniel eyes to concentrate. "About ten past nine."

"Is there someone who can verify that?"

"You mean like an alibi?"

"If you like."

"Well, Mr. Lawrey . . . What's this about?"

"You hear or see anything unusual?"

"Before I went to work?"

"Yeah."

"Ah . . . No. But I'm a pretty heavy sleeper. I used to have a place right up against the El tracks, and I barely noticed the trains. I used to sleep right through them."

"A woman was attacked in your alley yesterday morning."

"That sucks!" Lennox ran his hand through his hair. Left hand. "Who? Is she gonna be all right?"

"We're checking to see who might have seen or heard anything."

"I wish I could help you. Is the woman gonna be okay?"

Thinnes let the question hang.

Lennox looked toward the display on the VCR, and said, "Er . . . I'm afraid I've got to get going or I'll be late for work again."

Thinnes asked him a few more questions, but either he knew nothing, or he was a terrific actor. Thinnes handed him his card, and said, "Give me a call if you think of anything that might help us catch the rapist."

As he got to the third from last address on his list, mist drifted and eddied across the bright disk of the sun. His phone rang, and Franchi's voice reported that she was finished with her interviews. He gave her the next to last address and told her to meet him there.

She was waiting outside a typical Lincoln Park residence. Typical except for the Hummer parked in front. Too wide to keep from blocking the narrow street, it was half on the parkway, half across the near-side drive lane. It was a bit much, even for a yuppie.

Thinnes nodded as he approached, and Franchi climbed the steps to ring the bell. When the door opened, a man stepped out and walked past Franchi like she was a homeless woman in the subway. The guy was wearing an expensive suit and tie, and shoes Thinnes knew cost as much as his whole wardrobe. The man talked into his cell phone as he descended the steps.

"Hey," Thinnes said. He held up his star.

The man glanced at it, and said, "I don't have to talk to you. Excuse me." He closed the phone, climbed into the Hummer, and drove off.

Thinnes wondered if they made a boot big enough for a Hummer. He could tell from Franchi's body language that she was teed off, too, but she just pulled a notebook out of her oversize purse and started making notes, the plate number and vehicle description, presumably. She put the notebook back, and said, "Where to next?"

"Where to" was an older house with a rusty wrought-iron fence. A NO TRESPASSING/NO SOLICITORS sign hung on the unlocked gate. Thinnes held it open for Franchi. Before they could mount the stone steps to the porch, a kid in his teens wheeled a fancy, electric blue ten-speed around the corner. He was looking at something behind him and didn't notice them until he was about eight feet from Franchi.

When he saw them, he froze like a robber on a paused surveillance video, then shoved the bike at Franchi.

She was quick on her feet; Thinnes had to give her that. She dodged to the side, avoiding the front wheel, and jumped over the rear wheel as the bike tumbled into their path. Then, with her purse flopping out behind, she took off after the kid, who was running away.

Thinnes stepped around the bike and followed in time to see a large white male emerge from a side door at the back of the house, into the runner's path.

The kid stopped. Franchi crashed into him with enough momentum to send him sprawling at the big man's feet. Franchi landed on top. The kid grunted and squirmed.

Franchi said, "Police! Stop resisting!"

"What's going on?" the big guy asked.

Franchi's captive got curiously quiet. She said, "Dammit!" and rolled off him, into a sitting position. She looked at her knee, scraped and bloody from the fall. "Don't move!" she told the kid.

Thinnes showed the big man his star, and said, "That's what we'd like to—"

"Hey!" the man yelled, "my bike's gone!"

Franchi, who'd planted her undamaged knee in the middle of the kid's back, said, "Blue ten-speed?"

"Yeah. I had it chained to the fence. Now it's gone."

"Check in front." She pulled a pair of handcuffs from her bag.

Thinnes keyed the radio to call for patrol.

Franchi snapped the cuffs on the young thief's wrists. "What's your name, kid?"

"I ain't tellin' you! And I ain't talkin'!"

"Fine with me." She looked at Thinnes. "This is gonna be a big pain in the ass, isn't it?"

"You had to catch him. You *know* no good deed goes unpunished."

Back in the car, Thinnes realized he was humming the music Lennox had been playing when Franchi said, "You a Who fan?"

The only Who song he could think of was from *Tommy*—"The Pinball Wizard." He shook his head. "Why?"

"What you were just humming—the Who."

"No. It's just one of those tunes that gets in your head and drives you nuts."

SIXTEEN

Where're you going, Thinnes?" Rossi demanded. Rossi had ignored the goings-on in the squad room all morning. Now that Thinnes was ready to leave, he popped out of his office.

"The hospital just called. Our victim regained consciousness. Thought I'd take another crack at an interview."

Franchi stood up and whisked her coat off her chairback, putting it on so smoothly the whole operation seemed like a single motion. "I'm with you."

Thinnes didn't want to take her, but even more, he didn't want to give Rossi the satisfaction of seeing them feuding. He nodded.

Rossi's eyes darted around the squad room before he said, "You can't both go." Except for the three of them, the room was empty.

Franchi blinked several times.

She can't go because Rossi doesn't want to be the only one around, Thinnes decided. He might have to do some work. Thinnes could tell from the expression on Franchi's face that she was thinking along the same lines. He caught her eye and shrugged.

"Franchi," Rossi said. "You stay and get the phones."

Franchi said, "Yeah, boss."

North Michigan Avenue wasn't on the way to Illinois Masonic Medical Center—it was out of the way in fact. But Thinnes figured the delay would be worth the help he could get interviewing Katherine Lake. He called Caleb on his cell phone before he pulled out of the Nineteenth District parking lot, and the doctor agreed to help if they could be done and back in under two hours. "Piece of cake," Thinnes assured him. If necessary, he could use his oscillating headlights.

Caleb was waiting with two Starbucks coffees in front of the Art Institute.

He had known Caleb for three years—long enough that he'd stopped thinking of the psychiatrist's custom-made clothes and fifty-dollar haircuts. The fact that the doctor wasn't afraid to roll up his sleeves and wade into the fray made him okay.

The hospital was on Wellington, south of Belmont, so Thinnes took the Drive north. Traffic was light. He was able to fill Caleb in on the case and drink his coffee without losing time.

At the hospital, he parked in a space reserved for employees and threw his OFFICIAL POLICE BUSINESS card on the dash.

Inside, one of the intensive care nurses headed them off at Lake's door. She was middle-aged, short, and tough. She reminded Thinnes of the Nineteenth District patrol sergeant who'd worked the crime scene.

"Five minutes, no more, Detectives."

But not very observant, Thinnes decided, mistaking Caleb—in his tailor-made suit and silk tie—for a dick.

Caleb walked over to the figure in the bed and put a hand on her arm. "Miss Lake," he said. "Katherine? You're in a hospital."

She made a choking sound, trying to talk around the tube in her throat.

Caleb said, "Please don't try to speak. You have a tube in your throat to help you breathe. If you understand me, press against my hand with your elbow."

Thinnes noticed a slight movement of her right arm, and Caleb's nod.

"I'm Dr. Caleb. You were beaten severely, but you're going to mend. You're safe here." His voice was soothing, almost hypnotic. "There's a police officer outside your door, and the nurse is stationed twenty feet away. We're going to catch the man who did this to you, but we need your help. If you understand me, press against my hand."

Again there was a slight movement of her right arm. Caleb said, "Good. Can you move your feet?"

She could and did.

"Excellent," Caleb said. "I'm going to ask you some questions. I'll try to make them simple so you can answer yes or no. If that's all right, press against my hand."

Lake squeezed his hand between her side and elbow.

"Okay. If you want to tell me yes, squeeze my hand. For no, move your feet. Can you do that?"

Lake squeezed his hand.

"Thursday afternoon was the last time any of your friends remember seeing you. Do you remember going home from work?"

He repeated what he took to be her answer. Yes.

"Did you have a guest?"

Yes. And no.

"Did you invite someone over?"

No.

"Someone came uninvited?"

Yes.

"A man?"

Yes.

"A friend?"

No.

"An acquaintance?"

Yes and no.

"Someone you didn't know well?"

Yes.

"Can you remember what happened to you?"

Another arm movement was accompanied by a sound between a moan and a whimper.

Caleb stroked her arm, and said, "Katherine, we can stop if you like."

She wiggled both feet frantically. Caleb stroked her arm and told her to pace herself, then patiently continued his questions, backtracking to clear up a confusing response, then returning to his original line of questions. The story that gradually unfolded was familiar.

Lake had originally met her assailant in a bar, some months before, though she didn't know his name. She'd been surprised when he called—she didn't remember giving him her number. But he'd had it, hadn't he? So she must have. His name was John. She'd agreed to meet him at a nearby bar, a public place. It had seemed safe enough. She vaguely remembered having a beer. That was all. The last thing she remembered was being beaten. And raped. Then nothing.

Then the nurse came in to tell them Lake's monitor was screaming off the scale. They would have to leave.

They drove back to the Loop in silence. Thinnes used the time to plan how he'd run down the bar and add rohypnol to a possible MO.

Caleb left him alone with his thoughts.

As they turned onto Michigan Avenue, the doctor put a hand on his shoulder. "John, are you all right with this?"

Thinnes swerved faster than he needed to around a CTA bus and didn't answer until he'd curbed the Caprice in front of Caleb's office building. "The day I'm all right with something like this, I'm putting in for retirement."

SEVENTEEN

Thinnes knew he wasn't going to get out from under the mountain of unsolved cases without help. When he got back from the hospital, Viernes was in the squad room, reading the *Sun-Times*. Ryan, Ferris, and Franchi were working the phones. Thinnes divided the stack of rape files into five. He left one on his desk and set one in front of each of the other detectives.

"We're looking for any cases with the same MO," he said. "Blitz attack on the victim, severe beating and cutting. Offender may have used a condom or just raped her with an object—no semen. And he may have drugged her beforehand."

For the next half hour, the room was quiet as a study hall before finals. Then Viernes closed the file he was studying and handed it to Thinnes. "This could be the same guy. Victim, Greta Highlander, was a court stenographer by day, amateur hooker by night."

"That doesn't match the victim profile on these other cases," Thinnes said.

Viernes shot a glance in Ferris's direction, and said, "Look who caught the case."

Thinnes did. Ferris had been the primary. He was reading the *Sun-Times*.

"Hey, Ferris," Thinnes said. "What's with this?" He tossed the file onto Ferris's newspaper.

"What the—" Ferris looked at the file, then tossed it back to Thinnes. "Broad was puttin' out for anyone who'd buy her dinner and drinks. What'd she expect?"

"So you sleepwalked through the case."

"I did a routine investigation. There were so many suspects I didn't know where to start—none of 'em any good. They're all in there. They all had alibis."

Thinnes flipped through the file, glancing at the names and notes next to the names. Ferris's follow-up report was " 'Victim' moved—NFA." Thinnes put the file on top of his notes for the Lake case and went back to his in-box pile.

He'd eliminated two more cases when Franchi dropped a folder on the table in front of him.

"Ivy Jacobs. DePaul student," she said. "A party girl out on Rush Street on a Wednesday night. She turned up in an alley Saturday morning with a concussion, three broken teeth, and a smashed finger. And somebody cut her badly enough to require two hundred stitches."

"When was that?"

"May 8."

"They have any leads?"

"Nope."

"Any follow-up?"

Franchi flipped open the folder to the last page. "Says she moved back to her parents' home in Madison. Hasn't returned any calls, but as of the last interview, she claimed she couldn't remember what happened to her."

"Thanks."

Franchi went back to her place. Thinnes put the file aside and went back to skimming his own unsolved case files.

One by one, the others returned the folders, reporting that none of the cases fit the profile. Finally, Ryan closed her last file, and said, "What about that Asian girl that was raped last month. She was beat-up pretty bad. Think it could be the same guy?"

Coming back from the coffeepot with a refill, Viernes said, "She didn't see his face."

"She must've seen *some* part of him."

Viernes reddened. "Yeah." He flicked his free hand at his fly.

"My guess," Ferris said, "is she got a real good look before he shoved it down her throat."

"¡Jesus!" Viernes said.

Ferris laughed. "Not Him."

Franchi didn't seem the least bit bothered by the banter. "She say why she didn't bite it off when she had the chance?"

"Yeah," Thinnes told her. "She said he put a gun to her head and told her he'd blow it off if she even nicked him."

Ryan nodded. "That'd make a difference. So what color was it?"

"White, circumcised."

Ferris made a face. "Is that really something we needed to know?"

"I'd say they're fairly definitive details."

Ferris's face lit up. "Hey, we got mug shots of those things?"

Franchi's report on Eyes, born Alvin Eisner, eliminated him pretty definitively. His doctor confirmed his agoraphobia—a case so severe the shrink actually made house calls to treat him.

"Thanks," Thinnes told Franchi. As she started back to her phone, he said, "Were any of the eyeballs he had on display blue?"

"Yeah, I think so."

"Then they were probably human. You'd better talk to Columbo about whether he's breaking any laws."

"If he is?"

"Plain view evidence. And the ball's in Columbo's court."

"Very pun-ny."

A little later, Thinnes got a call from downstairs. One of the Nineteenth District patrol teams had arrested a suspect for aggravated assault when he threatened a Starbucks server with a bread knife. Since the server fit the general description—female, brunette, slight build—that Thinnes had circulated, they wanted a detective to question him before they finished the paperwork.

"Have them bring him up."

A clean-cut rookie and a heavyset veteran copper brought the arrestee up and put him in the interview room the assignment officer indicated, leaving him handcuffed to—"hanging on"—the wall. He was a skinny guy dressed in denim. He reminded Thinnes of Maynard G. Krebs from the old *Dobie Gillis* show.

Thinnes looked at the arrest report. "John Wherewolf?"

"Yeah," the rookie said. "He used to be John Smith but he changed his name legally."

The veteran laughed. "Sommabitch can't even spell!" He glanced at his partner and hooked his thumb toward the door. "We're goin' for coffee," he told Thinnes. "Have fun."

"Go get *us* some coffee," Thinnes told Franchi. "While I check something out. Then we can lean on this guy."

She sniffed. "Yeah, right." She walked over to look into the interview room.

When he got back with the joe, Franchi was nowhere in sight. "Dammit," Thinnes muttered. He stepped to the two-way mirror to see what Wherewolf was doing—just in time to see Franchi unlock the suspect's handcuffs. Before Thinnes could reach the door, Wherewolf produced a knife and slashed at her.

She blocked the move as Thinnes reached for the doorknob. As he jerked the door open, Wherewolf brought the knife over his head and drove it downward. Franchi bladed her body, grabbing his knife hand with both of hers. He jerked the knife upward, pulled her up on her toes. He grabbed her hair. She kicked his ankle.

Thinnes intervened. Shoving Franchi aside, he grabbed Wherewolf's knife hand and twisted until the wolf howled. The knife dropped. Thinnes shouldered him backward against the wall. Wherewolf grunted and stopped struggling. Thinnes spun him around, twisting his arm behind his back, and held him until Franchi snapped the cuffs back on. Then they slammed him down on the bench. They weren't gentle as they searched him for other weapons.

"What the hell is going on in here?"

Thinnes whirled to see Rossi filling the doorway. He was breathing as hard as Thinnes, Franchi, or Wherewolf, waiting for an explanation.

Thinnes nodded at the knife on the floor. "Somebody screwed up."

Rossi turned as white as the underside of an alewife. "Who?"

As he shrugged, Thinnes watched Franchi out of the corner of his eye. "The guys who brought this scumbag in."

In the old days—when Thinnes first came on the job, he would've taken Wherewolf to booking by way of the basement and given him a lesson in cop-shop etiquette. It was risky these days, but if Franchi were really Thinnes's partner, he'd take the risk to let the asshole know he'd crossed the line. Thinnes knew lots of ways to get a point across without leaving bruises. But Franchi wasn't his partner, and she'd asked for it. She should've followed directions. He decided to let Rossi call the play.

"Aggravated battery," Rossi said. "No! Make that attempted murder! And get him outta here. Now!"

Behind Rossi's back, Franchi made a face that said, 'Gimme a break!' Thinnes had to agree. Trust Rossi to overreact.

"We gotta question him first."

"Why?"

"He likes to cut women," Thinnes said, as if Rossi's question were perfectly reasonable. "Makes him look good for our rape."

"Make it fast!"

Rossi disappeared as quickly as he'd come

Thinnes decided to question Wherewolf himself. He picked up the knife and pointed at Franchi, then at the door.

She followed him out, closing the door behind her. They watched Wherewolf through the two-way mirror as Thinnes handed the knife to Franchi. "Log this. Then stay out here and

73

take notes." He forestalled any objection by adding, "You got good reflexes, Franchi, but bad judgment."

"You don't care much for women, do you Mr. Wherewolf?"

"They're the devil," Wherewolf said. "They make you do things."

Thinnes could sympathize. That was exactly how he felt about Franchi. "Tell me about it." When Wherewolf didn't elaborate, he said, "What kind of things?"

"Bad."

"Women make you do any bad thing today?'

Wherewolf pointed to the door. "She."

"Detective Franchi?"

"She was gonna make me do bad things."

"She didn't make you try to cut her."

"She was gonna. She was in my face. She wouldn't go away."

"Where were you today? Before you went in Starbucks?"

"In my den."

"Where's that?"

"Where I live."

"You have an address?" Wherewolf told him. "What time did you leave home?"

"Seven."

Thinnes stepped out of the interview room.

Franchi said, "What's up?"

"Unless he chartered a helicopter, Wherewolf isn't our man."

Half an hour later, the head shrink at Ravenswood confirmed Wherewolf's alibi, and Thinnes turned him over to the beat cops.

"If you ask me, that one wasn't wrapped too tight," Ferris said, as the coppers took him away.

Thinnes and Franchi said in chorus, "No one asked you!"

EIGHTEEN

The night shift caught the next rape.

It was another foggy Monday morning when Thinnes got the news. He felt the déjà vu even before the sergeant met him at the squad-room door. "Looks like the scumbag you're after's struck again." He handed Thinnes a paper with an address. "They got the scene secure, and they've started the canvass, but the boss wants you to handle it."

"Rossi's here this early?"

"Naw. Evanger's back. He wants a report as soon as you return from the scene."

"Where's Franchi?"

Before he could answer, Franchi pushed through the squad-room door carrying two radios and a set of keys. She handed Thinnes one of the radios, and said, "I'll drive." She started to back out the door.

"Nice try," Thinnes said. "Just give me the keys."

She stopped and stared at him. Thinnes waited. Finally, she said, "It's signed out to me."

"Go back down and sign it in again, if that's what you're worried about."

She shook her head, and said, "For God's sake!" but handed the keys to him before stalking out.

He looked to see if this latest salvo had been overheard. The sergeant, standing by the coffeepot, shook his head. "Lots of luck."

. . .

When Thinnes got down to the parking lot, he couldn't see the Dominick's store across the street to the north, or Western Avenue to the east. He found Franchi checking the car out—something everyone was supposed to do at each end of the shift to ensure no one had left any contraband or damage. Thinnes usually didn't bother unless he'd had to transport a prisoner. Or some jerk like Ferris had used the car last. Thinnes didn't razz Franchi about wasting time, though—the car was signed out to her. He also didn't help. When she finished—she'd even looked underneath—she got in the passenger side and sat staring out the side window. She didn't say anything until they'd turned onto Clybourn and stopped for the light at Damen. Disembodied headlights opened like yellow eyes in the gray face of the fog. Parkway trees and other nearby objects that normally receded into the background of his attention stood out against a backdrop of mist.

Franchi turned to him and gestured toward the steering wheel. "Is this some macho thing with you, or are you just a control freak?"

"I do the driving." He kept facing ahead, but he could see her roll her eyes and look back out the window. He said, "What have you got on this rape?"

She gave him a what's-with-you? look. "Hel-*lo. It's a murder.*"

"What have you got on this murder?" It took everything he had to keep his voice even.

The effort paid off. Franchi answered matter-of-factly, "The MO's the same as the bastard who nailed Lake, only this time he went all the way." She waited—maybe for something from him, then went on. "Beat coppers found her just before the end of shift—too late. We've got a tentative ID because she was reported missing two days ago, and she's wearing the clothes she disappeared in."

That seemed to be the gist.

They traveled in silence for the next few blocks.

. . .

The alley was between Kenmore and Seminary, just south of Dickens. Even in the clean, tree-lined streets of Lincoln Park, the damp air carried odors. Thinnes could smell the blood before he saw it. The victim lay in a pool of it, where the beat coppers had found her. Bloody shoe prints marked the path one of them had taken back to his car after checking for life signs. The car was still parked across the alley mouth.

At first glance, the woman had just been dumped. But as he studied the scene, Thinnes got the impression of careful staging. She lay in a semiprone position on her left side in the bloody puddle. Her left hand and right leg were stretched out. Next to her lay the broken bottle used to cut her—Thinnes was sure, though the damage was hidden underneath. The side of her face that showed was relatively undamaged. Her hair fanned out behind her head as if blown by the wind, but there wasn't any wind. Only fog.

Apart from the bloody shoe prints, the scene was undisturbed. The beat cops stood with their sergeant behind the yellow tape, waiting for instructions.

In all his years on the job, Thinnes had come across quite a few rapists and killers, offenders who'd kill without a thought, who'd sell their own kids. But none who'd made artwork of his crime scene. None like this guy. This was the kind Dirty Harry stalked in the movies and blew to perdition just before the final credits. This killer would fire up the press like no one since John Wayne Gacy's crawl space came to light.

Two dark-haired women victimized in the same way on consecutive Mondays was too sensational a coincidence. Thinnes didn't believe in coincidence, which was why he told the sergeant, "I'm calling the heavy artillery in on this one. And I'll use a pay phone so we don't have cell-phone skiers or scanner surfers selling this to the media. But stand by in case the ETs need reinforcements."

The patrol sergeant nodded. "What do we do meanwhile?"

"Just keep everyone out." The sergeant nodded. "I'll be back." Thinnes looked at Franchi. "You coming?"

They got in the car. After he'd turned north on Sheffield, he said, "You read the missing persons report?"

"Monica Nesbit, age twenty, five-six, one hundred ten pounds, blue eyes, black hair. Missing since Friday night."

"What did she do for a living?" He turned left into the alley across from the DePaul parking garage.

"She was a full-time student."

Thinnes turned left again and curbed the car in the NO PARK-ING zone in front of the Schmitt Academic Center on Kenmore. "Here at DePaul?"

Franchi said, "Yes."

He turned off the engine and took the key from the ignition. For a minute they just sat there, watching the students appear and disappear in the fog. Lots of them were small brunette women. Finally he said, "Yeah." He tossed the OFFICIAL POLICE BUSINESS sign on the dash and got out.

Franchi followed him through the double glass doors into an area with small tables and large vending machines. A dozen students sat around studying or visiting while they chowed down on Coke and Ding-Dongs. A university police officer was parked with his *Sun-Times* and coffee at a table within earshot of the pay phone. He followed their progress across the room but lost interest and returned to studying the paper when Thinnes nodded and continued past.

As Thinnes lifted the receiver, Franchi positioned herself between the phone and the campus cop, facing Thinnes.

Good move. The guy had to be curious, and who knew if he'd sell police secrets for his fifteen minutes in front of a mini-cam van.

Thinnes dropped coins in the phone and punched in the number. When he heard, "Area Three Detectives, Jenkins," he said, "Looks like we got a sequel. We need Bendix. And a few more bodies would be nice to help with the canvass. Oh, and let's try to keep this in-house."

As they walked out, Franchi asked, "Is there someone here we should notify?"

"Evanger'll take care of that."

The night-shift dicks had finished canvassing by the time the Major Crime Scene van arrived. Bendix got out with two flunkies, one with a camera. The techs were young and male. Bendix was balding, and as fat and out of shape as Jackie Gleason, but his mind was fit.

"This is Franchi," Thinnes told them.

Bendix leered. "You got a first name, Franchi?"

"Don."

"That short for Donna?"

"Nope."

Bendix looked at Thinnes. If he expected help, he was shit out of luck.

Thinnes had no reason to defend Franchi to anyone, but his feud with Bendix went so far back neither of them remembered how it started. "Body's in there, Bendix," he said, hitching his thumb toward the alley.

He could tell Franchi was pissed about something. Her body language was as unmistakable as a billboard. He felt like telling her, "You're *not* beautiful when you're mad. Get over it." It was probably just as well she was such a bitch, he thought. If she were even halfway nice, she'd be too damned attractive.

She said, "That body had a name! She's a victim, not just some piece of meat!"

"This your first murder, Franchi?" Bendix asked.

"No, of course not."

"You're not gonna last long if you take everything so personal."

"I should be like you guys and not feel anything?"

"Forget it," Thinnes said. He looked at Bendix and hitched his thumb toward the alley.

Thinnes had come on the job when affirmative action was

just starting to make inroads. The female cops he'd worked with—though he'd never partnered with one—worked hard to be one of the boys, putting up with shit so nobody would see them sweat. Those who'd lasted were like Ryan—tough and unfazed.

"Feel whatever you like," he told Franchi. "Just don't get in the way."

"Yes, *sir*!" she said, and walked back toward the car.

Bendix said, "What's eatin' her?"

The guy with the camera offered, "It's Monday. What do you expect?"

Thinnes looked up from studying the corpse. "I think it's gonna be Monday all week for me."

On the way back to the Area, Thinnes stopped at a red light, to the left of an aging black Volvo with a young Hispanic driver. Franchi rolled her window down and leaned out to stare at him. Rocking to a Latin beat that pulsed through the closed car body, the kid was oblivious.

"Tap the horn, would you?" she said.

"Why?"

"*Please!*"

Thinnes complied, then hit it again harder when the kid in the Volvo didn't notice the first time. The kid stopped rocking and rolled his window down.

Franchi leaned out and said, "Your taillight's out."

He gave her a blank look.

"*¿Lo entiende?*"

That he understood; he shook his head.

Franchi repeated what she'd said in Spanish. The kid nodded and waved. "*Sí. Gracias.*"

Thinnes said, "Franchi, why don't you tell him to renew his sticker, while you're at it?"

"Why don't you fuck off!"

She rolled her window back up and stared ahead. He noticed

she didn't point out that the light had changed. He hit the gas. The kid in the Volvo sped up to the next intersection, then peeled off to the right.

Thinnes let up on the accelerator. As he continued along on autopilot, he wondered when he'd stopped telling people that their lights were out.

Maybe about the time he'd stopped believing in God.

NINETEEN

Another Monday morning. Caleb stood at the window of his office staring out at Michigan Avenue and the fog that hid Grant Park beyond. He loved the mystery. When you were prevented from seeing what was beyond the next corner, you were free to imagine an entire universe out there, where familiar terrain faded into regions marked: "Here Be Dragons."

And it was a good metaphor for the way fears and misperceptions obscured a patient's worldview.

The intercom interrupted his reverie. "Doctor, your patient is here."

Caleb turned from the view and went to open the door.

She entered and walked briskly to the chair in front of his desk.

Caleb greeted her as she sat down. "How are you today?"

"Lonely. I can't really trust anyone. It's isolated me."

"You trust me enough to be here."

"A measure of my desperation."

She gave him a wry smile, and he could just glimpse the beauty that might have been. The silence stretched out. For most patients it was uncomfortable. He waited to see how she'd react.

The results of her physical exam had been normal. She was in excellent condition for her age. But he was struck by her lack of affect. She was logical and analytical, but apparently as without feeling as the sociopath who'd raped her.

Sociopath. He preferred the antiquated term, with its pejorative connotations to the more morally ambiguous antisocial personality disorder. It was the victim who was disordered, distorted, damaged. Perhaps—No! Very likely—her attacker had also been victimized, but we are all victims, of our parents or others, of circumstance. Your karma was what you made of it. And Caleb was dealing with *her*.

She said, "I suppose I'm also depressed." He nodded. "This weather makes it worse."

"Low pressure tends to depress some people," he agreed. "Or make them sleepy or irritable."

"A friend of mine told me her therapist says that if you're depressed and can't remember anything, it's because you've repressed it—something too horrible. Do you believe that, Doctor?"

"That's pretty Freudian."

"That doesn't tell me whether *you* believe it, Doctor. What do *you* think of Freud?"

"Freud was very creative, but there's virtually no evidence to support his theories. At best, I'd call his work a series of brilliant metaphors."

"Yes, but what about this repressed memory syndrome?"

"The theory that any unexplained depression is caused by abuse is criminally irresponsible. There's no question some people repress events that are too horrible to live with. But it's rare that people truly can't remember. Usually they make a conscious decision to not think about it."

"Not I *can't* remember, just I don't think about it?"

"Precisely."

"I've been having trouble, lately, not thinking about it."

"Why now?"

She'd answered the question before, but psychiatrists, like other types of detectives, built their cases on discrepancies.

"The news, I think. All the unsolved rapes. At least, I think they're unsolved. I read about them. I didn't read anyone was arrested." She got up and went to stare out the window as he had. The mist-softened sun was a shiny dime on the flat counter of fog. She turned her back to it. "I thought if I could just understand *why*, it would help somehow. So I studied rape. It made it worse. I just ended up filling my head with images of atrocities—things I couldn't have imagined human beings doing or surviving." She crossed her arms over her chest. "I learned a few things, but the real why still escapes me. How does destroying a perfect stranger make up for something someone else did to you?"

How indeed, Caleb thought. He said, "What do you think?"

"I think it's crazy. I tried that serenity prayer. You know— God grant me the serenity to accept the things I can't change, the courage to change the things I can, and the wisdom to know the difference?

"But how do I know what I have to accept? What I can change? God didn't help me when I was being attacked. Neither did the police. Or the neighbors, for that matter."

TWENTY

Acting Detective Commander Evanger had been at Area Six before the reorganization that turned it into Area Three. He'd been a good detective before he made lieutenant. He was even better as detective commander because he was good at politics and knew where the bodies were buried. With Franchi in tow, Thinnes tracked him to the Area Three Case Management office. He was watching out the window as a District tactical team with a drug dog tore a car apart in the parking lot below the window. Evanger was a light-skinned black, a fifteen-year veteran of the Department, well educated, ambitious, and smart. He turned away from the window, welcomed Franchi aboard, and told them to sit down. Then he turned to Thinnes.

"Report."

"Our serial rapist just crossed the line." Thinnes summarized what they had so far—practically nothing—and told Evanger his hunch. "This guy is too slick to be the disorganized offender he wants us to be looking for. He's chosen the circumstances too carefully—fog and apparently deserted alleys. But he didn't do the rapes there. He didn't leave a trace. Nobody heard anything. Nobody saw anyone suspicious in the area. The clincher's the physical similarities. The victims could've been sisters."

Franchi sat on the edge of her chair listening, not interrupting or arguing, but quietly fidgeting.

"What do you think, Detective Franchi?" Evanger asked.

Thinnes would've bet she was dying to get away for a smoke.

"It's as good a theory as any." She glanced at Thinnes, then asked Evanger, "What do *you* think?"

Evanger usually trusted Thinnes's hunches, but his face gave nothing away as he said, "Extrapolating quite a bit from just two cases, don't you think?"

Thinnes shook his head. "I'm betting two of the unsolved rapes we had in May were the same guy—same victim type, same MO."

Evanger said, "We're not going to start a panic by talking to the media about this."

"What about our duty to warn women that they're in danger?" Franchi demanded.

"Any woman over age 12, who's got an IQ above seventy, knows she's always in some danger in this city," Evanger said.

She scowled at him, then glared at Thinnes, who shrugged. "Sorry, but I think he's right."

"We'll see," Evanger said. "Keep me posted."

Franchi stood up—too fast—and started toward the door. Thinnes got up more slowly, and asked Evanger, "How was your conference?" at the same time Franchi said, "Excuse me."

Both men nodded, then watched her leave the room.

"It was all right," Evanger said, finally. He looked sharply at Thinnes, and said, "Spit it out."

"I'd like to work with someone else."

"Why?"

"She's a merit appointee."

"You sure of that?"

"That's the word."

Evanger shrugged. "So was Crowne. You didn't have a problem working with him."

"She's got an attitude."

Evanger shook his head. "She refusing to follow your orders?"

"No."

"Well someone at Eleventh and State seems to think she's got potential, so we're going to give her a shot. But Lieutenant Rossi said he thinks Franchi still needs some guidance and that you're the one best qualified to train her. I'm inclined to agree."

"Does that mean I get FTO pay?" Instructor's pay.

Evanger gave him a look he knew meant "Don't be funny." He said, "Keep me posted."

The victim's parents lived on Fremont, south of Webster. Lincoln Park. You had to have money to live there. The house was brick, faced with limestone, with carved stone railings and pillars supporting a porch roof that served as a second-floor deck. In another part of the city, it would have been divided into apartments.

There weren't any parking spaces in the block, but lots of half spaces left by inconsiderate drivers. Thinnes double-parked next to one and got out without a word to Franchi—they hadn't spoken since leaving the Area. There was nothing to say. They'd gotten into the habit of silence. It was uncomfortable but better than fighting.

As Franchi followed him up the steps, he noticed the security-company logo. You needed security when you lived in Lincoln Park, though it hadn't helped the Nesbits.

He knocked on the door. It was opened by a white male wearing a Bulls jacket, jeans, and Nikes. The man was big, with thick, curly, graying hair. His blue eyes were bracketed by crow's feet and softened by rimless glasses. He had a NOW button on his jacket lapel, and Thinnes was startled to see a Roman collar below his curly beard.

"Who are you?" Thinnes demanded.

"I'm Father Cannon." His voice was deep and cheerful. "Don."

Coincidence, Thinnes thought. What were the odds of meeting two Dons in two weeks? Behind him, Franchi didn't give any sign that the priest's name or outfit were surprising.

"Come in," Cannon said. When they did, he held his hand toward Thinnes. "I'm part of the rape crisis team."

Thinnes shook the hand. "Father."

"In" was a room that looked like an ad from a high-end

furniture store, with Tiffany-style lamps on maple end tables and a white leather sofa. The woman sitting on the couch was thin and blond and looked a lot like Goldie Hawn, one of Rhonda's favorite actors.

Franchi stepped forward to shake hands with the priest, then stepped back, and Cannon introduced the blond woman as Linda Seeger, Monica Nesbit's best friend and roommate. Seeger was dry-eyed but looked shell-shocked.

"Linda's also a member of the rape crisis team," the priest said. "Ironic, isn't it?"

"Unlucky, more like," Thinnes said. "That's something Detective Franchi and I will have to talk to you about later. Did you know Ms. Nesbit well?"

Cannon shook his head.

"Will you excuse us?"

"Certainly." Cannon left the room, closing the door behind him.

"Maybe we should sit," Franchi said.

Seeger nodded and settled back on the sofa. Thinnes took the chair opposite, Franchi a chair at right angles. She got out her notebook and pen. Good. She was getting trained.

Seeger's story was almost identical to that of Katherine Lake's roommate. Nesbit had disappeared without notice and had been gone an unknown period of time before her friend missed her and reported her absence. The only real difference in the two cases was that Nesbit had left a message on Seeger's answering machine saying she was at a bar, and, if she got lucky, she wouldn't be home for the night. As a result, Seeger hadn't been worried until Nesbit didn't show the following evening. Then, of course, Missing Persons couldn't do much. Nesbit had gone off on her own accord and, apart from her absence, there was no evidence of foul play. By the time her name and description were circulated, the evidence technicians were photographing her remains.

But she hadn't been dead the whole time her whereabouts

were unknown. So the question was, where'd she been in the meantime?

"Could you tell us the bar she called from?" She couldn't. "How 'bout the ones she usually went to?"

"She liked to do Mother's sometimes. She liked to have a good time."

"To party?" Franchi asked.

"Nothing heavy. Nothing more than booze and a little weed."

"What about men?" Thinnes said. "She have a boyfriend?"

"Nobody steady. She had a few friends who were men, but no one special."

"Any who might have thought *she* was special?"

Seeger shook her head. No jealous boyfriends, no stalkers or secret admirers.

When they ran out of questions, they asked her to send back the priest. He wasn't able to add much to what she'd told them. He'd known Monica slightly—she wasn't a regular at Mass. Her parents were members of the parish.

"Where *are* Ms. Nesbit's parents?" Thinnes asked. He'd sent Swann to break the news and ask a family member to make a formal ID, but Swann hadn't gotten back to him yet with the details.

"The police took her father to the morgue to make a formal identification. He didn't want to leave his wife alone—she's upstairs, under sedation—so he asked us to stay until he returns." Cannon looked down and seemed to notice for the first time how he was dressed because he said, "I don't usually make house calls dressed like this, but I was out running errands when the Center called. They wanted someone here when the detectives arrived to break the news."

Thinnes nodded. The usual procedure was to break the news, *then* call for grief support. "How did the Center find out so quickly?"

Franchi answered for him. "You have a very good connection at the Area."

Cannon smiled and nodded. "At the District, actually. Ordinarily, Linda could handle this by herself. Under the circumstances, though, *she* may need some counseling. And of course the Nesbits . . ."

TWENTY-ONE

By the time they finished interviewing Nesbit's parents and returned to the Area, the night shift had rounded up a few more known sex offenders living in Districts Eighteen, Nineteen, and Twenty-three. Rounded them up, interviewed them, and released them.

"A couple of the tac guys nailed a rapist in the act over on Halsted," the assignment officer told Thinnes. "You guys want to see if you like him for either of your cases before we get too far into things?"

Thinnes wondered how Franchi liked being one of the "guys," but he didn't ask her. "Yeah. Where is he?"

"They got him hanging on the wall at Eighteen, but they'll bring him over."

"Thanks."

"Does he have any priors?" Franchi asked.

"Oh yeah."

Half an hour later, Ferris and Ryan watched with Thinnes as the tac cops put Grover Cleveland in the interview room with the two-way mirror. Ryan was wearing a plain-looking suit over a man's dress shirt. Her red-blond hair was pulled back in a ponytail.

By the time Franchi—in her tailored suit and feminine blouse—got back with Cleveland's rap sheet, Thinnes had been watching him for half an hour.

"Busy boy," Franchi said.

Thinnes nodded. "How 'bout you go in there and ask if he needs anything to drink or something?"

"How 'bout *you* asking him?"

"Then I won't be able to see how he reacts to women."

Franchi gave him a dubious look but handed him her purse. "Keep an eye on my weapon."

She was at the door before he remembered to tell her not to get ambitious. "He hasn't been Mirandized yet, Franchi."

She closed the door behind her and took a position halfway between it and Cleveland, close enough to talk, far enough to step clear if he made a grab for her.

Through the mirror, Thinnes watched his face twitch. "Confusing, isn't she, Cleveland?"

Ryan and Ferris got up from their respective places and came up behind Thinnes to watch.

In the interview room, Cleveland leaned back against the wall, stretching his arms over the back of the built-in bench.

Franchi took a step closer. "Something to drink, Cleveland?"

A sly smile pulled up the corners of Cleveland's mouth. "How 'bout an Old Style?"

"Coke or Sprite? Or you could have coffee."

"How 'bout if I have you?" He lunged forward, like a WWF wrestler, swinging his arms like a gorilla to emphasize his muscles.

Franchi was obviously caught off guard. She jumped backward. "You—"

Cleveland laughed.

Thinnes opened the door, and said, "Franchi."

She came to the door. "What?" He shook his head toward the squad room. "I'll be back," she told Cleveland.

He leered. "I'll be waiting."

As she came through the doorway, Franchi must have noticed her expanded audience because she scowled.

"Ryan," Thinnes said, "what's the first law of detecting?"

"People lie."

"And the second law?"

"Everybody lies."

"Is there a third law?" Ferris asked.

Franchi said, dryly, "Follow the money."

Thinnes nodded and pointed to Ryan. "You try and see what you can get from Mr. Cleveland."

Franchi's scowl deepened, but she didn't say anything.

Ryan said, "Yeah, boss." Before Thinnes could respond, she added, "This guy's a rapist?"

"Caught in the act."

She nodded and took off her jacket, folding it over the back of a nearby chair. She reached under the edge of her shirt and pulled the little .38 she used as a backup weapon out of her waistband. She handed it to Thinnes, who slipped it in his pocket. She pulled off the band holding her ponytail together and fluffed up her hair. She unbuttoned the top buttons of her shirt, tucked the tails into her slacks, and rolled her sleeves to just below her elbows. She grabbed a clipboard and pen from a nearby table. Then she winked and lowered her head 'til her hair fell over her face. Before she pushed through the doorway, she looked back at them, and said, "Wish me luck."

Ferris laughed, and said, "Attaboy, girl. Sic 'em!"

Franchi said nothing, but by her body language she was pissed.

Thinnes turned his attention back to the two-way glass. Ryan had perched on the edge of the interview room's only chair, as far from Grover Cleveland as space permitted. She'd pressed her thighs together modestly, but splayed her feet to either side, pigeon-toed, the way young girls sometimes did. She put her forearms together, elbow to wrist, and rested them on the clipboard on her lap. This squeezed her chest between her upper arms, accentuating her assets. She turned her head slightly when she leaned forward so her hair fell over the left side of her face, and Cleveland was treated to a tantalizing view of cleavage.

When he licked his lips, Thinnes knew she had him.

Ferris guffawed. *"That's* why we don't videotape interrogations."

"Keep it zipped, Ferris," Thinnes said.

Inside the room, Ryan had acquired a Southern accent. "Mr. Cleveland?"

Cleveland nodded.

"My name's Kate, by the way."

"You a cop?"

"Don't I wish. I'm just the one who makes coffee an' straightens things up around here."

"You here to make me coffee?"

"If you like. You seem like a nice enough fella."

"Yeah. Surprise."

"Well, honey. The way Detective Franchi was when she come outta here—She called you a name!"

"She's a bitch!"

Ryan giggled. "Sometimes. But I won't tell her you said so."

"What do you want?"

"Don't be sore. I got a bet with my boss." She made a face. "Detective Thinnes. He bet me fifteen dollars you wouldn't talk to anyone. He said you're a real hard case. That you wouldn't even sign that you understood your rights." She gave him a curious look, as if waiting for him to confirm or deny it.

He did neither.

Ryan went on in her soft Southern drawl. "But even if you had some hard times, you're still a human bein'. And if you *had* done somethin' you shouldn't, I can't see how signin' that you understand your rights could hurt you."

She waited, as if really interested in what he had to say to that.

"You got a point. Gimme that. I'll sign it."

"Oh, hon. I couldn't let you sign this unless I know you had your rights read. I'll just read 'em. Okay?"

He shrugged.

She flipped to the bottom sheet on the clipboard. Thinnes knew that all the sheets were just blank typing paper, but Ryan pretended to read. "It says here, 'You have the right to remain silent . . .'"

She made it sound as if she were reading something unfamiliar, rather than reciting something she could say drunk or in her sleep. When she got to the end she flipped the top pages back in place. "Do you understand these rights I've just read you?" Cleveland nodded.

Without getting up, she scooched her chair across the intervening space and slid it around so she was sitting next to him. With her left hand she put the clipboard on his lap; she rested her right on his forearm. Cleveland reacted like a machine that's just had the power turned on. His eyes widened, and he suddenly seemed more alert. His tongue darted to the corner of his mouth.

Then he looked at the clipboard, and said, "This is blank."

"Yeah, I know. Would you believe they don't have forms for that here? They got forms for everything on Earth that you could think of—even ordering more TP for the ladies' room." She shook her head. "Dumb." Then she brightened. "You could just write, 'I was read my rights and I understand them,' and sign it."

He looked doubtful, but he took the pen she offered him and wrote with it. When he stopped, Ryan beamed. "You just made me fifteen dollars. Could I buy you a Coke or somethin'? Or a Pepsi?"

He licked his lips. "A Pepsi'd be nice."

Outside of the room, Thinnes pulled out his wallet and took out three dollar bills. "Ferris, go tell Columbo we need him. Then run down and get two Pepsis and an iced tea."

"Why can't Franchi—?"

"I need her to play bad cop."

Ferris shook his head but went.

Franchi said, "Do you think he's really dumb enough to fall for that?"

"We'll see."

The interview room door opened. Ryan came out and closed it and leaned against it. Her bright mood vanished. She pointed at Thinnes, and said, "You owe me fifteen bucks."

Thinnes took fifteen dollars out of his wallet and handed it to her. "You should have made it twenty."

"I only bet that much on a sure thing." She folded the bills and put them in the front pocket of her shirt, where Cleveland wouldn't miss them. "I'm gonna check the plumbing. Then I gotta get that asshole a Pepsi."

"It's on its way." Thinnes turned to Franchi. " 'Til she gets back, go stand just inside the door with your arms folded. And don't talk to him."

"Why?"

"You're the bad cop. Makes you look meaner."

It took Ryan just over an hour to get Cleveland to confess to aggravated sexual battery, and to satisfy Thinnes that he hadn't been anywhere near the alley where Monica Nesbit was found. It took an hour and a half to do the paperwork. After Ryan had turned Cleveland over to the guys in the lockup for booking, she said, "I need a shower," and took off in the direction of the female detectives' locker room.

Thinnes started the paperwork on Nesbit's murder.

For a while there was complete quiet in the squad room. Then Ferris said, "The gals have been gone a long time."

Too long, Thinnes decided. He'd better go see why.

The door to the female detectives' locker room was stuck about nine-tenths closed, so without trying, Thinnes could hear everything that was being said—or rather shouted—inside.

". . . of all the sexist crap," Franchi was saying. "How could you?"

"Hey!" Ryan said, "I've been on the job a lot longer than you, so don't get on me about sexism. And if you want to survive here, you better learn to use whatever you got."

Thinnes felt a stab of disappointment. He'd always thought of Ryan as just one of the dicks, not an undercover bra-burner.

"Including whoring for a bust?" Thinnes could almost see Franchi spitting the words out.

"That's the pot calling the kettle black!" Ryan's voice had dropped an octave—a sign, Thinnes knew, that she was about to hit a grand slam. "You might be able to intimidate Rossi with that harassment crap, but Thinnes and Evanger have always been straight shooters. There's not a man—or woman—in the Area who won't come to their rescue if you try it here. And I heard this'll be your third strike."

"You *bitch*!"

It sounded to Thinnes like they were about to come to blows. Much as he would've enjoyed watching a catfight, he knew both of them were carrying. He stepped to the door and hit it twice with his fist. "Ryan, Franchi, Evanger wants you!"

The second law of detecting. Or to put a spin on it that would keep him honest, Evanger *would* want them if he knew what they were doing.

As Ryan came storming through the doorway, Thinnes made his face as neutral as he could.

"How much of that did you hear?" she demanded.

"How much of what?"

She gave him a skeptical look and headed for the squad-room door. Thinnes didn't wait for Franchi to come out.

When Ryan came out of Evanger's office, she was frowning. She stalked over and told Thinnes, "Evanger wants to see *you*."

"What's going on?" Evanger asked.

"You ever try to break up a fight by getting in the middle?" Evanger waited. "Ryan and Franchi were getting into it in the locker room. They sounded ready to shoot it out, and I'm not wearing my body armor today, so I just provided a diversion."

"What were they fighting about?"

"Damned if I know." Thinnes shrugged. "Woman things."

TWENTY-TWO

The cops pulled me in for questioning the other day," Deacon said. He was wearing a leather jacket and motorcycle boots. Compensation? He went on, "For no reason except I'm a 'sex offender' now. If I had any idea what it was gonna mean for my future, I'd never have pleaded guilty."

He hadn't been born like this, Caleb thought, and maybe he could change. But the prospect of probing his psyche brought to mind the old caveat, *Whoever fights monsters. . . .*

Deacon scrunched up his face until he looked ready to cry. "It's just so unfair!"

"Do you expect life to be fair?"

"Huh?" Caleb waited. Deacon said, "What kind of question is that?"

"What do you expect to get from therapy, Mr. Deacon?"

"Off probation."

"Fair enough. Tell me about your family."

"Nothin' to tell. Ma's a housewife. My old man works for the railroad."

"In what capacity?"

"He supervises a track maintenance crew."

"How do you feel about him?"

Deacon shrugged. "Okay, I guess."

Caleb decided he would press him for details later. Now he said, "How long have your parents been married?"

"Thirty years."

"Do they get along?"

Deacon shrugged again and shifted in his chair. "Sure." Not true. "They're still together, aren't they?"

"You tell me."

"Yeah. Yeah, sure."

"When they disagree on something, how do they resolve it?"

"They don't."

"Disagree, or resolve their disagreements?"

"Disagree."

"Never?"

"Well . . . My old man wears the pants. He has the last word."

"When your parents argue, do they ever get physical?"

"Naw." Caleb waited. "Once in a while my old man used to pop her one."

"Used to?"

"The neighbors called the cops once. Now he's afraid to hit her."

"Did he ever hit you?"

"What do you mean?" Caleb raised one eyebrow, Deacon said, "Only when I got outta line." This time, Caleb could detect no indication he was lying. Another item to pursue later.

"Who was the disciplinarian in your family?"

"My old man."

"How did your mother deal with you when you needed discipline?"

"She'd always say, 'Wait 'til your old man gets home.' Half the time she wouldn't remember, though."

"Did either of your parents use drugs?"

"Naw, just booze."

"What's your earliest recollection of having been sexually aroused?"

"I dunno. Probably watching something on TV with my dad. He used to let me watch stuff— My ma didn't like it, but he was boss."

Caleb waited, signaled his expectation that there was more

by leaning forward and raising his eyebrow. He let his interest draw out Deacon's answer.

"I remember— I don't know how old I was, but I was in school because I was doing my homework at the kitchen table while Ma made dinner. She was on some kinda tear—banging pots and telling me I'd better not turn out like my old man. He musta been late for dinner again or something. She kept tellin' me if I didn't study hard and do good in school, I'd end up like him. She didn't say a drunk, but I was old enough to figure out that's what she meant.

"Then he came home and she started in on him for being late because he stopped in for a quick one at the Sail—the Sail Inn—on his way home.

"He got real quiet and said to turn off the stove so dinner wouldn't burn 'cause what he wanted was a *real* quick one.

"She looked at me, and I could tell she really didn't like the idea of that—even though I didn't know then what it meant. But he grabbed her arm and held it while he turned off all the burners. Then he told me to go watch TV for a while. I remember being really scared because she was so quiet but—I don't know—scared maybe, and my old man was so excited. I think he was even getting a hard-on. Then he sorta half dragged her into the bedroom and shut and locked the door.

"I just stood there for a long time trying to listen even though I was afraid. Most of what they said was too soft for me to understand, but I heard him say, 'Take it off, or I'll take it off you.' Just like a line from a movie. I couldn't hear if she said anything back. It was quiet for a while, then my old man started yelling, "Oh God! Jesus Christ!"

"When they came out of the room, my ma was wearing a different dress and she was real quiet. But the old man was in a good mood. He even asked me about school while my ma finished making dinner."

"How did you feel about what happened?"

Deacon thought. "Confused, I guess. They didn't talk about

it, but he was happy, and she didn't seem to be."

"Were you frightened?"

Deacon paused, then said, "Yeah, kinda. But it was exciting, too. Kinda like a movie."

TWENTY-THREE

Thinnes attended the autopsy without Franchi. They didn't both need to go, and he had something else for her to do. She didn't give him a hard time about being assigned to a follow-up.

In the PM room, the body lay on a stainless-steel gurney. Under its black-plastic shroud, it seemed very small and shapeless.

The assistant medical examiner, Dr. Cutler, was a thirty-something black man who obviously hadn't resigned himself to the city's level of carnage. As he pulled the plastic back, he said, "I'm looking forward to doing a post on the creep who did this." He meant it.

"Yeah," Thinnes said, "me too."

At first glance, it seemed impossible to tell the dead woman's race. Her clothing had been removed, sent to the crime lab, but she was completely covered with blood. Her face looked like roadkill.

"I have before me the body of a well-developed, well-nourished white female," Cutler began, dictating his observations into a miniature tape recorder. "Who appears to be between twenty and twenty-five years of age."

Thinnes had been to enough autopsies to be able to translate the doctor's description of her injuries into English—a shattered left cheekbone, smashed upper and lower jaws, broken teeth, and numerous bruises and contusions—all on the left side—the offender was right-handed, and jagged tears on her breasts, belly, and groin consistent with cuts from a broken bottle. Like the one found at the scene.

When Cutler had dictated all he had to say, he pocketed the recorder, and said, "Lisa."

A blond woman, who seemed too frail and feminine to be photographing corpses, stepped up to the body with a business-like Nikon.

"Detective Thinnes," Cutler said, "our new photographer, Lisa Littau."

Thinnes gave her a nod and got a brief smile in return. Then she was all business, shooting the body from all sides, climbing a small, mobile ladder to document the damage from above. She handled the camera with the familiar ease of a sharpshooter. When she'd finished, she pushed the ladder out of the way and stepped back.

"We did a rape kit," Cutler told Thinnes, "when she came in, but we'll check with UV in case we missed something." He got out an ultraviolet lamp and used it to examine the body, removing hairs and specks of glass and dirt with tweezers, putting each bit in a separate, small envelope that he handed to Thinnes to label. Thinnes marked each with the victim's name and the RD number and put it in the white-plastic mail tray they were using for a tote. Then Cutler and his helper turned the body over, and the whole process was repeated.

After that, they washed the blood away, so the particulars of the damage could be noted. It took a long time, longer than usual because Littau noticed a faint discoloration on the inside of the left forearm and had to go up to her office for special film to capture it.

After which, they opened the victim's skull and went through another round of descriptions and pictures. The internal damage was massive and probably fatal, consistent with the external trauma. The doctor took samples of vitreous fluid, bone, and tissues Thinnes couldn't identify. Then he went out for a smoke while his assistant replaced the skullcap and stitched the scalp back together. When Cutler came back, he finished the post efficiently.

"Cause of death: blunt force trauma to the head, though she

would certainly have bled out." He pulled off his gloves, tossed them in the trash, and threw his plastic gown in the bin.

Through it all, Lisa Littau had kept shooting with professional detachment. "I'll have copies for you by the time the preliminary report is ready," she told him after Cutler left the room. "I'll give you a call if anything develops from the mark on the arm."

Thinnes wondered if Franchi would have held it together as well.

By the time he'd dropped the evidence tote off at the crime lab and stopped in Little Italy for something to eat, his cell phone was ringing.

"Detective Thinnes, this is Lisa at the morgue. I've found something you might want to see."

The photo lab was on the second floor. Thinnes took the elevator up. Littau was waiting for him in her office doorway. He followed her in, to an orderly desk with neat piles of paperwork and a killer computer setup. When she poked the mouse, the screen saver disappeared, replaced by a life-sized color picture of the dead woman's left forearm.

"This is as close to the natural color as I could get with the film and equipment I had," she said.

"Looks dead-on to me."

She gave him a look that was almost a double take. "Punny!"

He shrugged.

She sat down and typed on the keyboard. Her fingers were small and agile, with short, trim nails. "I tried different exposures and filters until I came up with these."

She showed him three variations of her original shot, in three different colors. Each had darkened markings that were frustratingly close to a decipherable message, but each set was slightly different. After a few more keystrokes the monitor screen split in four, with one of the versions in each quadrant.

"When you combine them and enhance the composite . . ."

She gave the computer another command, and the divided view was replaced by a lifelike reproduction of the arm with an inscription that was clearly a phone number—three digits followed by a hyphen and four more.

"How does that work? Voodoo?"

Her laugh was much too delicate a sound for a computer nerd. "No, physics. Obviously someone tried to remove the number—either the victim or whoever killed her—but whatever it was written in—probably ballpoint ink—changed the light-absorbing properties of the skin."

"Which you caught with your magic film."

She smiled.

"Can I get a print of that?"

She handed him a manila envelope. "Copies of *all* the prints. And Dr. Cutler said to tell you he'd be done with the preliminary report by the end of business. He'll fax it to you."

Back at the Area, Thinnes laid out his case files on the conference-room table and began going over them one by one. There was a notation in the autopsy report about something illegible written on the wrist of a Jane Doe they'd found a month earlier. He grabbed the phone and called the morgue. "You still got that Jane Doe that came in on the third?"

" 'Fraid so."

"How 'bout I have someone come take a few pictures of her?"

"We got those."

"Not like what I need."

"Yeah. Well, if it'll get her ID'd and outta here, sure."

Thinnes called Lisa Littau next and asked her if at her earliest convenience, she could do her photo voodoo on the Jane Doe. "And let me know what develops."

He wasn't even finished going through the Missing Persons files when she called him back.

"I'm sending the pictures over with one of your detectives who's here for an autopsy," she said. "So far it looks like another phone number. The first three digits are 773. I'll keep playing with the negatives. Maybe I can tease something more out of them."

Thinnes said, "Thanks," and hung up. He jotted the numbers in his notebook and looked around.

"Franchi," he said, when she got off the phone, "how are you at puzzles?"

TWENTY-FOUR

They got to the funeral home early. No one was there yet but the Nesbits, Monica's roommate, Linda Seeger, and the priest—in uniform today, a black cassock and Roman collar. The cops hadn't come to pay their respects, though Thinnes noticed that Franchi did. He guessed she was probably Catholic, the guess confirmed when she went up and knelt in front of the closed casket and crossed herself.

Though they hadn't prearranged it, when the mourners started filing in, Franchi mingled while Thinnes stayed in the back trying to be inconspicuous. He noted who signed the guest book. And who didn't. At the funeral and at the cemetery afterward there'd be a cameraman documenting attendance, but there was no decent way to videotape a wake.

Thinnes had been to so many over the years that he sometimes felt like part of the funeral director's staff. Get murdered, and cops were part of the burial package. No extra charge. Unless, of course, you did it.

The firstcomers fit the profile—friends and family. They were mostly older, retired-looking couples and singles, middle-aged women, DePaul students with their books and backpacks. Nobody who looked like a violent rapist. They all dutifully signed the book, then homed in on the parents.

Monica Nesbit had been an only child. Her mother looked shell-shocked and drugged, her father like a fighter on the nine count.

The afternoon dragged into evening. More students came and

left. The retirees went home to supper, replaced as the day shift left jobs and stopped to pay their respects on the way home—teachers from DePaul and administrators, CAPS cops, the Nineteenth District CO. It was a tribute to the Nesbits' standing in church and neighborhood that there was a constant crowd in spite of the turnover. From time to time, the priest led prayers that most of those present joined in on—including Franchi.

By nine o'clock the crowd had thinned, and by nine-thirty, it was as it had been in the beginning—just the priest, the family, and the cops. Father Cannon offered to walk Linda Seeger to her car, and Franchi escorted the parents to theirs. Meanwhile, Thinnes photocopied the guest book on the funeral director's machine.

In the car, on the way back to the Area, Thinnes asked Franchi if she'd learned anything useful. He couldn't blame her for being smug when she said, "Just the names of a few bars Nesbit hit from time to time."

He looked at his watch. "You got anything pressing to do right now?" She shook her head. "Where to?"

According to Fodor's, the famous Chicago bar scene of Rush Street had faded, the action moved north to Division between Clark and State. The action hadn't changed.

Before shipping out to Vietnam, Thinnes had gone drinking on Rush a few times. He and a buddy had done the scene, finding enough bartenders who winked when they asked servicemen for their IDs to get totally wasted.

After Nam, he'd pretty much only visited the area in an official capacity, first as a probationary patrol officer, then as a detective. He hadn't done any drinking. The years or his experiences on the job had stripped the area of whatever attraction it had held. Now it was a two-block mug's game, entertaining only if you liked to watch people get drunk or separated from their money.

Monica Nesbit had been young enough to be fooled by the glitz and desperate to find "Mr. Right."

The bartender at Mother's didn't think she'd been in. But then—he told them—she wasn't a knockout blonde, so maybe he just hadn't noticed. Anyway, she would have been there a week and several thousand patrons ago. Maybe the bouncer would remember.

He didn't. He lit Franchi's cigarette, and asked her, "Did she look anything like you?"

Franchi shrugged and nodded. "Yeah. Well, kinda. My height and build, dark hair—long, though—and brown eyes."

The bouncer shook his head. "No, then. You I'd'a remembered."

Thinnes stepped between them at that point and handed the bouncer his card. "If you do remember anything, give us a call." He took Franchi's elbow and steered her toward the door. "Let's go."

"What was that about?" she asked, when they were back in the car.

"We got two more bars to hit, and I'd like to get home sometime tonight."

She put on her seat belt and sat back in the corner of her seat, watching him thoughtfully.

They remembered Nesbit at the Gin Mill. "But she hasn't been in here for a month," the bartender said. "I told her not to come back."

"How come?"

"The two clowns she was drinking with started a fight. So I told all three of them to get out and stay away."

Thinnes got the doorman to elaborate. "I remember those two—regular drunks. She must've been loaded to be seen with them. She looked like the type that has too much class to give losers like them the time of day. In fact, after Louie threw them out, she asked me to call her a cab."

"You remember what company or where she was going?"

"Some place nearby, I think. And it would be Yellow or Checker. I don't call nobody else."

"Franchi," Thinnes said.

"I know. Follow up on that for you."

"You're catching on."

The bartender who was on duty at McGee's, on Webster, the night Monica Nesbit disappeared was on vacation. The bartender who told them so was too busy to do more than glance at Nesbit's picture and shrug. Come back next week and ask Leo.

"Leo who?" Franchi asked.

"Leo Polo. He's the regular Friday night guy."

"Yeah?" she said. "Tall guy? Really hairy?"

"That's him. You know him."

"My cousin. Tell him Oriana sends her regards."

TWENTY-FIVE

On Friday morning, the parking lot and second floor of the building were lost in fog. Franchi was waiting in the Nineteenth District lobby with the car keys, a radio, and Bendix's techno-geek. She handed Thinnes the keys. Neither of them offered to help the technician with his equipment.

The fog was starting to lift when they left the car under the El tracks, just east of McGee's. Half a block west, the St. Vincent DePaul church was a large white limestone building at the corner of Sheffield, taking up the whole south half of the block. Thinnes didn't know enough about churches or architecture to identify the style, but it was tall, with the old stained-glass windows that showed saints and Bible stories. The inside was huge, but cozy somehow, the old wood pews ranked around a central fountain. Angels—guardian angels, Thinnes figured—flanked the front altar. He and Franchi took positions where they could watch the door while the tech set up in the choir loft with a videocam that worked in near darkness.

By the time the service started, the church was almost full. The Mass for the dead was in English, but the music was in Latin. Thinnes wasn't a classical music fan, but it sounded familiar, and he had to admit it nailed the occasion and fit the big church venue. Franchi said it was from Mozart's *Requiem*.

Father Cannon officiated. Or was it presided? Thinnes didn't know. In his sermon, the priest answered the inevitable question 'Why does God permit evil?' with 'Why do we?' Still, he was an effective speaker.

Thinnes didn't often think of a murder victim as anything more than the central piece in a puzzle he was solving. You couldn't unless you wanted to burn out or go nuts. But the combination of elements—the music that got into your head like a drug, the priest's simple eulogy, and the crowd of friends and sobbing students got to him. He knew Franchi felt it, too. He noticed she kept wiping under her eyes the way Rhonda did when she cried at movies and didn't want to smear her makeup. It wasn't fair or rational, but Thinnes felt like it was Franchi's fault he'd let the situation get to him. It had never happened when he worked with Oster.

By the time the service ended, the fog had thinned to a haze in the distance. They watched the casket load, and when people started heading for their cars, or back to the DePaul campus, Thinnes and Franchi didn't waste time joining the procession. They headed for their car with the tech in tow.

As they traveled North on Sheffield, Franchi reported that no one's behavior at the church had been suspicious. Thinnes cut over to Lake Shore Drive and headed north. When the funeral arrived at Calvary Cemetery on the Evanston border, he planned for them to be in position to observe the gravesite and both entrances.

They were already too late.

The grave had been dug earlier. The area around it, as well as the pile of excavated dirt, was neatly covered with what looked like AstroTurf. The gravediggers had disappeared, leaving the site to the mourners and the mocker: A single red rose lay in the center, where the coffin would rest.

"Shit!" Thinnes said. "I'll bet a week's pay that was our killer."

Franchi said, "No takers."

They left the geek with instructions to videotape the graveside ceremony and went to hunt for the workmen.

. . .

The two Hispanics were in the back room of the little stone office building north of the cemetery's main entrance. Neither spoke any English, but under questioning by Franchi, they admitted they'd seen the man who left the flower.

After they'd finished digging and were putting their tools in the truck, he'd stepped out of the fog.

"What did he look like?" Thinnes said. Franchi translated.

"No se, señor. No pudimos a ver su cara."

"They don't know," Franchi translated. "His face was hidden by a hat with a brim. But they *could* tell he was an Anglo. And he was dressed as a priest."

"We better run a check on Father Cannon," Thinnes said.

"You've got to be kidding!"

"Why don't you call the archdiocese and ask 'em how much they put out last year to defend priests against sex charges? This bastard's smart. He's not gonna make any big mistakes. And we're not gonna catch him on any little ones unless we have everything nailed down. So we're gonna interview every relative, neighbor, coworker, and acquaintance of every victim. And if one of them lives next door to God, we're gonna interview *Him*."

"Her," Franchi said.

"What?"

"If God's a neighbor, we're gonna interview Her."

"Whatever."

TWENTY-SIX

It took the rest of the morning and half the afternoon to canvass the cemetery employees and the businesses around the cemetery. They got takeout from Taco Bell on Western on the way back to the Area. They ate while they started their paperwork. Thinnes took his usual station; Franchi parked herself near the door, halfway across the squad room. The room was nearly deserted and unnaturally quiet. Quiet as Calvary. For the next hour and a half it stayed that way. When Franchi turned in her canvass reports, Thinnes invited her to watch the videos with him.

The window of the room—off the Major Case Crimes office—used for viewing tapes overlooked the north parking lot. While Thinnes loaded the VCR, Franchi took a chair near the window and stared out like a kid stuck in school on a summer day. The clouds had disappeared, and late-afternoon sun stroked the marked and unmarked squad cars. If he hadn't felt even more stuck, Thinnes would have been inclined to commiserate.

The first tape was of the funeral—a pigeon's-eye view. None of the mourners seemed to have noticed the cameraman. One familiar face was Mrs. O'Rourke's, and the guy with her had to be her husband. His alibi for Monica Nesbit's death was perfect if it checked out. Thinnes wrote himself a note to talk to O'Rourke's partner.

Another mourner Thinnes recognized was Lily Henderson, the old woman he'd interviewed after Katherine Lake was attacked. He couldn't identify the man with her. Though the guy didn't seem to be avoiding the camera, his face never showed clearly. Thinnes ran the tape to the end, then rewound it and forwarded to the best shot of Henderson's escort. He printed out a still and scribbled a note on the back for the lab guys asking if they could improve the image.

He and Franchi discussed others who'd been at the wake, the funeral, and both services, particularly the half dozen men between eighteen and forty-five who were unidentified or who hadn't had alibis. He printed stills of all six. It was a process of elimination basically, establishing that the killer either hadn't been at the services or was someone they didn't suspect.

By 5 P.M. Franchi looked as tired as Thinnes felt. She just nodded when he told her, "May as well knock off and start over in the morning." She left while he was packing the tapes and prints to send back to the lab.

He handed the pictures to the sergeant and had him sign the chain of command sheet, then gave him a list of people for the night shift to interview.

It was raining again when he stepped out of the Nineteenth District lobby. On the plus side, he hadn't run into Rossi all day. And the reporters had gone away.

When he came in the next morning, the sergeant handed him a pile of interview reports and phone-message slips. And Franchi, who'd been puttering with the coffeemaker, said, "No rest for the wicked."

He gave her a dubious look, and said, "Yeah," then went to his desk to sort out the calls.

Ferris walked into the squad room and came over to throw his *Sun-Times* on the next desk. He sat and put his feet up, his Starbucks coffee cup down.

Franchi walked over and put a cup of coffee in front of Thinnes. For him. "Don't worry," she said. "It's safe." He tasted it. It was fixed just like he liked it—two sugars, no cream. She must have been studying him. Simple observation, but it gave him the creeps to be on the receiving end. He kept his reaction to himself, though, and just said, "Thanks."

Ferris said, "That's not in your job description, Franchi."

She turned to look at him with a perfectly neutral expression. "I've got a *General Orders*, Ferris." She turned back to Thinnes, and said, "I'm going out for a smoke."

At roll call the sergeant asked how many more bodies Thinnes would need for the shift.

He looked around and said, "Swann and Ryan."

The sergeant nodded and assigned all his nonrape cases to the rest of the squad.

"Let's go in the conference room," Thinnes told his expanded team.

"Be right with you," Ryan said, and headed toward the door.

Franchi didn't say anything, but she had a cigarette in her hand as she followed Ryan out.

Swann said, "I'm gettin' coffee. Want some?"

Thinnes started to feel like he was trying to herd cats.

Twenty minutes later, Thinnes said, "Swann, take a picture of Monica Nesbit around to everyone connected with Katherine Lake. See if you can find any connection."

Swann nodded.

"Start with Mrs. Henderson. She's in the Lake file." Thinnes pointed to one of the five files he'd set out on the conference table while he waited for his team to reassemble. "And find out who she was with at Nesbit's funeral."

Swann said, "Right."

Thinnes turned to the two women, who were standing far enough apart from each other to make him think they might still be on the outs. Too bad if they were.

"Ryan," he said, "how do you feel about going to Madison?"

"Today?"

"Yeah. I think the same guy raped Ivy Jacobs. I doubt she'd open up to a man, but she might be willing to talk to you and Franchi. Why don't the two of you go up and see if she remembers anything."

Ryan gave Franchi a dubious look, and said, "Okay."

Franchi nodded without giving anything away.

After they left, Swann said, "Is that a good idea? They were ready to duke it out last week."

"Ryan's not gonna start anything. And if Franchi does . . ." Thinnes shrugged.

After they left, he walked around to the east side of the conference table, so he was facing the window. He put his five case files side by side and pushed them to the far edge of the table. He took the victim's photos—the before pictures—out of the files and put them below the files. The five women looked enough alike to be mistaken for each other from a distance.

He walked over to the chalkboard and wrote the names down the left side, then underlined the first letter of each name. He wrote the physical descriptions to the right of the names. Next to Lake and Nesbit's names he put the description of their roommates: nearly anorexic blue-eyed blondes. You didn't need a Ph.D. in profiling to see the similarities.

NAME	physical description	age	roommate	primary crime scene	dumped	injuries	misc.
JANE DOE	eyes? brunette	18–22	?	?	yes—alley	beaten raped murdered	writing on body
GRETA HIGHLANDER	brown, brunette	23	?	?	?	beaten raped	
IVY JACOBS	same	21	?	?	?	beaten raped	
KATHERINE LAKE	same	22	thin, blue-eyed blonde	?	yes—alley	beaten raped, cut	
MONICA NESBIT	same	22	thin, blue-eyed blonde	?	yes—alley	beaten raped, cut murdered	writing on body

The pattern reminded him of something. He picked up the phone and dialed Lisa Littau at the morgue. When she came on the line he said, "Lisa, you have any more luck with that Jane Doe?"

"The last digit is an 8, but that's all I think I'm gonna get," she told him.

"Thanks."

His next call was to the Area Three detective assigned to Missing Persons, a man who'd been a detective longer than Thinnes had been a cop. "You got a minute," Thinnes asked.

Kellog didn't get up from his cluttered desk when Thinnes handed him a cup of coffee and the Jane Doe file. Any adult reported missing, absent signs of foul play, eventually got shunted to his attention, so he had a lot of work, a lot of files, a lot of Post-it notes and message slips. There was a chair next to the desk, and Kellog shoved it at Thinnes with his foot. Thinnes sat down.

Kellog put down the coffee, shuffled through the file, and said, "I remember her. Dental records didn't match any of our missing persons, so there wasn't much we could do."

"You check with NCIC?"

"And asked VICAP for a profile." He shrugged. "There were half a dozen missing persons around the country that matched her general description that they didn't have dental records for. But given the damage to our Jane Doe's face, and that the possibles were in different jurisdictions, different parts of the country, there was no practical way to match any of them. Best we could do was narrow the list to a half dozen and wait 'til we got more to go on."

"I didn't see any list in the file."

"That's odd." Kellog sorted through the file again, turning over each piece of paper. "It gets nuts around here. Maybe I never wrote it up. Let me look in my notes and get back to you."

Kellog called back after lunch, by which time Thinnes had reread three of his five files and added details to his chalkboard grid. He jotted down all the names and NCIC numbers as Kellog read them off. None of them rang any bells.

When Thinnes came back from the printer with the NCIC data, the sergeant handed him a message slip. Lisa Littau was sending her latest photos over with the meat wagon crew that had just delivered a DOA. The message slip had "HAPPY HUNTING" in quotes.

Thinnes said, "Thanks," and went back to the conference room. According to the NCIC files, the closest fit came from Iowa, a sixteen-year-old, but Jane Doe's autopsy report said she was eighteen to twenty-two years old.

. . .

Swann came in around 2 P.M. and reported that none of the people they'd interviewed in the Lake case knew Monica Nesbit, but Mrs. Henderson knew her parents and had attended the funeral out of respect for them. The man with her at the funeral was her neighbor, Walter Lennox, who'd been drafted to act as her chauffeur.

"He told me he takes public transportation," Thinnes said. "Maybe you could check with the secretary of state on whether he's got a car. He doesn't have a license."

At 4:30 P.M., Ryan came into the conference room with her coffee mug that said, ONLY ROBINSON CRUSOE HAD EVERYTHING DONE BY FRIDAY. She stood in front of the chalkboard for a while, admiring Thinnes's handiwork. Then she pulled a chair out from the table and sat down, propping her feet on a chair across from her.

"Thought you'd want to hear right away—looks like Jacobs *was* victimized by the same asshole." She hitched a thumb at his diagram. "But it looks like you got that figured out already."

"What did she tell you?"

"She had too much to drink at a bar and passed out—though she doesn't remember having more than two. She woke up in the ER with a broken nose and cheekbone, and fifty stitches in her face, breasts, and abdomen. She'd also been raped."

He nodded. "Where's Franchi?"

"Working out something on her computer."

"You guys made good time."

"Well, with her driving and me navigating—"

"She drove?"

"You never let her drive? She's a good driver." She took a sip of her coffee. "Oh, I forgot. You never let anybody drive." She shook her head as if he were hopeless. "I'll have the report for you in an hour." She got up and started for the door.

Thinnes said, "You got a minute?" She put her mug down and sat. She made a face that said, "This better be good."

"What's your take on Franchi?"

She slouched onto a chair and thought a minute before saying, "Not as green as some of the new dicks we've had. I think she'll be okay if you just cut her a little slack."

"You think I'm being too hard on her?"

"Yeah, I do. And I'm wondering why. Crowne was a merit appointee, and you were never nasty to him."

"Crowne's dead."

Ryan looked at him as if he'd just announced a UFO sighting, and he realized his last statement was pretty far left of left field. He didn't bother trying to backpedal.

"Besides," he said, "Crowne never slept with anyone to get his star."

"Yeah! Right! You're so full of shit your eyes are turning brown!" She picked up her coffee cup and left, letting the door slam behind her on the way out.

TWENTY-SEVEN

Franchi came in fifteen minutes later with a sheaf of papers in her hand. She studied the chalkboard diagram as Ryan had. After a minute she walked over and tapped the notation primary crime scene, and said, "What's with this?"

"Lake wasn't attacked in the alley. Neither was Nesbit."

"You're clairvoyant now?"

"No, but I can read. Look."

He handed her Swann's report on an interview with the woman who lived half a block from the alley where Nesbit was found. The woman had been positive the alley was empty ten minutes before the time they estimated the rape occurred. She'd told Swann she was walking her dog past, and it would have reacted if there was anyone in the alley. It didn't.

"And this," Thinnes said, handing her a second report. "Nesbit was found fifteen minutes later, according to patrol, when a jogger spotted her and started screaming. Three neighbors dialed 9-1-1.

"And check this." He handed her a third report.

Ryan had interviewed an elderly woman who'd heard the jogger's screams and parked herself in her front window across from the alley to watch the goings-on. "She was still there when Ryan rang her bell. She didn't see anyone come or go except the jogger and the cops. There's no way this guy had enough time to go into the alley, rape and beat the victim, and get away without being seen by somebody. He must have done it elsewhere and dumped her."

Franchi nodded thoughtfully, then handed him the papers she'd been holding. She sat two seats down from him at the table.

"What's this?" he said.

"That partial phone number you asked me to follow up on. I looked up all the numbers in the 312 and 773 code areas that contained those digits and eliminated the ones that were NIS or not assigned. Then I ranked them in descending order of proximity to our crime scenes or our victims' residences."

She leaned forward to hand him another sheaf of papers clipped together. "This looks like our best bet."

Her jacket sagged away from her chest, giving him a glimpse of cleavage beneath the open neck of her blouse. Suggestive. She had to know she was doing that.

She said, "According to the owner, the phone went missing a week before Nesbit disappeared, but it wasn't reported stolen for another week."

Thinnes looked at the papers. The top sheet contained a 773 number, as well as the name Rick Meinke, the phone subscriber, his address, and the RD number of the police report on a stolen phone. The next was a copy of the report. The phone had been last seen at the Gin Mill twelve days before Nesbit's murder. The next few sheets were muds, phone company listings of all the numbers called from Meinke's phone for the last six weeks. Franchi hadn't highlighted any of them, though she had noted that one was a phone-sex line.

Thinnes grabbed the Nesbit file and pulled out the muds Franchi had gotten from Ameritech for Nesbit's phone.

"How did you get these so fast?" he demanded. Muds usually took weeks to obtain.

"You sure you want to know?"

"They gonna be admissible?

"Yeah."

He shook his head, then divided the list and handed half to Franchi. "See if Nesbit called that number."

The silence while they studied the lists reminded Thinnes of his cat, Skinner's, quiet excitement when he was ready to pounce on something. Franchi pounced.

"Bingo! Here it is! The night she disappeared." She looked up at Thinnes. "What now?"

Thinnes tapped the cell-phone ID sheet. "We ask this guy what he was doing while Nesbit was missing." He looked at the paper again. "I've seen this name before."

He reopened the Nesbit file. Inside he had a single-spaced list of the people they'd canvassed or interviewed. Meinke wasn't on it.

But he was on a similar list compiled for the Lake investigation. Thinnes had sent Swann to interview the guy who'd alibied Terry Deacon. "This'd be too easy," he said.

"What?"

He explained who Meinke was, then said, "Let's get some background on this guy before we bring him in."

Franchi got up, too. "I'll get on it." She pulled the door open, started through the doorway.

"Franchi."

She stopped and turned. "Yeah?"

"Nice work."

Thinnes brought Meinke to the station on the pretext of needing help with something and let him jump to the conclusion that the something had to do with his missing cell phone. By that time, Franchi had assembled enough information to make the interview uncomfortable. Thinnes had to give it to her—she was thorough. But he didn't.

Meinke and Terry Deacon went way back, had grown up together in Rogers Park, went to the same grammar and high schools. They'd gotten arrested together—misdemeanor stuff.

Thinnes put him in one of the Nineteenth District interview rooms and told him to hang tight. Out in the hall he asked Franchi, "You want to be the bad cop again?"

She shrugged.

"You push him," he said. "I'll sympathize. You go out for a smoke. I'll let him cry on my shoulder. Then we'll let him decide if Deacon's a good enough friend to do time for."

She nodded and followed him into the room. There were two chairs. Meinke was sitting in one; Thinnes took the other, pulling it close to the other man. It would have been comfortable if they were friends. For strangers, it was in-your-face proximity. Franchi leaned against the wall, at right angles to them, closer to Meinke. He had to turn his head slightly to face her.

"Tell me about your friend Terry," Thinnes said.

Meinke said, "He's not a bad guy."

"For a rapist," Franchi said.

Meinke turned and glared at her.

"Mr. Meinke came in here of his own accord to help us out." Thinnes tried to look annoyed. "You don't have to insult his friend."

"You know what they say about birds of a feather?" Franchi said. "If Meinke is Deacon's friend, what does that make him?" She sounded really disgusted. Maybe she was.

Thinnes answered her question with a look he hoped Meinke would interpret as "Oh, come on!"

Meinke looked from Franchi to Thinnes. "Terry just got a little rough with that broad. He's *not* a rapist."

"That's what he told you?" Franchi demanded.

"That's what I *know*." He twisted in his seat to face her. "I *know* Terry."

Reaching into her purse, she pulled out a cigarette. One of the facts Franchi had unearthed about him was that he smoked a pack a day.

His eyes followed her hand, lingered on the coffin nail. Right about now he was probably dying for a drag.

Franchi told him, "I'll bet you know what he *did*, *too*."

She tapped the smoke on her purse, holding his attention with it, while she gave Thinnes a questioning look. Thinnes nodded. She stood up and stalked out.

After a minute, Thinnes said, "Sorry about that."

"What's her problem?"

Thinnes shrugged. "You know. Broads. In this business they think they gotta be tougher than men. You're lucky. You don't have to work with her."

"Yeah," Meinke said. He seemed to be thinking about something besides what Thinnes was saying.

Thinnes waited.

"What is it you really want with me?"

"We got orders to find out where you were a week ago Friday night."

Meinke's relief was instantaneous and unrehearsed. "I was at the Gin Mill. I made— Listen, if this is going to get me in trouble . . ."

"You made a little money on the point spread." He could see from Meinke's reaction that that was exactly what happened. It would be easy enough to corroborate. "I don't care about that."

"Yeah. That's exactly what happened."

"Was Terry with you?"

"Yeah."

"All evening?"

"Yeah."

"He didn't go out for a while and come back?"

"Nah. He passed out for a while, but we just sat him in a corner 'til he sobered up."

"When was that?"

"Last call."

"Then what?"

"We went back to my place and crashed."

"Did he go anywhere else during the night?"

"It was morning by then. Just into the can. He spent a lot of time puking his guts out."

Thinnes nodded as if he'd known all of it all along and just wanted confirmation. "You want to tell me about the cell phone now?"

"I told Terry we'd never get away with it."

"How about you just set the record straight? Maybe we can amend your statement so you don't get hit with filing a false police report."

Meinke sighed. "I told the police it got stolen a week earlier than it did. So I wouldn't have to pay for all Terry's sex-phone calls."

"So it wasn't really stolen."

"No. It was. Only it was stolen the night Terry got shit-faced. He must have put it down, and someone noticed he was too drunk to know what he was doing. I didn't miss it for a week. I thought Terry had it. He thought I'd taken it back. When we finally compared notes, I figured I'd better report it stolen or I'd get saddled with any calls made by the asshole who took it. That's when Terry got the idea to say it was stolen a week earlier."

"So what happens now?"

"You'll have to sign a statement. And give me the names of people who can corroborate your story. Someone besides Terry."

Before he started the paperwork, Thinnes asked Franchi to get Ryan and go pick Terry Deacon up. By the time he got through talking to Felony Review and processing Meinke's statement, Deacon had been cooling his heels in the Area Three interview room for an hour. Thinnes sent Meinke on his way and headed upstairs.

Franchi was pacing in front of the interview room. She stopped when Thinnes came in.

"Ryan go home?" he asked.

"As soon as we got back. Rossi wouldn't authorize any more overtime."

"You got to stay because you're lower on the pay scale than she is?"

"I'm off the clock. I just wanted to see what this worm had to say for himself."

"If you're here, you're getting paid for it. And anyway,

Rossi's got no say in it. Evanger said to finish this thing." He looked around the room. "Where *is* Evanger?"

She shrugged. "At this hour, probably home."

"What did you tell this guy?"

"Nothing. Just that you wanted to talk to him."

Thinnes nodded and went into the room.

Deacon was sitting on the bench, in his work clothes—a T-shirt, painter's coveralls, and paint-splattered athletic shoes. He stood up. "This is harassment!"

"No, Mr. Deacon. It's a condition of your probation."

"Fuckin' A!"

"Sit down."

He sat. He said, "I don't know anything."

"About what?"

"About anything."

"Do you know where you were the Friday night before last?"

Deacon seemed to relax. "With a bunch of my friends, watching the game."

"Your friends are prepared to swear to that in court?"

"They're not prepared for anything." He grinned as if he thought he'd said something clever. "But you ask em. They'll tell you. The bartender, too."

Judging by his nervousness, and because his story agreed with Meinke's, Thinnes believed they would. He said, "That's not what I wanted to talk to you about."

Deacon tensed. "What, then?"

"Tell me about Rick's cell phone."

Deacon squirmed. "It was stolen."

"When?"

There was a long pause while Deacon considered his options. Thinnes weighted the decision in the direction of the truth by saying, "I'll give you a hint. Your buddy's already come clean and amended his police report."

Deacon looked like he'd just been gutshot. "Oh, shit. Shit! Shit! Shit! What can I say?"

"The truth if it's not too foreign a concept."

"Look, I don't know what he told you, but the phone was stolen, just not when he said." Thinnes waited, let Deacon's own worry prod him for details. Eventually, with a few words of encouragement—"Yeah, I could see that"; "That makes sense"; "Most guys could relate to that"—Deacon told him the truth.

"I'm trying to stay away from broads, you know, stay out of trouble. But I got this sex jones . . . I'm getting help for it, seeing a shrink. It just didn't take yet. But I'm trying. It's just sometimes I get so horny I can't take it. So sometimes I call one of those numbers—you know—"

Unable to admit verbally to jacking off, he made a cylinder of his right fist and jerked it forward and back to pantomime what he meant. "Just for a little relief. You know?"

"Go on."

"It's just that they charge so damn much. And I racked up a couple hours on Rick's phone before I even knew it. So when it got stolen, I thought what the hell, let the thief take the blame. Rick wasn't gonna argue."

Thinnes took out his notebook and pen and handed them to Deacon. "I need the name and address of everyone who was in the Gin Mill the night the phone was stolen."

Deacon took them. "Yeah, sure."

It took him about fifteen minutes to write down everything he could remember, which wasn't much. About halfway through the list he admitted to having been shit-faced. When he handed back the notebook, he said, "Denny was tending bar that night. I don't know his last name."

Thinnes nodded. "If this doesn't check out, you'll be hearing from me."

"That mean I can go?"

"Yeah. Get out of here."

Franchi was scowling when Thinnes came out of the interview room.

Thinnes said, "What?"

"You let that rapist walk."

"He hasn't raped anyone lately that I know of. If you want to do all the paperwork just to nail him for ripping off a phone-sex provider, go right ahead. I'm going home."

TWENTY-EIGHT

Louis A. Weiss Memorial Hospital was located on Marine Drive, in Uptown, which was still one of the armpits of the city to Thinnes's way of thinking. The hospital was shabbier and more congested than Illinois Masonic—like the neighborhood it was located in.

Thinnes had been paged at home, and was at the entrance, congratulating himself on getting to work a case without Franchi, when she caught up with him. "What've we got?" she asked, as if they'd been partners for years.

He shrugged. "Rape complaint. Battery for sure." He got close enough to the door to trip the sensor, and it slid open.

"For sure? What does that mean?"

"It means the patrol officers who got the call could only confirm the woman was beaten. She hadn't been seen by a doctor when they called it in."

"You pig!" Franchi's voice was low enough so only he could hear—he said/she said if he beefed her. No independent witnesses. "If she said she was raped, she was raped!"

He shrugged. "Yeah. Right."

He thought he heard her mutter, "Asshole," as he walked through the doorway. He didn't stop to ask her to repeat it.

Inside, there were two beat coppers holding up a wall, sucking down machine coffee, shooting the breeze with a good-looking, young black nurse. The cops were black and Hispanic. The black cop noticed Thinnes and Franchi and tapped his partner with the back of his hand. He nodded toward the detectives.

The Hispanic—obviously the rookie—pushed off the wall and tossed his coffee in a nearby can. He pulled a notebook out of his pocket as he approached them. "Detectives."

Thinnes nodded. "What've you got?"

"Female. White. Kristen Berkeley. Came running out of an alley screaming she'd just been raped. She said he did her, then beat her 'til she passed out. When she came to, she flagged us down. We got a flash out on the guy."

"You got a description?"

"Yeah. Male black, medium height, medium build, medium complexion. Bald."

"Sort of a generic black offender?" Franchi asked.

"Yeah." The rookie grinned sheepishly.

"You getting all this, Franchi?" Thinnes said.

"What am I, your secretary?"

"No. You're the junior *dick*."

She scowled, but repeated what the cop said verbatim.

He wondered how she did it. He said, "Good," then asked the cop, "How 'bout the victim?"

"She's in there." The rookie hitched his thumb toward the interior of the ER.

Thinnes stifled the urge to be sarcastic. "What does she *look* like?"

"Not bad."

Behind his partner, the veteran grinned.

The rookie caught Franchi's expression and reddened, dropping his eyes to his notebook. "Ah, white—I already told you that. Blond, hazel eyes, five-seven, 130 pounds. Says she's twenty-eight."

"Is she?"

He shrugged. "She looks older to me but . . ." He glanced at Franchi. "What do I know about women?"

The veteran grinned. "He's learnin'. She's forty if she's a day."

"What was she doing before the attack?"

"Said she was waiting for a bus."

132

"What about the alley? You call for evidence?"

"Not yet. We got a car securing it. Sergeant said to let the detectives make the call—in case it looks like your Lincoln Park Loony."

Thinnes nodded. "Ask them to send an evidence tech. Then you guys can go back to work." To Franchi, he said, "Let's go hear what the victim has to say."

The bruises looked new. There were judges in domestic court who swore they could tell to the minute how long ago a bruise had been inflicted. But they saw a monotonous variety of victims. Thinnes usually just saw the ones whose attackers went too far, and he could only say recently. Franchi didn't say anything.

Kristen Berkeley was dressed in a standard-issue hospital gown, with one flap of the open-backed gown pulled around and tucked under her arm to keep it shut. She sat sideways on the gurney with her feet dangling, toenails painted red. She looked as described by the rookie cop. If she was twenty-eight, she'd led a *very* hard life. She had the beginnings of a dandy shiner, a nasty scrape on her right cheekbone, and a split lower lip. The right side of her mouth was swollen. She wasn't a natural blonde, but her roots weren't a whole lot darker than the rest of her hair.

Thinnes could see bruises on her arms, no track marks. She had her hands nestled in her lap, her legs slightly apart, and she was swinging her feet like a bored kid. The last rape victim he'd interviewed had had trouble looking at him and had sat hugging herself tightly with her legs clamped together and her feet tucked under her chair.

When they got close enough to Berkeley for a private conversation, Thinnes introduced himself and Franchi, then asked what happened.

"I told the cops who brought me here," Berkeley said.

He nodded. "We have to hear it, too."

She sighed—more like it was an inconvenience than a trau-

133

matic rerun—and repeated almost word for word what the rookie cop had told them.

Thinnes said, "Think you could recognize him again? Do you feel up to coming to the station to look at some pictures?"

"Oh, I didn't see his face. It was too dark. He grabbed me from behind and dragged me— The alley was really dark."

He nodded and glanced at Franchi. Was she getting this? Her face gave no sign. He wondered if she was still too pissed off to think about what Berkeley was saying. "What *could* you see, Miss Berkeley?"

"Ah, almost nothing."

"Did he say anything to you?"

"Yeah. 'Take off your clothes and spread your legs.' I told him, 'Go to hell.' That's when he hit me."

She seemed to be finished, so Thinnes said, "Then what happened?"

"What do you mean, what happened? He raped me!" Thinnes waited. "He forced himself between my legs and put his thing in me."

Thinnes could tell Franchi was still seething. Trying to keep his voice neutral and his face impassive, he said, "Detective Franchi, maybe you could explain to Miss Berkeley how important the details are if we're ever going to make a case."

Franchi's face softened a little. Maybe that was the secret to getting along with her—let her do the talking. He watched Berkeley as Franchi went over the clinical details, using anatomical descriptions to keep it impersonal. But as she questioned the victim further, he could see she wasn't getting anywhere. The story was the same—no more detail, no discrepancies, no inconsistencies. Berkeley seemed to be reciting a well-rehearsed part.

Thinnes said, "Detective Franchi, could I have a word with you?"

He pointed to the hall. Franchi followed him out and waited, finally saying, "What?"

"What're you pussyfooting around for?"

"You just want to get home and watch the Bulls!"

"Yeah, as a matter of fact. Something wrong with that?"

"The woman was raped!"

"I don't think so. She maybe got cheated by a john, or she's trying to use us to get to her boyfriend, but she wasn't raped. Trust me."

"What are you, God? In God we trust?"

"No, but I'm the primary."

"You think a hooker can't be raped?"

That sounded as if she might be willing to at least consider what he was trying to say.

"No. But most of the time when a hooker cries rape it's a case of theft of services, not sexual assault. And when it's not, it's almost impossible to get anyone to believe her. It's the price she pays for being in that line of work."

"Bullshit!"

Thinnes shrugged and gave up.

Back in the ER, Berkeley was sitting where they'd left her. "Where do you work, Miss Berkeley?" he asked.

"Why do you have to know that?"

"It's possible this wasn't a random crime. Maybe someone where you work or someone you pass on the way to work's been stalking you."

"I never saw him before."

"I thought you said you couldn't see him."

"I did! I didn't— I mean, I didn't see him. I couldn't."

"Doesn't mean he didn't see you."

She shrugged. "I work for an insurance agency, Byron's on Lawrence. But it's a small company. There's no way this creep ever worked there."

"Have you ever been arrested, miss?"

"No! Why?"

"Standard question. We're going to have to have your prints for comparison."

"I get assaulted, and you want to fingerprint me!"

Before they put Berkeley in a cab, they got her reluctant promise to come into Area Three and look at mug shots. "Tomorrow," she said. "I'll call first."

"Want to bet she doesn't show?" Thinnes asked.

"She'll be in," Franchi said. "If I have to pick her up myself." She dragged a set of keys out of her purse and stalked toward the parking lot.

Thinnes pulled out his cell phone as he watched her let herself into a red Corvette. Her bumper sticker said: HARASSING ME ABOUT SMOKING COULD BE HAZARDOUS TO YOUR HEALTH. She started the engine and laid rubber pulling out of the lot.

Inwardly he shrugged. He was pretty well convinced that the rape complaint was just something for Berkeley to hold over a john or her boyfriend. Her blasé reaction to the whole thing, her evasiveness about where she worked, and her indignation at the prospect of being printed weren't credible reactions for a rape victim. Berkeley's use of the word *assault* clinched Thinnes's theory that she was a hooker. Cops and attorneys used the term, and women who'd been in the system. Civilians mostly used *rape*.

He'd met a lot of hookers. Whatever turned women down that path apparently only went one way. Their appetite for the life seemed to be endless. Maybe it had to be. The job didn't pay much, and like professional athletes—another kind of whore come to think of it—career life was limited. And most of them had a jones to support or a lazy, greedy pimp who demanded more even when he didn't need it.

Thinnes had never paid for sex, never even taken it for free when a quid pro quo was offered. And he'd had plenty of offers since coming on the job. Fact was, though, he hadn't really wanted another woman since he met Rhonda. She was his center, his lover, and in the twenty-five years since they'd first made love, she'd never refused him. Most of the few times when they weren't speaking, they'd still made passionate love. And if he *could've* brought himself to break the vow he'd made to be faithful, he knew better than to screw up what they had going.

He punched the number for the Area into his cell phone and asked for the sergeant. When he came on the line, Thinnes told him, "I'll be in shortly to write this one up."

He put the phone away and got out his car keys.

Funny, he'd never thought of Rhonda as being the same species as a hooker before meeting Franchi. He wondered if Franchi had ever put out for money or anything else besides the desire to jump some guy's bones. It wasn't something he could ask—even without her track record.

God, he missed Oster! They hadn't talked much about personal stuff, but if they'd wanted to, they could have.

TWENTY-NINE

Thinnes didn't sleep well. The unsolved cases flashed through his dreams like scenes from bad movies, with subplots about Franchi's hostility projected into them. Or maybe reflected. He was honest enough to admit their inability to get along was more his fault than hers. Admit to himself. He woke without the alarm.

Beside him, Rhonda slept soundly, beautifully. The sleep of the innocent. He rolled toward her and kissed her bare shoulder—the closest point to him. Then he got up.

Traffic was light—one of the advantages of coming in so early. It was only six-thirty when he got to the Area. He didn't have a problem finding parking. He made coffee and spent the next hour looking at mug shots.

Kristen Berkeley hadn't been arrested recently, but she did have a record. For prostitution. So his radar was still okay. He printed out her arrest record. Even if she had been raped—which he still doubted—and they tracked down an offender and made an arrest, given the politics of prosecution it was going to be nearly impossible to bring a case to trial.

Which is what he told Franchi when she came in.

"Look," she said. "I don't care if she's a prostitute. I don't care if she did time for murder. If she was raped, she deserves the same effort on our part as you'd expect for your wife if she were raped." She didn't add, "asshole," but he heard it in her voice.

"So while we waste time on a BS beef, a real rapist is staking out his next victim."

"*You* can't be sure it's not the same man."

"Our killer does brunettes."

"You can't be sure from just two victims."

"Five, but who's counting?"

Looking behind him, Franchi swallowed whatever she was going to say. Thinnes turned around to find Evanger watching. His expression gave away nothing, but Thinnes knew he wasn't happy. Well, fuck it!

Thinnes looked back at Franchi, and said very deliberately, "This is a test, Franchi, to see if you can follow orders. You go pick her up and don't talk to her about anything but the weather. Capische?"

"Perfectly."

Thinnes didn't miss that Evanger was standing in his office doorway when Franchi escorted Berkeley in.

The squad room was busy. Three Property Crimes detectives were working the phones. Viernes was translating something into Spanish for Swann. Ryan was sitting near the coffee machine with her coffee mug and a *Sun-Times.* Thinnes waved Franchi toward the interview room and waited while she escorted Berkeley inside.

Franchi came back out, closed the door, and leaned against it. "I want to do this interview."

"Next time."

Franchi paused, glanced at Ryan, then told Thinnes, "You've been dumping on me since I got here. I'd like to know why. And why you're taking it out on her." She hitched her thumb at the interview-room door.

"You want to beef on me, go ahead," Thinnes said. "Meantime, I'm running this show."

"No!" Evanger was suddenly on top of them, glaring from one to the other. "I'm running the show! And I've heard enough. Get back to work."

Thinnes read fleeting fear, then dismay in Franchi's expression. Then she stared at Evanger. "You're not gonna let *him* question her are you?"

Evanger rolled his eyes. "Why not?"

"He's already made up his mind about her."

"So?"

Franchi just kept staring. Acting 101, lesson two—incredulity.

Evanger shook his head. He looked around the room and said, "Ryan, you busy right now?"

Ryan looked up from her *Sun-Times*. "Depends."

"Go in there and do this interview. The woman claims she was raped and beaten. Franchi believes her; Thinnes thinks it's bogus. You sort it out."

A polite and sympathetic Ryan took only fifteen minutes to get Berkeley to contradict herself, another twenty to get the whole story. As Thinnes had figured, she'd had a falling-out with her pimp. He'd knocked her around, and in the heat of the moment, she'd called the cops. When they arrived, she didn't want to press charges. And she didn't want them to arrest him for domestic violence on the evidence of her battered face, so she'd sent him packing and cooked up the rape story from details she'd read in the paper.

Ryan walked out of the interview room with a smug look on her face, which pissed Franchi off. Ignoring Franchi, Ryan caught Thinnes's eye and pointed back at the conference room. "I'm still on my break. *You* can write all this up."

THIRTY

Someone told me you're gay." She was slightly more animated today, wearing a floor-length cotton dress with a high neck.

Caleb said, "How do you feel about that?"

"Relieved. I think. *Are* you?"

"You can think of me that way if it makes you feel more comfortable."

"It does."

Caleb nodded. "Are you having problems with sex?"

"No problems." When he raised his eyebrows, she added, "No sex. I haven't been able to let a man get close enough." Caleb waited. "I tried masturbating, but I get no pleasure from it. It just reminds me—

"And once I let a woman make love to me." She shrugged. "I'm just not wired that way."

What a joyless existence, Caleb thought. He said, "After you were raped, did you get help? Counseling?"

"No. I didn't want to think about it. And I couldn't stand the thought of being pitied.

"I can't stand myself—what I've become . . ."

Caleb let his silence ask what.

"Short-tempered. Irritable. Rude. I have no patience with anyone who's not as intelligent as I."

"Ever feel sad or depressed?"

"Once in a while. We discussed this before."

Caleb ignored the comment. "Ever feel you can't cope?"

"No. I've reached the point in my life and career where I

know I can deal with whatever comes along. But sometimes I wonder why I should."

"Have trouble sleeping?"

"Not anymore." She didn't elaborate until the silence had stretched painfully long. Finally she said, "I just keep going 'til I'm ready to drop.

"I used to watch TV a lot. Can't anymore. Can't watch *National Geographic,* Holocaust stuff, world news. My consciousness has been raised as high as I can stand."

"How do you fill your time?"

"Work. Mundane activities—cleaning, shopping . . ." She shrugged. *"Where can we live but days?"*

A quote. Philip Larkin. Caleb finished it for her. *"Ah, solving that question Brings the priest and the doctor In their long coats Running over the fields."*

She smiled. A sad smile. "I keep thinking of that old chestnut 'the best revenge is living well.' I just can't seem to pull off the 'well' part."

"Sometimes the best revenge is just living."

"It's *so* hard. I've come to associate rape with sex. Sex is everywhere. They use it to sell vacuum cleaners, for God's sake! And rape is a major theme in half the movies that come out. It's implied in print ads, even on billboards. You'd have to go to a cloister or an Amish community to escape it."

Caleb couldn't argue. Most people didn't notice. If you weren't turned on by that kind of message or victimized by it, you tuned it out along with all the other irrelevant stimuli the modern world threw at you.

She said, "Why *is* that? If the majority of men didn't buy it—at least subconsciously—it wouldn't sell."

"You've heard of *Fear of Flying?*"

"Erica Jong's novel?"

"Yes."

"I read it in a former life."

"Andrea Medea and Kathleen Thompson said, *In our society, the rape fantasy is* normal. For the average man—who

142

wouldn't dream of actually committing rape, rape fantasies are like Erica Jong's *perfect zipless fuck*."

"That's supposed to make it okay? And what about the men who aren't average?"

THIRTY-ONE

Hey, Thinnes, somebody grabbed a rapist in the act down on Clark. Before we get too far into things, you want to see if you like him for any of your open cases?"

"Yeah. Where is he?"

"They got him hanging on the wall over at Eighteen, but they're bringing him over. Along with the good citizens that nailed him. I'll let you know."

The witness was one of those large women, like Camryn Manheim, who manages to be sexy, even glamorous in spite of her generous proportions. She had light brown, shoulder-length hair and perfect makeup—as far as Thinnes could tell. Her clothes were expensive-looking and flattering, her purse and shoes real leather. Sitting with her legs crossed at the ankles, she was fanning herself with the information-for-witnesses sheet—folded into accordion pleats—that the beat cop gave her. Her hand was wrapped in gauze.

Thinnes went into the interview room and introduced himself, then said, "Mind giving me your name and date of birth?"

"Micki—with an 'i'—Hoover. I'm thirty-nine."

"I need your date of birth, Ms. Hoover."

"Who's going to be seeing your report?"

"My supervisor. And the State's Attorney."

"Not the press?"

"No."

Hoover thought about that, then said, "All right. I fibbed. I was born April 17, 1956." Which made her forty.

"You got some ID?"

She sighed and dug an insurance card—for an M. Hoover—out of her purse.

"You don't have a driver's license or state ID?"

"Not with me. I didn't know I was going to be interrogated by the police."

Thinnes shook his head, noted the particulars on the card, and returned it. "So what happened tonight?"

"I told the other officer . . ." The beat copper, obviously.

"Tell me."

Hoover sighed. "My horoscope *said* it would be a trying day." Thinnes waited. "My girlfriend and I were slumming tonight. Just for something different, we thought we'd catch the show at the Baton, at Clark and Halsted. Do you know it?"

"The club that features female impersonators?"

"Very good. Anyway, after the show, I'd just put my friend in a cab—she lives in Printer's Row; I'm in Lakeview. So I was trying to get a cab for myself. And just as one pulled up, I heard a woman scream in the alley beside the theater. I told the driver to call nine-one-one and ran to see who was being murdered. The poor girl was lying in the alley with that—bastard!—on top of her, raping her.

"I was so angry, I didn't think—just pulled him off and punched him. That's how I got this." Hoover held up the gauze-wrapped hand. "I told him if he moved a hair, he'd be singing soprano in the choir.

"And he must've believed me, because he didn't budge until the policemen carted him away."

"And then?" Thinnes said.

"Then I helped the young lady cover herself up. And I held her hand until the ambulance came. The rest, as they say, is a matter of public record."

The story jibed with what the beat cop had told Thinnes, and with the preliminary statement by the cabby. Still, there was something a little off.

"We're having your statement typed up," Thinnes said. "When you've signed it, we'll have an officer drive you home."

"Is that really necessary, written statements and all?"

"Standard procedure. Sometimes these things don't go to trial for months. We don't want to have the case thrown out because a witness forgot some incriminating detail."

"I see. But I don't see why you need my testimony. You've got the victim's and the cab driver's."

"At this point, you're our best witness. The suspect's lawyer'll no doubt try to make a case that the victim consented. And the cab driver's Pakistani. He doesn't even speak English real well."

Hoover nodded sideways, almost like a shake of her head, but she didn't argue.

"We appreciate your cooperation," Thinnes said. "Plenty of people wouldn't even have dialed nine-one-one."

The suspect took one look at Thinnes and demanded a lawyer. So Thinnes backed out of the interview room, leaving him hanging on the wall, and sent Franchi to check Hoover's story. Meanwhile, Thinnes started on the paperwork. Franchi—for once—didn't give him any lip.

"I hate to admit it, Thinnes," Franchi said, late the next morning, "but you were right about Hoover not telling us everything."

"Like what?"

"Like she's a *he*."

"A female impersonator?"

"More like your garden-variety transvestite. Micki's short for Michael. He's a producer for Wellworn Favorites Recording Company. And he fills a suit out nicely. I got to see him in his work clothes."

"A real versatile guy."

"Apparently. But everybody I talked to seemed to think he was a regular Joe."

"They know about his extracurricular activities?"

"Nobody said anything."

"Did you find out anything else about him?"

"Just that he contributed his fair share to the United Fund, remembers his secretary on Sweetest Day, and buys Girl Scout cookies, Boy Scout popcorn, and Varsity candy bars."

"You check on his girlfriend?"

"*She*'s a real girl. I interviewed her. She swore me to secrecy before admitting that she knows about Michael's *hobby*. She said she's known him for years and he's a real teddy bear. And she's prepared to swear—if she has to—that except for his fondness for women's clothing, he's completely normal—normal equipment *and* urges."

"Humpf," Thinnes said. "Why don't you run them both through the secretary of state and check with LEADS and NCIC. If they're clean, we'll just file our reports and let the States Attorney figure out how to dress Micki for the witness stand."

"Oh, Lord! Do we have to tell Rossi?"

"You're catching on." Thinnes could imagine the fallout—not to mention twenty-five-year-old J. Edgar jokes if Rossi found out. "The best way to hide something from Rossi," he said, "is to bury it in a report. I swear he never reads them. If he wants to know something, he asks for a summary. But just make sure it's neat—no typos or erasures."

"*You're* gonna write this report," Franchi said.

"I can do that."

147

THIRTY-TWO

Evanger was in by the time Thinnes finished his report, so he decided to give the lieutenant a heads-up on Micki Hoover. Evanger was in uniform—white shirt and dress blues. Probably going to have a TV interview or photo-op. Better him than me, Thinnes decided. There was a new picture of the family on the desk. Evanger's wife was a knockout, and their daughter favored her. It was a measure of how much the other cases were getting to Thinnes that he thought, Lucky they're black. Lucky they didn't live in Lincoln Park. Lucky they didn't fit the victim profile. *That* was another thing he hated about rape. It wasn't personal like murder. The victim usually didn't do anything more specific to provoke it than be there, or say no. It made you feel all women were at risk, not just the victim. *Your* woman. And your friends' wives and daughters. It gave some asshole who didn't have the balls to raise a finger to you a way to get you by the short hairs.

Evanger's take on the Hoover case was "Good job. We'd be in deep shit if you two hadn't picked up on that."

Thinnes grinned. "I doubt the State's Attorney would've caught it—at least not the men. But the asshole's lawyer might."

"You got anything new on the ripper cases?"

"Not yet. The guy's smart enough to make it look like he's a disorganized offender and to not leave anything we can use. If we get him, it'll be as much luck as anything or because he's decompensating."

Evanger was pretty good at playing it close to the vest, but Thinnes could see he wasn't happy to hear that. "I'm authorizing whatever you need in the way of personnel or overtime."

"What I need is a different partner."

Evanger shook his head. "Cut Franchi some slack. She's got a brand-new star."

"And a chip on her shoulder the size of a CTA bus."

"I'm counting on you to convince her it's interfering with her aim."

"Word is she filed sex harassment complaints against two detectives and a sergeant. Just what we need around *here*, a broad with an attitude. What's her problem?"

"Why not ask her?"

"Yeah, right."

"Those complaints were upheld by IAD."

"So now she's a smug broad with an attitude."

"She's a good cop, Thinnes, smart, principled. With a little on-the-job training, she'll be a first-rate dick. Anyway, what're you complaining about? You've just got to work with her. I'm the one that's gotta wonder every time I give her an order whether she's gonna beef on me."

Thinnes debated whether to repeat what he'd heard Ryan tell Franchi about everybody backing Evanger. Instead he said, "It was so much simpler when we didn't have female dicks."

"But it's worse having to supervise 'em," Evanger said. "If you tell 'em they look nice, it's either sexual harassment or a criticism of how they looked yesterday when you didn't say anything. And heaven help you if you point out they're dressed too suggestively or too casually! Either way, you're a sexist pig—either for noticing they're built, or for suggesting they're dogs if they don't look like Sharon Stone on Oscar night."

Thinnes laughed, and said, "Except Ryan." And Rhonda, he thought. Thank God! She'd never pulled any of that shit on him. But then he wasn't her boss. And she wasn't a dick.

THIRTY-THREE

Rhonda made Irish stew for dinner—one of those things you could reheat indefinitely. Rob was gone for the evening, and except for Toby, sitting hopefully by the kitchen door, they were alone. Rhonda didn't seem to mind that he was preoccupied through dinner. Afterward, in bed, when he missed her more subtle cues, she told him, "You'll feel good about yourself later if you make love with me."

He didn't. Much as he adored Rhonda and wanted to please her, he couldn't seem to rise to the occasion. He did everything he knew she liked—except the most obvious—and there was evidence he succeeded partially, but it was more duty than fun. He finally kissed her on the collarbone, and said, "Sorry."

Rhonda sighed and stroked his cheek. "Next time."

He rolled off of her, onto his back, and laced his fingers behind his head. "This case is driving me nuts. Franchi's a pain in the butt and has Evanger on my ass. I've got a murder victim who was a coed at DePaul—no pressure there—and a surviving victim who can't tell me what she knows or even if she remembers anything. And I haven't got a clue about how to question her without making things worse."

Rhonda shifted to face him and put her hand on his chest, twirling a finger through the fur. "Didn't you tell me she's expected to make a complete recovery?"

"Physically."

"Then what's bothering you?"

"What that asshole did to her makes me almost ashamed to be the same sex."

"Just be patient. Explain to her what you need to know and why. Let her help you."

Thinnes shook his head.

"Right now," Rhonda said, "she's feeling terrified, and helpless, and probably stupid. Giving her a chance to help you get the bastard will make her feel more in control."

"How do you know all this?"

She pulled away and rolled on her back.

Thinnes felt his question had put her off somehow, made her back away mentally. He rolled on his side and propped his head on his hand. "What did I say?"

"Nothing."

"Come on, Ronnie, something's bugging you. You really pissed 'cause I couldn't get it up?" It was weird that it would bother her more than him.

"*No*, John."

If it was something else—"*What?*"

"*Nothing!*"

She was lying! He'd seen it in too many suspects in his career to miss the signs and, out of reflex, he shifted sideways, into her personal space, and said, "Cut the crap! I ask you a simple question, and you get all distant on me. If you're pissed at me for something, say so!"

"I'm not mad at you."

Maybe, he thought, but . . . "Then it's got to be something to do with how you know this woman'll recover."

She pushed him away. "I've been there."

"What?"

"*I* was raped."

He felt like he'd been sucker punched. He stared at her and he could tell she'd told him something she hadn't meant to. "When?"

"When you were in Vietnam."

"You never . . ."

"I couldn't. How could I write something like that?"

"Who was it?"

"When he came by the house, I thought he was safe, so I let him in."

"Who!?"

"Mark Ashley."

"Chuck's oldest brother?" Chuck was Rhonda's brother-in-law.

Rhonda nodded.

Mark was dead. Killed in Nam. "You never even hinted . . ."

"I never told anyone. I went to a Planned Parenthood clinic and got a test for VD. And I held my breath until I got my period. When he was killed, I felt that it was justice. Maybe God's punishment. And when you came home safe, I knew I was forgiven."

"For what, for God's sake."

"He told me it was my fault. That if I hadn't wanted it, I wouldn't have let him in when I was alone."

Thinnes grabbed his pillow and punched it across the room. "Fucking A!"

Rhonda rested a hand on his upper arm. "It was twenty-three years ago, John."

"You never told me!"

"I couldn't put that in a letter. You'd have let it eat at you. And what if you didn't come home? It would've been the last thing you remembered."

Thinnes just looked at her.

"When you came home, you were so happy. I couldn't spoil that. I wasn't damaged. So I just forgot it."

"For twenty-three years?!" Thinnes's heart was racing, and he couldn't get his breath. He couldn't think. It was his worst nightmare come to life. "You didn't tell me."

"I didn't think you'd understand." She rolled on her side, turning her back to him.

He felt like he had in the aftermath of a firefight in Nam, and he didn't know why. He felt the way he had when his first partner, Frank, was murdered. He wanted to cry.

He thought about what she'd said. She was right. He didn't understand. His defenses kicked in—he recognized them for what they were. She was still Rhonda, he rationalized, no more damaged than she'd been five minutes ago when they were making love. And it was twenty-three years ago.

He couldn't think of anything to say that wouldn't make things worse, so he said nothing. He shifted on his side and slipped his arms around her. She stiffened. He waited, and she relaxed a little. He took deep, slow breaths and tried to calm his thoughts. It took a long time, but Rhonda finally seemed to be asleep. Thinnes felt everything slowing down. But the last thought he had as he drifted off was *You didn't tell me . . .*

THIRTY-FOUR

Thinnes came awake slowly, aware he was depressed without remembering why. When he did, it hit him like a kick in the crotch. Rhonda's place was empty, and he felt a vague panic. *What if she's left me?* He pushed the thought away and headed for the john.

When he found her in the kitchen twenty minutes later, Bill Withers's song, "Ain't No Sunshine When She's Gone," was pounding in his head. She had the *Sun-Times* spread out on the table and was leafing through it while she sipped her coffee. She looked up and said, "Good morning. Coffee?"

"Yeah. Don't get up. I'll get it."

There was a mug on the counter by the stove and a pot of five-minute oatmeal simmering on the front burner. Next to the coffeemaker were bowls and spoons, a sugar canister, and a half gallon of milk. Thinnes filled the mug, then shifted everything to the table.

Rhonda folded her paper and began to serve. "Do you want something more substantial?" she asked.

"No, thanks. This is fine." He looked around. "Where's Toby?"

"Rob took him to work."

Rob worked in the AV department at school. "Schools've sure changed since we were kids."

Her quiet, "Yeah," told him he'd brought up a sore subject. Twenty-three years ago.

He looked at her, wishing he could think of something clever or even tolerable to say, but Rhonda's no-longer-secret hung in the air between them, and his own accusation echoed in his head: *You didn't tell me.*

When Irene Sleighton announced a Lieutenant Evanger to see him, Caleb ushered him into the inner office, closed the door, and offered him a seat.

Evanger sat in the chair opposite Caleb's desk. Caleb sat behind it, and said, "What can I do for you, Lieutenant?"

"You do marriage counseling?"

"Occasionally."

"I got a couple a dicks squabbling like two cats in a gunny-sack. I'd like you to straighten 'em out for me."

"Why not just let them work with different partners?"

"One of them's a merit appointment that nobody wants to work with, Thinnes is the other. He can make something of her if anyone can."

"Her?"

"Yeah."

"Do you think this animosity is sexually motivated?"

Evanger shrugged. "Maybe. She's drop-dead gorgeous and she's filed sexual harassment complaints. And rumor has it she slept her way into the job. But Thinnes's always seemed okay working with women. I'll let you sort it out."

"Detective Thinnes and I are friends. It wouldn't be appropriate."

Evanger held his hands out in front of him, palms parallel and fingers splayed. "Just talk to them. If you think counseling would help, set them up with someone. Please."

Just before lunch, Caleb was proofreading an evaluation he'd done on a consult when Irene Sleighton rang him to announce,

"A Miss Morgan." He put the report away and crossed his office to the reception-room door.

Linny Morgan, fifteen, was the daughter of his dearest colleague. She was studying the reception-room fish tank as if she'd never seen one before. In the six months since Caleb had last seen her, she'd let her hair grow out and changed it back to its natural auburn color. She was dressed in what Caleb presumed was the latest fashion, showing her developing curves and tidy, bare midriff. She still had rows of earrings down the edges of her ears, and silver rings on every finger. When she noticed Caleb and turned to greet him, he caught the flash of silver at her neck, an ornate Celtic cross.

"Jack!" she said, and ran to throw her arms around him.

With his peripheral vision, he registered Irene Sleighton's shocked reaction. After cautiously returning Linny's embrace, Caleb disengaged himself, and asked, "To what do I owe this visit?"

"I happened to be in the neighborhood and said to myself, 'Self, we've never seen Jack's office. Maybe if we drop by, he'll give us a tour.' "

Her smile reminded Caleb of her mother, a dragon lady as fierce as any crocodile in the swamp. "We?" he said.

"Me, myself, and I. Kinda schizophrenic, don't you think?"

What he thought of was Haley Mills's performance in *The Chalk Garden*, though he doubted Linny was disturbed. "I think you may mean dissociative identity disorder—multiple personality disorder as it's commonly known."

"Whatever." She raised her eyebrows.

"I think it could be arranged." To Irene, he said, "Could you possibly stay a little longer, Mrs. Sleighton?"

"Certainly, Doctor." Her tone conveyed that she understood how inappropriate it would be to leave him unchaperoned with a histrionic minor.

As he held his office door open for Linny, he shot Irene a look he hoped conveyed his appreciation.

. . .

Linny examined the office with the air of a cat taking possession of a new territory. There was an intensity to her movements that suggested fear or excitement. She studied the Jason Rogue lithograph over his desk and read the titles on his bookshelves. After she'd crossed to the window to peer down at Michigan Avenue, he invited her to sit and bare her soul.

She perched on the center of his couch—again like a cat—then settled her purse on the cushion beside her, manipulating the moment by taking her sweet time. Amazing how like her mother she was in certain ways.

Caleb sat in the chair opposite and waited.

"I think my father's gay," she said, finally. Her relaxed posture suggested she wasn't particularly disturbed. It was a test of some kind.

"What leads you to believe that?"

She shot him a look he interpreted as annoyance, then her mood changed and she seemed saddened. "He's gentle. My mother accused him of being a gutless wonder, but he's not. He just . . . not pushy. And since he met *you*, he's been happy."

"Perhaps he's just relieved . . ." Caleb paused to work the phrasing out—the girl's mother was dead after all—"to be out of an unhappy relationship."

She thought about that. "No. It's more than relief. He's gay, isn't he?"

"You'll have to ask him."

"Talk to my father about his sex life? Surely you jest!"

Caleb gave her a look.

She shrugged. "You don't have to tell me. If it's not you, it's someone else. He's in love. I know it. And he never goes out. Except with you."

Caleb waited for her to get to the point.

"Not that I object," she insisted. "I looked up homosexuality on the Internet. It's just a variation of regular sex—only like being double-jointed, or having perfect pitch."

He wondered how many people would appreciate the analogy. "Is that what you came here to tell me?"

"Not exactly."

"What, exactly?"

"Uh. I was almost raped."

He raised his eyebrows and waited.

"There's this guy at school. He's supposed to be one of the 'in' crowd. He's in the drama department, but he's really a jock. Only I didn't know that.

"Anyway, he asks me to go to this party at a friend of his's house in Highland Park. He told me his name, but I forget. I thought it would be way cool because this guy is supposed to be really hot. And he picked me up in a Mercedes convertible!"

"Did you introduce him to your father?"

"As if! I didn't even tell Martin I was going. *He* would've wanted to have a background check on him."

"Go on."

"Well, we drive to Highland Park, to this really high-rent district on the lakefront and pull up in front of a house that makes mine look like a shack."

Linny's house was itself on the lakefront, in Kenilworth, one of the most exclusive suburbs on the North Shore.

"But there's no sign of a party, no other cars on the street. When I point this out, he says, 'Oh, this isn't the party. This is my uncle's place. I forgot I have to pick up some drinks.' He turns off the car and gets out, and says, 'C'mon in.' Well, what do I know. I go inside and take off my coat. He says would I like something to drink, wine, beer, scotch. I thought he was kidding. I say, 'Yeah, right. How 'bout a Coke.' So he brings me a Coke—with booze in it. I ask myself, 'What's wrong with this picture?' Duh!"

Caleb raised an eyebrow.

"I tell him I think he'd better take me home. He says, 'In a little while.' Then he tries to kiss me. I push him away. He tries to put his hand up my skirt. I say 'Don't. This isn't funny. Take me home!' He grabs my wrists and pushes me down on the couch and gets on top of me. "He says, 'You know you want it. You wouldn't be here if you didn't want it!' He holds my hands together over my head with one hand while he starts tearing off my blouse with the other."

Caleb waited. She had a flair for drama and dragged the suspense out until he caught his cue, and said, "But he didn't succeed."

"I hit him with an ashtray. On the side of the head. I got one hand free and felt around for something to hit him with, and I grabbed on to this big old solid glass ashtray. And I just let him have it." She giggled. "That got his attention. I never— My parents never let me fight or anything, so I didn't know how. But I just smashed it into the side of his face, and he let go. He kept calling me a prick-tease and a cunt. I pushed him off, and told him I'd kill him if he touched me again."

"Good for you." Linny looked shocked. "Sometimes it's best to make yourself perfectly clear. What happened then?"

"I got my coat and ran out the door. I didn't wait to see if he'd come after me. I kept running 'til I got near the downtown area. Then I found a phone and called a three-oh-three. My mother always told me never to go out without cab fare. She was right."

"And?"

"The jerk told everybody at school that he wiped out on his brother's skateboard."

"And all this happened when?"

"A month ago."

"Have you told anyone?"

"No. Who could I tell?"

"Your father."

"Are you kidding? He'd ground me 'til I'm twenty-seven. Besides, it's hard enough telling you."

"I think you underestimate him." Linny had no response for that. "Why did you wait until now to tell me?"

"I sort of felt it was my fault. I shouldn't have gone in his house. Maybe I gave him the wrong idea." She couldn't meet his eyes. "But then I found out I wasn't the first girl he did it to. The others weren't so lucky."

Caleb waited.

"The guy used to live in Highland Park, so I called a friend of mine who goes there. She asked around and found out he got kicked out of school because he got some girl pregnant. And there was talk that it wasn't voluntary on her part. Then I asked the reference librarian how to find out who owns what property. She said call the township office, so I did, and guess what?

"His uncle doesn't own that house in Highland Park, his father does. They're just renting their house in Wilmette so he can go to New Trier."

"So why are you telling me? And what are you going to do?"

"I thought you could tell me."

"I'm flattered, but I think you know I can't." Linny made a face that told him he'd hit the mark. "How old is this individual?"

"Well, he's graduating this year, so I guess he's eighteen."

"And what would you advise a friend who told you this story?"

She looked sheepish. "Tell your dad."

"And?"

"And maybe go to the police?"

"And perhaps encourage the girls who were raped to press charges?"

"He told them no one would believe them."

"That's possible but unlikely if all of you come forward."

"I thought you'd be able to tell me something easier."

Caleb smiled inwardly and nodded. "That's magical thinking. If wishing could solve our problems, we'd never have any."

Catching her lower lip between her teeth, Linny echoed his nod. "But how'm I gonna tell my dad?"

"Just the way you told me."

THIRTY-FIVE

The sergeant at the Nineteenth District front desk told Caleb that Detective Thinnes was out but would be back momentarily. Caleb could wait in the detectives squad room. When he got upstairs, he took a seat near the coffeemaker, at the table reserved for visitors who had paperwork to do. There were four men working in the room. They had the aloof indifference to his presence of cats unwilling to abandon an intriguing prey solely to greet a visitor. Except one. Detective Ferris was a dog at a cat show. When he looked up from the *Sun-Times* he was reading he said, "Hey, if it isn't Dr. Butt-in-ski. How's business, Doc?"

"Not bad, Detective Embarrass."

Ferris laughed the way an insecure man does when he's been put down and can't think of a comeback. He went back to studying the paper. Pretending to study it. When Thinnes came in, Ferris immediately announced, "Thinnes, your shrink's here."

Thinnes walked toward Caleb.

Ferris said, "Where's your girlfriend, Thinnes?"

"Jealous, Ferris?"

Caleb could tell Thinnes was a good deal more agitated than his words indicated. Perhaps Ferris had hit a nerve. Or maybe the rape case Thinnes was working on was getting to him.

Thinnes said, "What can I do for you, Doctor?"

"I need some information about a rape."

"What unlikely coincidence brings you in asking about rape?"

Caleb had never known Thinnes to be so sarcastic. Usually

he left the bad-cop role to his current partner. Caleb gave no indication of being put out. "Coincidence?"

"I just happen to be up to my ass in rapes at the moment."

"I have a patient who was raped some years ago. The recent assaults have brought up some unfinished issues for her."

"She think it might be the same guy?"

"That would be too much to expect, but there are enough similar elements to cause her distress. She needs to know whether the man who raped her was ever caught."

"She should contact the detective who handled the case."

"He retired. It was fifteen years ago."

"I'm right in the middle of a heater case right now. And besides the statute of limitations has run out."

"I understand that, and I'm not asking you to drop everything. Just look into it when you can."

Thinnes shrugged. "You got an RD number?"

Caleb handed him an index card with the case number, a date, and a detective's name on it. Thinnes put it in his pocket, and said, "Don't hold your breath."

Caleb nodded. "Thank you." He looked around. There was no sign of Thinnes's new partner, "the knockout," or any indication that she'd be returning soon. He could think of no plausible excuse to tarry. But judging by Thinnes's behavior, *something* was wrong. Caleb decided to call Lieutenant Evanger from his office and set up an appointment for the sparring partners.

Thinnes knew better than to imagine females were a weaker sex. He'd grown up with the knowledge that it wasn't so. His dad had never made any pretense that he could go it alone. Thinnes had come to have the same feelings about Rhonda.

So he was nervous about going home that evening. He called ahead, then stopped and got Chinese on the way.

Their conversation over dinner was strained. After they'd

cleared away the dishes, he asked her point-blank what was wrong.

"You never asked what he did to me."

He felt betrayed. She'd never trusted him enough to tell him! And he felt the outrage he'd seen so often in the boyfriends and husbands of women who'd been raped. He said, "You told me. He raped you."

"You didn't ask for the details."

"I don't need details. It's bad enough I gotta know some asshole raped my wife, and there's nothing I can do to him."

"Just what would you do to him? If he were still alive."

"I'd kill him."

He must've sounded like he wasn't kidding because Rhonda looked at him as if he were crazy.

"What're we arguing about this for," he demanded. "It's over. More than twenty years ago."

"I'm starting to think it's only just begun."

THIRTY-SIX

When he and Franchi arrived at the scene, Thinnes had a déjà vu. The alley was open at the south end, but was otherwise nearly identical to the alley where Katherine Lake had been dumped. The beat cops had cordoned it off and were standing in front of the yellow crime-scene tape with two women and three dogs—a black-and-white border collie, a black Labrador retriever, and something else—Thinnes wasn't sure what. The third dog was taller than the Lab and rangier, with red-blond hair that lay flat everywhere except along its backbone. The dog's eyes, ears, and muzzle were black; and its ears flopped down, slightly less than most hounds. The border collie had blood on its face and chest, but from the women's lack of concern, it either wasn't the dog's, or the animal wasn't badly hurt. When Franchi and Thinnes got close, the patrol officer noticed him and made introductions.

"Detectives, this is Ms. Grube . . ." He indicated the thinner of the two women. She was about five-seven and dark-haired, and had enormous eyes, like Franchi's, that gave her a waiflike look. She was wearing a flowered dress that was mussed and missing a button.

"She just missed bein' victim number three," the copper said.

Both women were pale, but Thinnes thought they turned a little paler when they heard the mention of the near miss. He made a mental note to chew the goof out later. Franchi glared at the copper. Maybe, Thinnes decided, he'd just sic Franchi on him.

He didn't seem to notice. "And this is Ms. Romanelli. She

was walkin' her dogs an' heard screamin' an' came runnin'—just in time. I'm gonna put her in for a Good Samaritan award."

An inch shorter than Grube, Romanelli also had dark hair, though hers was shoulder-length. She was wearing a sleeveless blouse, slacks, and Reeboks.

"Let's get first things first," Thinnes said. "You call the paramedics?"

Grube said, "I'm not injured, Detective . . . I'm sorry, I didn't get your name."

"Thinnes." He introduced Franchi, who was standing with her hands tucked into her armpits. Franchi nodded at them.

"I'm just a little shaken, Detective Thinnes," Grube said. "This lady and her dogs chased the creep away before he could do any real harm."

"I'm glad to hear that," Thinnes said. "But I'd still feel better if you'd let a doctor look you over."

"I'm fine."

Thinnes nodded. "Mind telling me what happened?"

"I'd just left the home of a patient, and—"

"Patient?" Thinnes interrupted.

"I'm a visiting nurse. Anyway, I was walking toward Armitage to get the El when this man— He was walking towards me, and he moved to the outside of the sidewalk. I didn't think anything of it— My mother always said a gentleman walks on the outside . . ."

Only this was no gentleman. Thinnes said, "Go on."

"He walked past me. He had his head down and his hands in his pockets—"

"What was he wearing?"

She looked up while she thought about it. Ms. Romanelli stood listening intently with her hands in her pockets. The dogs sat quietly at her feet.

"I never saw his face, but he was dressed like someone who'd live around here. He had on a hat and raincoat, a tie, and shoes like yours." She pointed.

"What happened next?"

"He grabbed me. He put something over my face that had ether on it."

"How do you know it was ether?" Franchi asked.

"I've smelled it before. It's used occasionally . . ."

Thinnes nodded. "Go on."

"I tried to fight, but he was really strong. I think I managed a 'No!' or something like that, but he would've— Whatever he was planning to do to me, he would've succeeded if this lady and her dogs hadn't come along. They chased him away. And I think one of them bit him."

"What's your first name?"

"Sally."

"Address?" She told him. "Okay, Ms. Grube—"

"Sally."

"Sally. I'd like you to go with this officer to the hospital and have one of the doctors look you over, then he'll bring you back to Area Three Headquarters so you can make a statement."

"Well . . ."

"It would really help us to get this guy," Franchi told her. "And we'll drive you home afterward."

"All right."

Thinnes turned to the beat copper and told him to take Grube to the Illinois Masonic ER, wait while they checked her over, then bring her to Area Three.

The patrolman nodded and took Grube's elbow. "This way, miss."

Thinnes turned to Romanelli. "What happened?"

"It's like Sally said—"

"I'd like you to tell me in your own words."

"Well. I was walking my dogs— Actually only Kitty is mine." She pointed to the border collie. "This is Kitty. And the Lab is Hank. And that's Rage." Rage was the smooth-coated dog. "I walk them for their owners."

Franchi pointed at Rage. "What kind of dog is he?"

"A Rhodesian Ridgeback."

"Okay," Thinnes said. "Go on."

166

"We were just coming down the street and the dogs started to get excited and then I heard Sally cry out—"

"Do you know her?"

"No. I just met her."

"Go on."

"Kitty and Rage started growling, and I looked. I could see Sally struggling with a man. That's when I realized he was trying— I don't know what he was trying to do, but I knew it was against her will. So I let go of the dogs' leashes, and *they* went to her rescue. I'm afraid Kitty bit him."

"Good for Kitty," Franchi said. "Where?"

Romanelli smiled. "On the arm, I think. Near his elbow."

"We're going to have to get samples of the blood that's on Kitty, and some samples of her blood for comparison."

Romanelli didn't seem quite as keen, suddenly.

"And we'll need a statement from you." She nodded. "I'll have to ask you to wait here until the evidence technicians get here. They'll get the suspect's blood off Kitty here, on the scene, to avoid any future allegations that our sample was contaminated in transit. Then we'll take Kitty somewhere to get a little of her blood."

Romanelli nodded, more to signal that she understood, Thinnes would've bet, than because she was enthusiastic about it. "What about the other dogs?"

"I'm afraid we'll have to get samples from them, too," Franchi said. "But we'll see you all get home safely when we're done."

THIRTY-SEVEN

Thinnes had been a cop before the term *serial killer* was invented, so he knew whatever you called them, men who killed again and again weren't like they were portrayed on those slick, sick movies. They weren't rich geniuses who could outmaneuver whole PDs or the entire FBI. They were usually just smart enough to learn from their mistakes and experience. And it was ruthlessness more than smarts that gave them the upper hand. Even so, a victim who was unpredictable had a chance. Or a lucky one, like Sally Grube. Romanelli's timely arrival was lucky for the cops, too, because the chance of two rapists hitting the same upscale neighborhood at once was slim to none. So now they'd have DNA. If their luck held, the asshole would be in the database. If not, he'd slip up sooner or later. Thinnes called for a mobile crime-scene unit.

They sent Bendix again. When he spotted the dogs, he said, "Not again, Thinnes. It's harassment."

"What's he talking about?" Franchi asked.

Bendix said, "Thinnes's got a thing for dogs."

Thinnes pointed at the border collie. "Kitty bit the offender, Bendix. That's his blood on her. Evidence."

Bendix took a cigar out of the inside pocket of his jacket and put it in his mouth. He looked from Thinnes to Franchi and back, then stared at the dogs. Trying to figure out if this was some kind of joke. "If it bites me, the evidence will be contaminated."

Kitty stretched out on the ground and started licking the blood off her paws.

Thinnes said, "The dog's destroying the evidence, Bendix!"

Bendix swore, but put the cigar away, and told Romanelli, "Make him stop that."

"Her," Romanelli said. "Kitty's a girl. And she won't bite you."

Bendix rolled his eyes and started getting out scissors and a tray with a collection of small envelopes and vials. When it came to actually collecting the blood from the dog, he handed everything to his assistant, and said, "You do this." Digging his cigar out, he stalked toward the perimeter of the crime scene.

"What's his problem?" Franchi demanded as they watched Bendix light up.

Thinnes hid his smile. "Guess *he*'s got a thing about dogs."

It took two hours to find a vet who could take blood samples from the three canines and then to take them and Romanelli home. By the time they got back to Belmont and Western, minicam vans from cable news and Channels 5, 7, 9, and 32 were parked out front.

And Rod Manly, a WGN radio reporter was parked inside the Nineteenth District lobby. Manly was decent enough as reporters go, and Thinnes nodded but didn't stop to talk. He took the stairs up to the Area two at a time.

The squad room was crowded. Thinnes's usual place was occupied by a night-shift Property Crimes dick, and Ryan was sharing her space with a tall, heavy black woman Thinnes had never seen before. Ryan introduced her as Detective Orella from Area One. Whatever Orella thought about being pulled out of an Area with, probably, ten or twelve unsolved rapes to help out here with two, she kept to herself.

Thinnes said, "Orella," then to Ryan, "Don't tell me. Rossi's gone off the deep end with this and called for reinforcements?"

"Yeah," Ryan said.

"Where's Evanger?"

"Downtown."

"Who tipped the press?"

"Who knows? By the way, Thinnes, we took Ms. Grube's statement and sent her home an hour ago."

"Thanks."

"And Evanger wants to be brought up to speed as soon as he gets back."

The headline in the *Sun-Times* afternoon edition read KILLER RAPIST STALKS LINCOLN PARK. It was a great story for the media. Sex sells. Kinky sex is even better. Trying to ignore something like that in Lincoln Park was like pretending the elephant parked in your living room was a beagle. Six or seven rapes in Englewood wouldn't have generated as much heat.

The meeting was held in the conference room. In addition to Ryan, Ferris, Viernes, Swann, and Franchi, there were five Property Crimes detectives and three dicks on loan from other Areas. Evanger, the Property Crimes guys, and the visitors got chairs around the table. Everybody else stood against the walls or window. After making introductions, Evanger asked Thinnes to bring everyone up to speed.

Thinnes had been organizing his notes and updating his chart ever since Ryan gave him the heads-up. Now he crossed to the chalkboard and turned it around to show off his diagram.

"I think we caught a break with this latest abduction attempt," he said. "The victim fits our profile—at least physically—and thanks to our good Samaritan, we got a blood type—O negative—and DNA although it'll be a while before we can check it against the database.

"What we know about this guy is that he's organized and smart enough about evidence and profiling to try to pass himself off as a disorganized offender. His signature: He targets slim, brown-eyed brunettes, who, it looks like, have blond roommates or close friends.

"We're not sure how he locates his victims, but organized offenders often stalk their prey before making contact. From what we could get out of Katherine Lake, and from the message

170

Nesbit left for her roommate, we think he meets, or at least spots, his victims in a local bar. Maybe he grabs her off the street if she won't leave with him, maybe slips something in her drink. Once he's got her, he rapes, beats, and cuts her, then dumps her in an alley.

"I think we can also safely say he's white and middle class—someone who blends."

"An invisible man," Franchi said, "like the Father Brown story." That got her a few strange looks.

Thinnes continued. "It looks like he grabs them Thursday or Friday, holds them for the weekend, and dumps them Monday morning. So he's probably employed with weekends off."

"Looks like he's working his way through the alphabet," Viernes observed.

"Yeah," Thinnes said. "Ryan and Franchi interviewed Ivy Jacobs." He pointed to his diagram. "We're trying to run down Greta Highlander, or at least her former roommate, see if either of them can add anything."

"But this woman today's all wrong," Viernes said. "She should be 'O,' 'P.' And today's Wednesday, not Thursday or Friday. I think we got an unrelated mugging or rape attempt here."

"I think it's the same guy," Thinnes said. "He's getting rattled and couldn't wait to find a woman who fit all the criteria."

Evanger said, "You got anything to back that up or is it just wishful thinking?"

"A hunch," Thinnes said.

"Thintuition!" Ferris put in.

Evanger gave him a stern look, then asked Thinnes, "What else don't we know for sure?"

"We don't know how he finds his victims, or how he transports them. We don't know where he keeps them before he dumps them."

"Then get out there and find out."

Detective Orella said, "You check NCIC for an A to F?"

"Yeah. Nothing. But it seems like he must've started sooner—maybe smaller. Maybe he didn't kill them—just roughed them up a bit or raped them. He seems to be getting more violent."

"What about our known sex offenders?"

"None of them has an alibi for both attacks, but they've all got someone to vouch for their whereabouts for at least one. My gut tells me that our offender started somewhere else and got interrupted. Then he moved here and took up where he left off."

Evanger said, "Did you check the graduation lists for Wisconsin, Indiana, and Michigan?"

"Yeah."

"Then maybe it's time to send this to the Feds for a profile."

"Give me another day or two."

"I'll give you 'til next Monday—if nobody turns up missing in the meantime."

There was a collective groan.

"Lieutenant," Franchi said, "what are we doing to warn the public?"

"What we can: We got a flash message out to the beat cars, and we're bringing it up at roll call. We've notified the campus cops and hospital security people. And News Affairs is going on all the stations."

"We *could* put it out that brown-eyed brunettes need to be extra careful."

"And warn our offender that we're on to him? No." Evanger got up.

Franchi had the sense to let it go, for once, but Thinnes could see that some of the others were giving her funny looks. Rookies!

He said, "Anything else?" to no one in particular.

There were a few headshakes as they all filed out.

Out in the squad room, the sergeant handed Thinnes a phone-message slip: Rhonda was having dinner with the girls from work.

Except for the front hall light, the house was dark when Thinnes entered. Toby stood on the mat and signaled his joy by wiggling every part of his body.

"Just you and me, eh, boy?"

Toby sat down and listened intently.

"Guess we might as well get your walk over with."

At the word *walk* the dog jumped up, crooning with delight, and whirled to grab his leash off the stair railing. Thinnes took it from him, but didn't bother to clip it to his collar. On the sidewalk, Toby ran to the end of the block, then waited at the street for Thinnes to signal him to cross. Once across, he checked out hydrants and tree trunks, leaving his own messages for other dogs.

There wasn't any hurry, so Thinnes walked him all the way to the park. It was dusk. The night was warm and humid, perfumed by fresh-cut grass. The park was populated by strolling couples and a group of teens just hanging out. A single firefly signaled its availability. Insects buzzed the streetlights. A car cruised past with stereo booming.

Thinnes found himself slipping into beat copper mode, although he hadn't worked patrol in a dozen years. Stupid. Sauganash was as safe as Lincoln Park. But that was the problem, wasn't it?

Nowhere was safe. And no one.

And there was nothing he could do about it twenty-three years later.

THIRTY-EIGHT

The light flashed on Caleb's phone, and when he picked up, Irene Sleighton told him, "There's a woman on the phone who won't give her name. She called earlier and wouldn't leave a message."

Caleb said, "Thank you," and when Irene hung up, said, "Hello. This is Dr. Caleb."

"Jack? It's Rhonda Thinnes. I came downtown to see the special exhibit at the Art Institute. If you're free for lunch, would you join me?"

It took him a moment to remember her—John's wife, whom he'd met only twice and didn't really know well.

The invitation was more likely a plea for help than anything, one his curiosity wouldn't let him ignore.

"The cafe?" he said.

"Wonderful. Shall I meet you by the lions?"

Rhonda Thinnes was thirty-nine, Caleb recalled. Standing below one of the museum's landmark lions, she looked younger. She was naturally blond, with the corollary blue eyes and coloring, and she wore a summer suit that showed off both to advantage. Her body language signaled that she'd seen him, but she hesitated as if unsure of her welcome. But when Caleb got close enough to say, "Rhonda," she offered her hand in a businesslike way. They walked to the restaurant in companionable silence.

The café was a small outdoor garden settled within the walls of the Art Institute. Sparrows flitted among the tables, cheeping and squabbling. Sunlight filtering through the branches of the locust trees overlaid the pattern on the tablecloth with a filigree of shade.

When the waiter had left with their orders, Caleb said, "Now what's this about?"

She hesitated, tracing a pattern over the filigree with the end of her spoon. Thinnes had told him she was the only honest woman he'd ever met. So she wasn't prevaricating, just ordering her thoughts. Finally, she looked up. "I need some advice."

He stifled the urge to give it—Get counseling—and said, "Why me?"

"Because you're wise." Before he could protest, she added, "John's said, several times, he thought you were way ahead of everyone else."

"Even supposing that were true, why me?"

"You're John's best friend."

Caleb felt himself blink with astonishment.

"His best male friend, anyway," Rhonda said. "Since Carl Oster left the Department."

He could think of nothing to say to that, so he said, "Go on."

"I was raped. A long time ago. Before John and I were married. But I never told him. I guess I was afraid it would come between us, and it has."

"Why did it come out now?"

"These cases he's been working lately—rapes. He hates working rape. And Rossi—one of his supervisors—has him studying all the unsolved rape cases. It's making him crazy."

"He's had problems on the job before. What's different about this time?"

She took a sip of water from the glass in front of her. She kept her eyes on the glass after she'd returned it to its place. "Maybe it's sexist to say it, but I think women are constitutionally more monogamous than men."

"We might quibble about *constitutionally*," Caleb said, "but traditionally that's been true, even if it's only due to socialization."

She shrugged. "I've always thought the difference between men who cheat and those who don't is just that the latter have a sense of fair play and well-developed self-control."

He laughed. "I've never heard it put that way, but you're probably right." He could've speculated where she was going with this, but he waited. Better to let her get to her point. He had a one o'clock appointment, but he tried to react as if he had all the time in the world.

Finally, she said, "I don't know for sure if John's ever been unfaithful, but I don't think he has. His old partner, Frank, the one who was shot to death, told me once—we used to have him over for dinner a lot after his first wife died, before he remarried—he took me aside once, after John and I had a fight, and said, 'You two gotta make up. John couldn't live without you and he knows it. And he's the straightest man I ever met. That's why I know he would never cheat on you.'

"I can't even remember what the fight was about, but I do remember making some crack about John catting around. I didn't believe he would, but I knew it would push his buttons." She smiled wryly, and added, "Too soon old; too late smart."

"Some people never get smart. What are you trying to tell me?"

"Just that John's at that age. . . . And just because he's never cheated doesn't mean he hasn't been tempted."

Caleb raised his eyebrows and waited.

"He's got a new partner."

"So?"

"I understand she's gorgeous!"

He gave her a wry smile.

"And half my age, and with him eight hours a day. And they've been working together for weeks, and he hasn't even mentioned that she's a woman."

"Why do you suppose that is?"

Rhonda's brows crept together. "Obviously he's afraid."

"Obviously, but of what?"

Her expression softened. "I'm not sure. Am I being silly?"

"It's a perfectly logical fear."

"But it doesn't help the situation. What do I *do*?"

"What would you do if his new partner were a man?"

"Invite him to dinner?"

"Well?"

THIRTY-NINE

Excuse me, Doctor." Irene Sleighton's voice interrupted his patient's monologue.

"Yes, Mrs. Sleighton?"

"Dr. Morgan's here."

It was an odd habit and not an endearing trait that Martin never failed to show up without notice.

"Please ask him to make an appointment or wait until I'm free." Caleb hung up before Irene could say, "Yes, Doctor."

"I apologize for the interruption," he told the patient. "Please go on . . ."

To the casual glance, Martin presented a tranquil façade, but Caleb had learned to read his reserve. He sat studying a magazine until Caleb had escorted the patient out and closed the door. Then he stood and offered Caleb his hand saying, "Hello, Doctor. How are you?"

His handshake was firm enough, but he'd put on weight—not much—but with the slight puffiness and shadows beneath his eyes, and the deeper frown lines, it indicated stress. There was a hint of urgency in his movements, too: haste or anxiety. Caleb wasn't sure which.

"Come into my office," Caleb told him. "No interruptions, please, Mrs. Sleighton."

Inside, Caleb gestured toward the couch, and said, "Have a seat, Martin."

He shook his head. "I'm too angry." He stalked to the window and stared out.

Caleb sat in one of the chairs in the center of the room. Michigan Avenue and Grant Park weren't visible from his point of view, and the tops of the Art Institute and the Goodman had vanished in the mist.

A pigeon materialized and fluttered toward the windowsill. When it spotted Martin, it veered away. Martin turned and leaned his back against the sill. Caleb thought of augers and wondered what it signified.

They had become lovers very slowly, over the course of a year. Intimate, but not yet intimates. They hadn't yet come to trust one another as soul mates must.

"Start at the beginning," he said neutrally, countering his urge to provide comfort with the knowledge that finding resolution would be more productive. "What's made you angry?"

"Linny told me she was nearly raped." Caleb nodded. "After she told you."

"And you're angry with me because . . . ?"

"Jealousy. Pure jealousy. That she'd come to you instead of me."

Caleb smiled. "What teenage girl talks about sex with her father?"

"Helen did."

Caleb felt a profound sense of irony. "Linny isn't Helen."

Martin clenched his jaw and fists. "But sometimes she'll toss her head or laugh at some order I've given her, and I see Helen mocking me."

Caleb shook his head. "She's the best of both of you."

Martin walked over and sat on the couch. He put his elbows on his knees and rested his head on his hands. "My daughter was nearly raped." He looked up at Caleb. "What am I going to do?"

Hadn't someone once called children hostages to fortune? Linny wouldn't be held easily. But what father wants to admit his children no longer need his protection? Certainly not Martin. Martin lived for his children.

Caleb smiled ruefully. "What are your options?"

"I don't know. My first inclination was to call the police, but she threatened to run away if I did."

"You think she was serious?"

"I think she was being dramatic, but she made her point. She'd be embarrassed to death. Nevertheless, I can't see letting that punk get away with it."

"From Linny's description of the incident, he hardly escaped unscathed."

"What can I tell her?"

Caleb had seen Martin work. He was a physician of extraordinary skill and sensitivity, but in his personal life he was perversely insecure.

"What would you tell a teenage patient who came to you with the same question?"

"But Linny's my daughter!"

"You say that as if being your daughter should confer some special protection from the hazards to which other young women are prey."

"I should have warned her."

It seemed to Caleb that guilt was unfairly apportioned. Some—like his three o'clock appointment—seemed congenitally lacking, while others, like Martin, were overburdened.

"Do you remember the story of Sleeping Beauty?"

Martin looked confused. "Yes, of course, but . . ."

Caleb let him think about it.

Martin leaned forward. "Are you telling me I should accept her fate? I don't believe in fate!"

Caleb leaned back, deliberately increasing the distance between them. Giving Martin his point. "Not fate, karma. The interaction of event and character."

"But *I* need to do something." Martin sat back and relaxed slightly. "For me, if not for her."

Caleb felt an urge to take Martin's face between his hands

and kiss it. But Martin feared gossip more than anything. And although Mrs. Sleighton would never enter a room without first knocking, anytime a door is unlocked, there remains the possibility that someone will enter.

Michael Ondaatje's words came suddenly to mind:

> *Love arrives and dies in all disguises*
> *and we fear to move*
> *because of old darknesses or childhood danger*
> *So our withdrawing word*
> *our skating hearts.*

So beautifully stated. So apropos.

"I know you don't give advice, Jack, but what can I do to make *me* feel she's safe?"

"Karate lessons?"

"Helen tried to get her into karate when she was ten. She hated it."

"She may have matured enough to have a new perspective. You could offer."

"I'll do that. Thank you." Martin gave a great sigh—as if the problem of the millennium were solved. He seemed about to say something more.

Caleb felt the charge that crosses a room when lovers exchange glances.

Then Martin stood. "I've interrupted your work. I should go."

Inwardly, Caleb acknowledged that the anger that stabbed him was from frustration.

Martin stopped at the door. "Will I see you Sunday? Eileen has the children."

"Yes, of course."

He could wait until Sunday. He would wait until Martin was ready to stand shoulder to shoulder with him against the world.

FORTY

The news reports generated a lot of tips from the public—most worthless, some obviously nuts. Thinnes sorted his share of phone messages into "promising," "doubtful," and "check out after New Year's." He got himself coffee and settled down at his phone to answer them. Except for Viernes, who was doing the paperwork on a gang-related incident, the rest of the squad seemed to be doing the same.

Franchi was wearing a pantsuit again. Come to think of it, she hadn't worn a skirt since she skinned her knee. He wondered if that meant something, or if all the rapes were making her think defensive dressing.

By the time she went out for her second cigarette of the morning, Thinnes had answered all the "promising" calls—false promises—and was starting into the stack of "doubtfuls." He noticed that as soon as Franchi was out the door, Ferris went over to her desk and slid a magazine under one of the files she'd been reading.

Thinnes wasn't curious enough to get up and investigate, but when Franchi came back, he finished his call and disconnected, but kept the receiver cradled between his ear and shoulder so it would look like he was still on the phone. With a pen in his hand and a notepad under it, he pretended to be hard at work. Instead, he watched and listened.

Franchi sat down and shuffled her papers around, immediately finding what turned out to be a copy of *Playboy* folded open to a playmate who fit her general description and had an identical haircut. Her first reaction was to roll up the magazine and shake it at Thinnes, giving him a look that would bring a Marine to attention.

Thinnes dropped the pen and held both hands out in a take-it-easy gesture. Simultaneously, he shook his head and mouthed, "Not me."

"Who did this?" Franchi demanded.

Thinnes took hold of the receiver and held it against his shoulder as if to prevent his imaginary caller from hearing him say, "Rossi hasn't been in here for an hour, so who do you think?"

"Ferris?"

"Bingo!" He noticed that Ryan was suddenly tuned in. He figured Ferris was laughing his ass off behind the sports section of the *Tribune*.

"That's it. This is harassment. I'm filing a grievance!"

"You got any idea how much satisfaction it would give Rossi to know you're teed off?"

"Yeah," Ryan said. "Relax. Real harassment is when they slip a Kotex in your briefcase, or a dead rat in your locker, or put used condoms on the backseat of your car.

"How did Rossi get to be a lieutenant?"

Ferris came out from behind the *Trib*. "Same way you did, Franchi. He knows who to sleep with."

Franchi turned to Ryan. "Why do I have to put up with this shit?"

"You don't have to put up with it," Ryan said. "You have to put up with *Ferris* because the only thing we got going for us out on the streets is that when someone calls for backup, we all come running. Even a jerk like him."

"Hey," Ferris said, "you broads want to be equal, but when we treat you like one of the guys, you go postal."

Ryan turned to him, and said, "If that were true, someone would have blown you away years ago."

Ferris retreated behind his paper.

Ryan turned back to Franchi. "Arm yourself. When someone starts in, let him have it."

"For instance?"

Ryan raised her voice to say, "Hey, Ferris!"

"Yeah?"

"What do you call a man with half a brain?"

Ferris stayed behind the paper. "What?"

"Gifted."

Ryan's lip curled at one corner. She raised her voice again, so Ferris couldn't miss her saying, "Franchi, what do you have when you have two little balls in your hands?"

Franchi played along. "I give up, what?"

"A man's undivided attention."

Franchi laughed, then asked Ryan, "What does a man call a seven-course meal?"

"Tell me."

"A hot dog and a six-pack."

"There you go," Ryan said in a normal tone. "I think Ferris's had enough."

Thinnes made a mental note never to fuck with Ryan.

"What about Rossi?" Franchi demanded.

"Rossi's a type-A. And the A is definitely for asshole." Franchi waited. "Keep a perfectly straight face and say, 'I'm not sure I understand. Would you mind putting that in writing?' "

FORTY-ONE

Y ou ever been sent to this guy before?" They were on Clybourn Avenue, on their way downtown. Franchi was waiting for his answer like a cat sitting on a mouse hole.

"No," Thinnes said. "But he's helped me with a couple cases—as a consultant."

"Helped?"

"Yeah."

"How?"

"He muscled his way into the first case—the victim was his patient. But he's good. He knows how people think. And he moves in circles I don't have access to, so after that I asked him to consult."

As she thought about it for a while, she reminded Thinnes of Skinner. When the cat first moved in, he'd alternated between paranoia and curiosity about his new digs—sometimes changing from one mode to the next in a heartbeat. Franchi wasn't as obvious, but her questions proved a promising curiosity. Promising because Thinnes knew Evanger wasn't going to back down on the subject of them working together. Somehow or another they were going to have to work things out.

"Can I have a minute alone with you, Doctor?" Franchi asked.

Caleb looked at Thinnes, who shrugged. Caleb said, "All right."

Thinnes said, "I'll wait out here."

Caleb nodded and held his office door open for Franchi.

After he closed the door behind her, Caleb offered Franchi a seat. He wasn't specific, waving in the general direction of the conversation area, with its couch, chairs, and coffee table. The subject's choice of seat often told him volumes about her character. Franchi planted herself in the center of the couch. He took the chair opposite and waited.

"Thinnes told me you and he are old friends, Doctor. Doesn't that make your counseling us a conflict of interest?"

"It would if I were counseling you. Your lieutenant asked me to talk to the two of you and see if you need counseling. If I think you do, I'll refer you."

"You and Thinnes are old friends?"

"We haven't known each other long, but we've worked together. And we *are* friends. If that's a problem for you, I could ask Dr. Fenwick . . ."

"No. That's okay. I checked you out with a couple people I know. They said you're okay."

Caleb nodded. "Very prudent. Anything else?"

She shook her head. Caleb got up and went to summon Thinnes, who sat in the chair opposite Franchi.

"What did you two talk about?" he asked. He glanced at Franchi, then stared at Caleb.

Caleb said, "You'll have to ask Detective Franchi."

Thinnes looked at her; she just smiled.

Caleb took a chair at a ninety-degree angle to the two of them, and said, "What did you hope to get from coming here?"

There was a stubborn silence, during which Thinnes merely shook his head. Franchi finally said, "Nothing." They were both sitting back as if maximizing the distance between them.

"Then why did you come?"

"Orders," Franchi said.

Caleb looked at Thinnes, who reluctantly agreed. "Evanger sent us."

Caleb waited a long time, but neither elaborated. They were cops who knew how the game was played. And according to the information Evanger had sent, both were very good. He probably wouldn't outwait them. "Why?" Neither responded, so Caleb added, "Detective Franchi?"

"We don't get along."

She didn't elaborate. Caleb said, "Detective Thinnes?"

Thinnes said, "Yeah."

"Why?"

Thinnes shrugged. "Chemistry?"

"What are your specific objections to working with Detective Franchi?"

"She's got an attitude."

Caleb waited until he was sure Thinnes wasn't going to say more, and said, "Explain."

Thinnes showed signs of exasperation as he thought, then said, "First day of work she shows up late, then gets all sarcastic because I didn't hold up a rape investigation for her."

"He takes off without even asking for me!" Franchi leaned toward Thinnes, and said, "And you knew I was around! You gave me the eye when you walked in!"

"I didn't know who you were!"

"So," Caleb interjected, "you got off to a rocky start. Then what happened?"

"Then he ticks me off for being late and sends me to baby-sit a brain-dead victim while he does the investigation!"

"Detective Thinnes?"

"She shows up late, an unknown quantity—for all I know a loose cannon—and I don't have time to drop everything to check her out. So I gave her something to do I knew she couldn't screw up. Anyway, she's the new dick on the squad. So I don't see what she's complaining about."

Caleb looked at Franchi, who said, "He'd already decided I was a loose cannon!"

"Not at that point!" Thinnes leaned sideways to look at Caleb, resting his elbow on his knee. "With most men, you can hate each other's guts and still work together. But with a woman—" He glanced at Franchi, then looked back at Caleb. "Franchi sulks."

"I don't!"

Thinnes gave her an 'Oh, yeah' look.

"So do you think *all* woman sulk?"

"No. I never worked with all women."

"Name one," Franchi demanded.

"Who doesn't sulk?" She nodded. "Ryan."

"So why don't you work with her?"

"I wasn't given a choice."

Time-out, Caleb thought. He said, "Peace, children!" He leaned into the space between them, and said, "Did Lieutenant Evanger tell you what would happen if you don't come to some working agreement?" They shook their heads. Caleb looked at Thinnes. "You've had a number of partners in the last three years. How did you get along with them?"

"All right."

"Immediately?" Thinnes shrugged. "All of them?"

Thinnes squirmed, and, with his peripheral vision, Caleb could see Franchi smirk.

"Crowne took some breaking in, I guess."

"He objected to being assigned all the grunt work?"

"At first."

Caleb waited, but Franchi jumped in with, " 'Til you wore him down?"

"We worked out a division of labor."

Franchi snorted.

"What's stopping you from working with Detective Franchi?" Thinnes shrugged. Caleb said, "Why don't you just say it? Whatever you're reluctant to say is likely to be less inflammatory than what she's probably thinking."

Thinnes looked at Caleb, and said, "I don't want to have to watch my back and hers, too."

Franchi surged forward until she was half-standing over the table. Only Caleb's outstretched hand prevented her from head-butting her reluctant partner. "I knew it! It's the same sexist crap I've been getting since I came on the job!"

Thinnes just glared at her.

Caleb said, "So you object to working with a woman?"

"No! I've worked plenty of cases with Ryan."

"In what way does Detective Franchi differ from Detective Ryan?"

Thinnes hesitated, but Caleb—and Franchi—waited until he added, "Ryan's never beefed anyone."

Franchi shook her head vigorously. "I knew it! You guys are worse gossips than any ten *Star* reporters alive. And you're great detectives—you always check your sources."

Caleb put his hand up in the universal HALT sign. He kept looking at Thinnes while he asked Franchi, "To what gossip are you referring?"

Franchi said, "Ask *him*. Nobody'll tell me to my face."

Caleb said, "Well?"

"Word at the Area is she slept her way into the job, and it caught up with her. So she filed a beef."

"Did you check on this information yourself?"

"No."

Franchi made a sound that sounded like "Huhn" that managed to convey the maximum contempt.

"How do you feel about working rape cases, Detective Thinnes?"

"I hate it."

"Is it possible you took some of this aversion out on the new person who had the misfortune to be assigned to work with you?"

"Maybe." It sounded grudging but honest. Caleb looked at Franchi, who was studying Thinnes as if she had never considered anything like him before.

"There's something else," Caleb said. "Beyond working with someone you don't necessarily admire. What?"

"My last three partners are all off the job."

Franchi had apparently caught on, because she waited with Caleb until the silence drew the rest out of him.

"It's superstitious, but it gives me the creeps. I don't want to work with anyone else. Except maybe Ferris."

Franchi guffawed. "You'd kill him yourself."

"And you don't think Detective Franchi could assess the risk and decide for herself if she wants to work with a jinx?"

Thinnes looked at her without raising his head. "Now she probably thinks I'm nuts."

"No, just a—"

Caleb held up his hand to interrupt. "Can we agree that you and Detective Thinnes don't bring out the best in each other?" Franchi snorted. Caleb turned to Thinnes. "What would it take for Detective Franchi to get in your good graces?"

While Thinnes thought about that, Franchi drummed the arm of her chair with her fingers. Caleb pretended he had all day.

"We start over," Thinnes said, finally. "If I'm the primary on a case, and I ask her to do something, she does it without the attitude and without arguing. Not because she's a woman, but because she's the new dick."

"Detective Franchi?"

Franchi looked at Thinnes as if he were offering to sell her Navy Pier, but, finally, she said, "You're on!"

FORTY-TWO

As if by mutual agreement, they were silent on the trip back to the Area. After they turned onto Clybourn, Franchi took out a cigarette and started turning it around between her fingers as she stared at the Cabrini-Green residents they were passing.

Thinnes was annoyed. He started to warn her not to light up in the car, then stopped himself.

Three blocks farther, she said, "What do you think he's going to tell Evanger?"

"You got me."

She tapped the end of the cigarette on her knee, getting shreds of tobacco on her pants leg. "I gotta quit these." She reached for the package and shoved the cigarette back inside.

Thinnes had a sudden flash—her rage at being left at the hospital her first day was really due to four hours without a smoke—nicotine withdrawal. "Maybe you better wait," he said, "until we're done with this case."

Her laugh was loud and genuine and—he was startled to note—very attractive.

"You used to smoke," she said. Not a question.

"I quit fourteen years ago. When I found my two-year-old trying to light up one of my Marlboros."

"He your only kid?"

"Yeah. You got any?" It was a roundabout way of asking, Was she married? She didn't wear a ring.

"Not yet." She looked out at the action on the street or maybe the antiques in the storefront windows they were passing.

He thought she sounded wistful. She shook herself and glanced at him. "Haven't found the right father."

Thinnes watched her watching the street like any veteran street copper. Then he looked back at the road. Without paying particular attention, he noticed the car in front of theirs had a tag that had expired in March. Patrol's problem.

He stopped at the three-way intersection at Western and waited for a green. The light changed, and he started forward. "We gotta tell Evanger something. Can you think of anything we might've overlooked?"

"We?"

Thinnes turned into the Nineteenth District parking lot and pulled into a space. "If he said we're working together, the only way to get out of it is to quit the job." He put the gearshift in park and turned off the engine.

"He's that bad?" She took out a cigarette and put it between her lips.

"He's fair. Just don't cross or embarrass him."

She nodded, then got out of the car and lit up. She closed the door and leaned against it while she took several deep drags.

Thinnes got out and faced her across the roof.

"About what you said back there—" Franchi stuck her cigarette in her mouth and hitched her thumb in the direction of downtown, and Caleb's office. "I'll do the scut work—at least for now. But I won't get coffee."

He shrugged. "We can take turns."

She nodded. They stood there while she finished her smoke, then headed toward the building. Thinnes got to the door a step ahead and held it open for her. "Working with me might not be good for your health."

She accepted the courtesy without comment, but said, "Yeah, like you said—Ferris warned me, too—you're a jinx."

They both nodded at the coppers in the square ring of the District desk as they passed them. On the stairs, Franchi said, "Two of my last three partners got canned, so maybe we'll cancel each other." She reached inside the front of her blouse and pulled out a gold chain with a St. Michael's medal. "Anyway, I got protection."

FORTY-THREE

Area One Detective Headquarters was at 51st and Wentworth, upstairs from the Second District. The District lobby was like the neighborhood it served, stressed and overextended. Most of the people in it, on both sides of the desk and wandering the halls, were black. Thinnes took the elevator up and got the same feeling he always did that it was going to quit and strand him between floors.

The detective's squad room was long and narrow, with far too many desks and too much clutter. All the people in it were white and male. Most, Thinnes suspected, were meat-eaters. He nodded to them as he made his way down the room.

Detective Gordon McIntosh looked up from the file he was reading and nodded. "John, what brings you here?"

McIntosh looked more like a successful businessman or lawyer than a Southside detective. He was wearing the kind of suit most dicks wore to testify in court, though he couldn't be at this hour. His shirt was crisp, not a silver hair on his head was out of place.

"I need a little background information—off the record."

McIntosh took off his rimless glasses and rubbed the bridge of his nose with his thumb and forefinger. He put the glasses back on and waved at an empty chair at an adjoining desk.

Thinnes sat.

"On who?"

"Don Franchi."

"Ah."

"Ah?"

McIntosh looked around, causing Thinnes to do likewise. Three men were sharing a joke near the elevator. Another was watching a rap sheet roll out of the printer. No one was paying any attention to McIntosh or his visitor. "She got a bum rap. She was shit as a decoy—a blind man could make her for a cop three blocks away—but she's a good cop."

"And?"

"And you know how it is for a woman on the job. If she gets a promotion, it's because she's blowing someone. If she beefs on someone, even if he's hit on every woman in the house, she's a bitch, or a poor sport, or whatever."

"What, specifically, went down?"

McIntosh shrugged. "There were a couple versions, but the one I believe is her sergeant propositioned her and when she told him to go to hell, he started a bunch of nasty rumors about her. So she filed a grievance. He got disciplined, but I guess it was easier to transfer Franchi than housebreak all these old dogs."

"Why wouldn't she tell me that?"

"Why bother? Who's gonna believe where there's smoke, there's no fire?"

"Good point. But you'd work with her?"

"Sure. There a problem?"

"We're working it out. Thanks."

"Anytime."

FORTY-FOUR

For the first time in a donkey's age, morning sunshine shone into Caleb's office, warming the pale fabric of his couch, polishing the cherrywood table, brightening the splashes of red in the Oriental rug. It wasn't improving the mood of the man sitting on the couch. A man not a client. Someone Caleb had come in early to see.

"My father is dying, Doctor," the man said.

"And?" Caleb was sitting in a chair at right angles to him. The sunlight warmed his legs and feet.

"Don't you think it's just a little unethical to take money from a dying man when there's nothing you can do for him?"

"What makes you believe that?"

"Oh, for God's sake. You just agreed that he was dying!"

"But he's not dead."

"*And where there's life there's hope?*"

"Do you think he doesn't need help to come to terms with his situation?"

"Well, my God! You can't *change* anything for him."

Caleb waited.

"*He* can't change anything! He's just wasting his money coming to you!"

Caleb said, "Excuse me," and squinted as if the sun were getting too bright, letting the man think the sun was the reason when he got up and moved to the chair opposite the couch. He settled himself, and said, "Do you get along well with your father?"

"What kind of question is that?" Caleb waited; eventually the son said, "Of course!"

Not true. Caleb merely said, "Why don't you ask *him* what he's getting from therapy?"

"I did. He said it was 'None of my business.' "

"Did you ask as if you wanted to know the answer, or as if you wanted to know why he was wasting his cash?"

Caleb knew he'd hit his mark when the man stood, and said, "You're full of shit! You'll be hearing from my lawyer."

Caleb doubted he'd find a lawyer who'd be willing get involved, but he didn't argue.

He let his breath out slowly as the man slammed his way out, and gave himself ten minutes before asking Mrs. Sleighton to send his next patient in.

When he opened his door he gestured toward the entire office, and said, "Please have a seat," giving her the choice of where. As usual, she took the chair opposite his desk and sat upright with her arms pressed tightly against her sides and her legs clamped together.

Without preamble, she said, "I keep looking at young women, noticing them the way a rapist might, thinking they're asking for it."

"What made you think of that just now?"

"There was a *Trib* on the table out there." She gestured toward the waiting room. "I couldn't help but notice the headline on the Chicagoland section: Dog bites attacker.

"I want to know why. Freud said it was all about sex, but why?"

"He was wrong. It's about power, not sex. And rape is almost exclusively about power. Members of other species seem able to sort themselves into hierarchies and live with it. Humans apparently are the only animals with issues."

"I've purposely avoided reading any of those feminist things about rape," she said. "—*Our Bodies, Ourselves* and that kind of thing. It would make me more anxious and more outraged. I couldn't read *Soul on Ice*, either. Eldridge Cleaver was a rapist. That's something you don't hear mentioned much.

"My mother always gave me the impression that it would be better to be killed than raped. I think she was right even if for the wrong reason. I have all this anger. And I was raised not to express my anger. What do I do with it?"

Caleb waited for her to answer the question herself.

"Even if they caught the guy who raped me, they couldn't lock him up. I found out that the statute of limitations for rape is only three years. It ought to be when the victim gets over it. And when they're convicted, rapists ought to be locked up until their victims recover."

"That might be never."

"So?"

"Do you think the arrest of the man who raped you would give you closure?"

"Castrating him would give me closure."

She shifted slightly in her chair, but didn't seem much more relaxed.

"I'm not afraid anymore. I can't even remember what it's like to feel fear. All my fear has been replaced by anger. It might be almost nice to feel fearful again."

She looked straight at him, aggressively. "What do I do with my rage?"

"What would happen if you let it go?"

"I don't know."

She did know. He waited.

"I'd be empty. There'd be nothing left."

"It's familiar," he offered. "Better the devil you know . . ."

"It keeps me going. No, that's not right. It's become who I am."

"You've taken the first step. You've admitted this great anger exists."

"And?"

"You need to mourn your loss."

"Loss?"

"A good part of loss is anger. You've lost a great deal."

She nodded.

"Rage is a powerful force. You could learn to use it to fuel any number of worthy causes."

FORTY-FIVE

Thinnes wasn't sleeping well. Rhonda had been cold lately when he tried to touch her. She wasn't mad, she'd said. She asked him to give her time. What choice did he have?

But he wasn't used to sleeping alone on the far side of the bed.

She stopped him in the doorway as he was on his way out that morning. "John, do you mind if I invite someone from work for dinner tonight?"

"I don't have to cook, do I?"

"No."

"No, why should I?"

He came into the squad room with the feeling he'd overlooked something. The night shift had unplugged the coffeepot, leaving a half cup of cold sludge in the bottom. Thinnes turned the cases over in his head while he took the pot into the men's room and scrubbed it out. He left it perking, with his empty LONE STAR mug next to it.

In the conference room, he turned the chalkboard so his diagram faced the room and laid the rape files—Doe, Highlander, Jacobs, Lake, and Nesbit—out across the table with the victims' pictures on top. He'd just started rereading the various reports in the Jane Doe file when Franchi came in.

She had on a new suit, loose-fitting like the ones Ryan wore, with a high-collared white blouse. She was carrying his coffee mug and one for herself that said DEATH BEFORE DISHONOR. NOTHING BEFORE COFFEE. She put his mug in front of him. She put her mug two chairs down along the table. Then she took off her jacket and hung it on the back of her chair.

Her blouse looked like cotton, and it hugged her upper torso in a way that was more suggestive than revealing. Too damn suggestive. He grabbed his coffee and took a quick swig to hide his reaction. For the first time he couldn't smell cigarettes on her. What he could smell was a subtle, attractive perfume. He wasn't sure it was an improvement considering he had to work with her day after day because Evanger was right. No matter what you said to a woman under such circumstances, it would bite you in the butt.

He realized Franchi was offering him a stack of papers, and said, "Sorry. What was that?"

"Printouts. Just for kicks I ran the names of our suspects—males eighteen to thirty-six—through a search engine last night."

"Here?"

She gave him a "be serious" look. "On my PC at home. Wish I could afford some of those subscription sites."

He didn't ask what those were. He had heard of a search engine—Rob mentioned searching the Web for something with one—but the Internet was pretty much a new frontier for him.

"The jerk with the Humvee—got his name from the SOS, from his license plate. He's not our rapist. Turns out he spent the weekend in County for contempt—refused to pay $8000 in back child support."

"Figures."

Franchi tapped the top sheet. "Anyway, there was an interview with Erik Last, the photographer, in which he alluded to being in trouble as a kid before he discovered photography. So I called the cops in his hometown. They told me—'off the record because it was a juvenile beef'—that he was incarcerated for rape as a teenager."

Thinnes had already determined that Last had no adult arrest record.

"He's beginning to look like an excellent suspect," Franchi said.

Thinnes remembered Last's surprised look when first told of the rape. "It's not Last."

"Another hunch?"

"Was I wrong about the hooker?"

"No."

"Well then." He figured he'd made his point, so he added, "Let's run a check on him anyway."

An hour later, they hadn't found out anything more about Erik Last but decided to pick him up for an interview anyway. Thinnes pulled out of the lot onto Belmont and turned north on Western, behind a dark red, late-model Chevy S10 that had two bumper stickers. One said, THE NATIONAL SAFETY COUNCIL IS A BUNCH OF CRASH DUMMIES, the other, GM PUT THE IDIOT LIGHTS ON THE OUTSIDE.

Franchi pointed to the truck, and said, "What do you suppose that means?"

"The driver must not like daytime running lights," Thinnes said. "I'll bet he's got 'em disconnected." He turned on the headlight flashers. The Chevy's driver obligingly signaled right and curbed the truck. Thinnes waved a thanks and glanced in the rearview as he pulled past. There were no headlights showing on the Chevy. The driver, a middle-aged, white female with short, dark hair and wire-rimmed glasses, waved back. Thinnes checked the road ahead, then glanced sideways at Franchi. "See?"

"Yeah. But aren't running lights supposed to be a safety thing?"

"Advertising hype. I think they're a hazard. You're driving along with those when it gets dark. You don't put on your headlights 'cause you can see fine so you think you have them on. And you get slammed from behind by some semi driver who can't see you because you've got no taillights showing."

"I never thought of that."

"Trying to idiot-proof cars just puts more idiots on the road."

Erik Last was only marginally more cooperative than he'd been when Thinnes first interviewed him. On their promise that if he'd come back to the Area and sign a statement, they'd never darken his doorway again, he reluctantly agreed to accompany them. He was wearing a long-sleeved white silk shirt. He refused to roll up his sleeves; refused to say why he wouldn't. They grilled him for an hour in one of the claustrophobic Nineteenth District interview rooms downstairs, without getting anywhere.

When Thinnes asked if he'd ever been arrested, he said, "You know the answer to that. You have access to every arrest record on the planet."

"Not quite. Would you mind answering yes or no?"

"Yes, I mind. Am I under arrest?"

"No."

"Then take me home."

"What about your juvenile arrest?" Franchi asked.

Perfect timing, Thinnes decided.

"If you know about that, you must have gotten the information illegally."

Touché.

"I don't have any information," Franchi said without missing a beat." Good girl! "You mentioned it in an interview on the Internet—common knowledge."

"Take me home!"

He hadn't finished his report on the interview when the desk sergeant called out, "Phone for you, Thinnes."

The guy on the other line said, "Thinnes, Jackson, Area Five. We got your rapist. You want to come down and watch us peel him?"

"Peel him?"

"Like he was a grape. Sommabitch tangles with the wrong broad, and she drilled him. They're doing the post in an hour."

"That might be entertaining. How do you know he's *our* rapist."

"How many rapists we got working the North Side?"

When he'd hung up, Thinnes said, "Franchi, Five caught an attempted rape. I'm going to check it out. You with me?"

Franchi had her jacket on before he finished "me."

The autopsy was pretty standard. The deceased, "a well-nourished white male of approximately twenty-five years of age," died of a gunshot wound to the left chest. A bullet had ripped through his heart and exited through his back. The manner of death would be listed on the death certificate as homicide, but nobody was suggesting it wasn't justified.

According to Jackson, the man had been trying to rape a woman in her own bedroom after breaking into her apartment. It was just his bad luck that she was a security guard who kept her gun in a drawer next to the bed.

Though her description fit the victim profile for the rape cases, the MO was wrong. And her name was wrong too, Selma Ala.

Thinnes and Franchi stood back from the autopsy table, behind Jackson and Dr. Cutler, the pathologist. Franchi had put a blue smock on over her new suit, but it wouldn't keep the morgue smell from seeping into it. Thinnes didn't say so. He was beginning to think the odor would be less distracting than her perfume.

"Doc," he said, "this guy have any damage that could've been done by a dog?"

"Not that I can see."

"What was his blood type?"

"Don't know yet. Call back before end of business."

"I don't think this was our guy. Check him against the blood type we got from the dog bite."

Jackson shook his head. "Tryin' to make a molehill into a mountain. They warned me about you, Thinnes."

The squad room was full, the whole team working the phones when Thinnes called the morgue to get the blood type report— AB positive. He wasn't an expert, but he knew enough to be sure the dead rapist wasn't the O-negative offender they were looking for. "Area Five didn't get our guy," he announced. "Let's keep working."

"Thintuition!" Franchi said.

"No, Murphy's Law."

FORTY-SIX

At least we're narrowing down our suspect list."

Franchi handed Thinnes the printout on Father Cannon—showing no arrests, no wants or warrants, and a clean driving record. Cannon was outside the age range of their offender profile, but they were running out of leads and not making any assumptions.

"You a Catholic, Franchi?" Thinnes asked.

"Sort of—raised Catholic anyway."

"Father Cannon strike you as a normal priest?"

She shrugged. "What's normal? He's not like the priests my mother grew up with—to hear her tell it. But Linda Seeger told me he practices what he preaches . . ."

Thinnes waited.

"From what she told me, he must've been a hippie in the early seventies. You know—some of 'em grew up to be aldermen or businessmen. And Father Cannon became a priest."

They went to the entrance marked RECTORY and asked for Father Cannon. The young priest who answered the door had them wait in the foyer. Two minutes after he disappeared, Father Cannon appeared, and their first question was answered without them having to ask it—his short-sleeved black shirt let them see he had no bite wounds on his arms.

In his priest costume, he inspired confidence. His cheerful expression suggested optimism—even before he spoke—and his size gave the impression he could handle anything—sort of like the burly coppers who headed off trouble just by the weight of their presence. As far as Thinnes was concerned, he wasn't their man. But he still might know something.

The priest kept a running commentary on DePaul, University and Church, the rape-crisis center, and points of interest along the way back to the Area. He even mentioned Riverview, the amusement park that had occupied the land now taken up by the police station, Cook County's First Municipal District Circuit Court, and the shopping mall to the north.

Most people who talked so much were trying to cover their nervousness, but Cannon gave the impression he soaked up information about everything he came across and was eager to share it. He seemed to take for granted that everyone else would be as interested as he was.

By the time they got to Belmont and Western, he'd answered half the questions Thinnes had for him without having been asked.

Since he wasn't a strong suspect, they took him into the Neighborhood Relations office and offered him a chair and coffee.

When they were all settled, Franchi started the ball rolling. "Why rape counseling, Father?"

"It's one of my pastoral duties. And it's something I can do. Not everyone can."

Most men couldn't stomach it, Thinnes thought. He said, "You got some kind of degree for that?"

"An MSW."

"So you do counseling?"

"Yes. In addition to crisis counseling, marriage and family counseling, and personal counseling."

"But you go out of your way to counsel rape victims," Franchi said. "Why?"

"I feel it's my duty as a man—all men benefit from rape."

"How's that?" Thinnes said.

"Those of us who aren't rapists are heroes by default."

"You ever counsel a rapist?"

"Yes."

"The guy who killed Monica Nesbit?"

"I don't know who killed her."

"You didn't answer my question."

"If I had, I couldn't tell you."

"You ever been arrested?" Thinnes asked.

Cannon seemed surprised by the question but seemed to recover his balance. "Yes."

"For what?"

"Trespassing. Disorderly conduct. During the war." Thinnes waited. "Vietnam. I was a protester."

"What would you do if the guy who killed her came to you and confessed?"

"I'd urge him to surrender to the police."

"What if he came to you for counseling, Father?" Franchi said.

Cannon looked at her. "Then I'd have to go to the authorities because I have no doubt, if he's not caught, he'll kill again."

Later, driving back to the Area after dropping Father Cannon at the rectory, Thinnes said, "How old are you, Franchi?"

"Twenty-nine. Why?"

"You been a cop how long?"

"Seven. I joined right after college."

"College?"

"Yeah. My dad was a cop, and he wanted us to go to school and get a career. He didn't want us to be cops."

"Figures."

"Well, he warned me." She stared out the window for a while, then added, "Patrol wasn't so bad."

"So why not stay there?" Thinnes knew there were women sergeants in patrol, even a few watch commanders. "Why put yourself through this shit?"

"Somebody's got to break the glass."

The glass ceiling, he presumed. Rhonda had mentioned it.

Franchi went on. "You know how it feels when you're assigned to work with someone, and he picks up the phone—right in front of you—and calls his CO and asks him to send up a 'real detective'?"

"Like working for Rossi."

FORTY-SEVEN

Toby was waiting at the door when Thinnes got home. He greeted Thinnes with his usual excitement, then wriggled off toward the back of the house. Thinnes slipped the holstered .38 off his belt and put it on the top shelf of the closet by the stairs. He called out, "Ronnie?"

"We're in here, John."

He followed her voice to the kitchen.

She and Toby weren't alone. The woman seated at the table with a half-filled wineglass acted like she'd been friends of the family forever.

Franchi!

She turned her head and gave Thinnes a smug little smile. Her body language said, "Gotcha!"

He registered his adrenaline flood, the prickling it caused on his arms and shoulders. At the same time his brain was forming his response—Shit! He felt as if his newly forged truce with Franchi had been broken by this invasion of his territory.

He caught Rhonda's eye, and she flashed him a sad little smile, the one—he'd learned over the years—that meant she was disappointed. He didn't cross the room to kiss her as he would have if they'd been alone.

She had him! He'd agreed to let her invite "someone from work" and her failure to specify who, or from whose work, was Rhonda's way of letting him know how she felt about being kept in the dark.

He couldn't throw Franchi out, and he'd have to be civil. He wondered, though, why Franchi had come. Curiosity, maybe, or a chance to put him on the spot?

Nodding in her direction, he said, "Franchi."

"Call me Don." The laugh lines around her eyes deepened, though the smile didn't get to her mouth. She was wearing a red silk shirt open at the neck and tucked into tight black slacks. Her black leather sandals showed off toenails painted to match the shirt, and a heavy gold necklace and bracelet. Next to her, Rhonda looked dated and domestic even though the flowered dress she was wearing was Thinnes's favorite—both for how she looked in it and how quickly he could get under it when she was in the mood.

Thinnes nodded to Rhonda, and said, "Hi, Ronnie. Where's Rob?"

"Working. Would you like some wine, John?"

"Yeah. Sure." As she poured for him from the bottle of imported Italian that Franchi must have brought, he asked, "You need help with anything?"

"You could set the table."

"Okay."

They ate on a set of Corelle ware that Rhonda had admired once when they were shopping at Sears. They didn't have company dishes. The wedding china they'd never used because it was too expensive to replace, Rhonda had sold when Rob was twelve so they could send him to Space Camp. They no longer invited people who were too good to eat on their family dishes.

Thinnes got out what he needed and made three trips back to the kitchen for other things Rhonda set out for him. Meanwhile, Rhonda and Franchi continued the conversation they'd been having before he got home—woman things.

Then Franchi started asking Rhonda about her job, listening carefully to every answer. She was a good interviewer when she wasn't pissed, though Thinnes wasn't about to say so.

He was standing over the table, trying to decide if he'd missed any essential equipment, when Rhonda came in with the salad. Alone. He said, "What *is* this, Ronnie?"

"This is payback, John. I hate being lied to."

"I haven't lied to you."

"You don't say! You *didn't* say. Why is that?"

He looked to be sure the kitchen door was closed, then said, "I thought I'd get rid of her before it got to be an issue—I don't tell you about every dick I'm assigned to work with."

"You told me about this one. You just omitted the most important fact."

"Yeah. I'm sorry."

"I don't want to hear it. I thought we had it worked out that I'd never have to hear 'sorry' again." She went back into the kitchen, leaving him trying to recall what he'd been doing when she came in.

The meal was nerve-wracking. Rhonda's lasagna was fine, and the wine Franchi brought very nice, but he was too uptight to enjoy either. The women chatted like old friends. After a couple of attempts to include him in the conversation, they gave up and went on without him, discussing their respective family histories, Rob, recent movies they'd enjoyed, Franchi's lack of a "significant other." In the half hour it took to finish off the pasta, Franchi's wine, and a bottle of good California Merlot they'd been saving for a special occasion, Thinnes learned more about Franchi than he had since they first met.

He noticed she hadn't excused herself for a cigarette since he got home. "You quit smoking, Franchi? Don."

She gave him a Mona Lisa smile. "I decided it's not good for my health." She turned to Rhonda. "I'll bet you never smoked."

Rhonda laughed. "Not cigarettes. I tried marijuana when I was in college." She looked at Thinnes, gave him a look that acknowledged she'd brought up a topic he'd rather not think about. College. When he was in Vietnam. Then she looked back at Franchi. "It was like standing downwind from a trash fire. What a disappointment."

"Forbidden fruit," Franchi said.

Rhonda nodded, then said, "How about dessert?"

"None for me, thanks."

"John?"

"No room." He pushed away from the table, and said, "I'll clear."

"Is he always this domestic?" Franchi asked.

"Only when he's trying to get on my good side."

When he came out of the kitchen, he asked, "Coffee?"

Rhonda said, "Yes, please."

"That would be very nice," Franchi said.

He nodded and collected another load of dishes. In the kitchen, he started the coffeemaker, stowed the food, and scraped the dishes and loaded them in the dishwasher. When he went back for the last of the clearings, the women had left the table.

He put the coffeepot, mugs, creamer, and sugar bowl on a tray, and brought it into the family room. They were working on the five-thousand-piece jigsaw puzzle that Rhonda had going on a card table kept for such projects. The box picture showed the Chicago skyline at night, and all the pieces that weren't part of the Standard Oil or the Stone Container Buildings looked the same—small and dark with white or yellow splotches. Thinnes set the tray down and poured.

"Help us with this, John," Rhonda said. It was a request she'd never have made but for Franchi. He hated doing puzzles. The ones he solved at work had some point. But he figured working the puzzle would be less stressful than trying to make conversation, so he sipped his coffee while he looked for edge pieces.

Franchi dived into the middle, where all the bits looked alike. She kept on with what she'd been talking about when he came in the room: "My dad was a great sportsman. He used to take me with him sometimes, hunting or fishing. The best part was sitting in the bar with him, afterwards. He'd buy me a beef jerky and a root beer and let me sit next to him listening to the stories and watching the Hamms—'Land-of-Sky-Blue-Waters' display."

Thinnes remembered those. His father was also a fisherman, and they'd always stopped on the way home from the lake to get a burger and a beer—Coke for Thinnes—before calling it a day. Thinnes would always worm his way onto a stool by the Hamms light where a translucent plastic drum, with a lake scene, rotated around a lightbulb. Something inside made the water in the picture seem to move like wind-driven waves. The effect was mesmerizing.

Weird coincidence.

"I think I was his favorite," Franchi continued, " 'cause I wasn't afraid of him. I would always tell him 'Someday I'm gonna be a policeman, just like you.' And he'd say, 'Don't be silly. Girls can't be cops.'

"I'm the only one in my family on the job. My oldest brother made it almost all the way through the Academy, but one day he just walked away from it. I've got cousins who're on the job, but no brothers."

"I had a very nice time," Franchi said as she was leaving.

Thinnes had the feeling she was saying one thing to Rhonda and something altogether different to him. She held his eye as she told him, "See you in the morning."

Later, when Franchi had gone home and they were getting ready for bed, Thinnes said, "What did you two talk about before I got home?"

Rhonda stepped close and said, "Oh, I told her that you're mine, and that I know where you keep your backup gun in case she forgets it."

"Ah-hunh."

"Really, I told her I love you dearly." She leaned against him.

Thinnes folded his arms around her and rested his chin on the top of her head. "That's all?"

She put her face against his chest. "I think she's a person of integrity. That's enough. If she were trash, nothing I could say or do would make any difference."

He held her at arm's length, and said, "You're really jealous!" Her expression told him it wasn't a joking matter. He put his arms back around her, and said, "When I look at her, I see her pissed-off expression and her attitude. And even if she quits smoking, she'll never smell as good as you.

"Besides, she's young enough to be my daughter."

"I thought that's what middle-aged men were looking for."

"Middle-aged!"

FORTY-EIGHT

The detective who'd investigated the rape of Greta Highlander had summarized her medical record in his report:

> Victim had a superficial transverse cut across the throat which was deeper on the left side indicating a cut from the rear by a right-handed offender, also had numerous cuts to the breasts, vulva, and lower abdomen consistent with cutting with a broken bottle. Bruises and contusions on the inner thighs and genital area were consistent with forcible penetration. Tests showed no sign of semen or seminal fluid.

Highlander had been found naked and bleeding in a Dumpster by a homeless woman who'd flagged down a passing patrol car. The investigating officer noted that the victim wasn't able to be much help in identifying her attacker as she'd been comatose for two weeks and was semihysterical subsequently.

When detectives tried to follow up on the case, they found she'd moved and left no forwarding address.

Thinnes and Franchi looked up Highlander's former roommate, who turned out to be a slight, ditzy redhead of an unnatural shade, almost maroon. She was still living in the place she'd shared with Highlander, a long narrow garden apartment in a three-flat in West Lincoln Park. The front room appeared to have been furnished from a Salvation Army store. Though it was clean, it was incredibly cluttered. They told her they were trying to track down her old roommate, reinvestigating the case. As she cleared a place on the couch for them to sit, Thinnes wondered how the woman ever kept track of anything.

"Tell us about Greta," Franchi said.

"She was totally paranoid after the attack," Ditzy told them, "wouldn't go out or anything. And she was scared of men. She was never scared of a man before. I guess I'd be scared, too—she was in the hospital for two months. And they couldn't fix her completely. They couldn't do much about the scars, and she had to have a hysterectomy. One day I came home and she was gone—no good-bye, no forwarding address."

"Do you have any theories about who the guy was?" Franchi asked.

Ditzy shook her head. "She had lots of guy friends, but she didn't string any of them along. They were all nice.

"She used to be a lot of fun." She got up and pulled a photo album out from under a pile of newspapers. She flipped it open and showed them a picture of herself with the dark-haired Highlander. Ditzy was blond in the picture.

"Aren't you afraid, living here?" Franchi asked.

She shook her head. "No sense in moving now. Lightning doesn't strike twice, ya know."

They got back in the car, and Franchi said, "When I meet someone that stupid, I just want to shake her."

They tracked Highlander down with considerable difficulty. She was living above a pediatrician's office in a small town in Indiana, working as the doctor's receptionist. She was reluctant to talk to them, but when they told her the rapist had struck again, she agreed to see them on her lunch hour. She led them up to her spartan living room and offered them seats on the couch after displacing her two cats. Two gray-striped short-hairs.

Physically, to an astonishing degree, Highlander resembled Katherine Lake and Monica Nesbit. But she was much thinner. She didn't sit, but leaned against the side of her recliner and held one of the cats as she told her tale.

"I was walking down the street, about four o'clock in the afternoon when I was grabbed from behind by someone very strong. He put one hand over my mouth and used the other to hold a cloth with some chemical on it over my nose. When I breathed it in, I blacked out.

"When I woke up, I was naked. Cold. In someplace that smelled like a damp basement. On what must have been a cement floor. My hands were taped together in front of me, and my eyes and mouth were taped. I could hardly breathe. I was so terrified and freezing. I think I must've been in shock.

"I was able to get the tape off my mouth, but he must've been watching me, waiting for me to wake, because when I tried to pull the tape off my eyes he spoke. He told me if I saw his face, he'd have to kill me.

"I begged him not to hurt me, to let me go.

"He laughed.

"That really scared me. I thought, he's going to kill me anyway, I might as well try to escape. But I couldn't see to run, so I reached up to remove the tape. That's when he hit me, slapped me hard. I panicked, and even though I couldn't see, I tried to run. I smashed into things. He laughed, and all the while chanted, 'Run! Run! Run!' Then he tackled me, brought me down with as little feeling as a wolf bringing down a deer.

"I fought him, but he held my arms over my head and laughed, and when I kept struggling, he slapped me until I nearly lost consciousness.

"Then he raped me."

She had to stop, taking little hiccuping breaths like someone who's cried herself out. Tears seeped from her eyes, and she wiped them with her sleeve.

Franchi leaned over and put a hand on her arm, and asked, "Would you like to take a break?"

Highlander took in a long shuddering breath. "No. I'd like to get this over with.

"After he raped me, he rolled me over and pulled me up on my knees and raped me in the rear. I think I screamed. I heard screaming, and I heard him laughing. Then I passed out.

"When I woke up, he raped me with a thin, hard object. Smaller in diameter than his penis and longer—like a broom handle—until I passed out again from the pain.

"That's all I remember until I woke up in the hospital. I never saw his face."

"The detective who investigated this initially said you had a number of boyfriends," Franchi said. "Could any of them have had a reason to want to hurt you?"

"I admit I used to enjoy sex. Maybe I could even be called promiscuous, but I was always careful. About diseases and about not leading anybody on. The guys I went out with were fun. None of them would hurt me."

"Anybody you refused to go out with who might want to hurt you?" Thinnes asked.

"Don't you think I would've said so?" Thinnes waited. Highlander said, "No."

Franchi asked the next obvious question. "Why did you leave Chicago without leaving a forwarding address?"

"I was afraid. After I got out of the hospital, my roomie brought me home and sort of took care of me. But she had a job and a life—you know. I was a wreck, physically and— I couldn't go out with her, and I couldn't ask her to stay home with me all the time. It was scary. I must've been home a week when I noticed the earrings I'd been wearing when I was attacked were on my dresser with the rest of my jewelry. I know the police told my roommate to change the locks, and she said she did, but I freaked. I got paranoid and started to think she was in on the attack. So I just ran. I left her a note saying I couldn't live there anymore and just packed a few things and walked out. I didn't tell her where I was going or where to forward my mail in case he might find out where I was and come after me. I went to stay with an aunt in Rensselaer. She took care of me, got me a job here. I started seeing a therapist . . ."

FORTY-NINE

When they got back from Indiana, the sergeant at the Nineteenth District desk told Thinnes that a guy waiting in the Neighborhood Relations office insisted on talking to the detectives in charge of the rape investigations. "He's been here a couple hours," the sergeant added. "He swears he's not a reporter, but he's driving 'em nuts in there with all his questions." Questions they wouldn't answer even if they could.

The visitor was old and white-haired, with large ears and bushy brows over large brown eyes. He was wearing a plaid cotton shirt, tan slacks, and canvas loafers, carrying a black-nylon briefcase.

He introduced himself as Calvin Witt and told them that he was retired, with time on his hands, but seven years earlier he'd been a reporter when a couple of rapes occurred in Waukegan. He'd covered the stories for the *News-Sun*. The perpetrator's—his word—MO was identical to the attacks in Lincoln Park. "We had information we couldn't put in the paper—like the exact damage done and the victim's names. Even had a picture of one of the victims—of course we couldn't use it. And there was a girl who disappeared who was reported as a missing person, who bore an uncanny resemblance to the girl in that picture—the rape victim. What'd you think of that?"

"Interesting."

"If I'm not mistaken, the perp's back in business. Check this: The victim's attacked on her way home. She's dragged into a semiprivate place—alley or deserted street, where the chance of interruption is small. Her mouth is taped. She's taunted, stripped, sodomized, and beaten. The perp takes her money and credit cards, her keys. Then he chokes her half-unconscious and tells her, 'I'll be back.'

"She either gets found and taken to a hospital, or she drags herself home and calls the cops. Either way, when she gets back from the hospital or cop shop—whenever—she discovers someone's been in her place, messing with her things."

It sounded too much like Greta Highlander's story to be coincidence. Thinnes glanced at Franchi, who looked politely bored. He wondered if she was on some kind of tranquilizer—she hadn't gone out for a smoke all day—or if she was just hiding her interest from Witt.

Witt continued, "The attacks stopped as suddenly as they began. The cops wouldn't say so, but I think they ID'd the rapist but couldn't nail him for some reason. He may have been arrested and sentenced for something else, or have been in a serious car accident—something that put him out of circulation for a good long while. At the time, I thought he might even have killed himself. But now, with these new cases here . . . I think he may have just gotten cold feet because the cops were getting too close."

Witt took a folder out of his case and handed it to Thinnes. "You can keep these. I got the originals at home."

The folder was full of neatly typed notes and photocopies of newspaper articles.

Thinnes said, "Thank you, Mr. Witt. We appreciate the input."

Witt didn't make any move to leave.

"We'll definitely follow through on this." Witt still wasn't taking the hint. Thinnes waited.

Finally, the old man said, "You'll keep me posted?"

"As soon as we've made an arrest, we'll call you." He stood up. "Detective Franchi will show you out."

Franchi threw him a look, but just said, "This way, Mr. Witt."

When the door had closed behind them, Thinnes opened the file and skimmed the articles. Most were typical—short on useful information, long on speculation. On the face of it, though, the cases did have a lot in common with their own.

Franchi was gone long enough for him to get through the whole file. She must've gone out for a smoke while she was at it. Thinnes met her in the squad room and handed her the folder. "Check these out, will you? Maybe call up and find out who handled the cases. See if they're still on the job." She nodded. "What did you think of Mr. Witt?"

She shrugged. "We checked all the recent graduates—nothing. I think Gramps needs to get a life." She waved the folder up and down. "You want me to do this now?"

"Unless you got something more urgent."

"Right." She gathered up her purse and jacket. "You want the results today." He shook his head. She nodded, and said, "*Ciao*, then."

FIFTY

As soon as Franchi left, Thinnes went into the conference room and read through the file, then turned the chalkboard so his diagram faced out. He expanded the grid, adding rows for the names of the two rape victims in Witt's file. He wrote aka Coral Davis?, the name of the missing person, under "Jane Doe."

NAME	physical description	age	close friend or roommate	primary crime scene	dumped	injuries	misc.
ABBY BURTON?		16			?	beaten raped, cut	suicide
JANE DOE aka CORAL DAVIS?	eyes? brunette	18– 22		?	yes—alley	beaten raped murdered	writing on body
ELAINE FRANKLIN?					?	beaten raped, cut	
GRETA HIGHLANDER	brown, brunette	23	thin, blue-eyed blonde	?	yes—alley	beaten raped, cut	
IVY JACOBS	same	21	?	?	?	beaten raped, cut	
KATHERINE LAKE	same	22	thin, blue-eyed blonde	?	yes—alley	beaten raped, cut	
MONICA NESBIT	same	22	thin, blue-eyed blonde	?	yes—alley	beaten raped, cut murdered	writing on body

After studying the results, he decided it was time for a break. Time to find out what the National Crime Information Center had on Coral Davis. He turned his diagram back facing the wall before he left the room.

To his surprise, NCIC had nothing. Thinnes called the ME to give them Davis's name, then headed for Evanger's office.

"Let me make a few phone calls," Evanger told him, when he'd finished laying out what they had.

Half an hour later, Evanger met him at the coffeemaker. "You and Franchi go up to Waukegan tomorrow morning. Early. See a Detective Hogencamp. They said you'd better plan to spend some time if you want to read everything they've got. May as well make a day of it."

Next morning, Thinnes and Franchi killed time doing paperwork until 9:00 A.M., when rush hour was slackening, then they headed north. Thinnes had been to the Waukegan station just last summer while checking out an arson suspect. The police department occupied the west end of the two-story limestone-faced building it shared with the Waukegan municipal government.

As they pulled past the building, Franchi asked about the human-sized replica of the Statue of Liberty at the southwest corner.

"Gift from the Boy Scouts," he told her, as if that explained it, and turned into the police parking lot.

The reception area inside the station was the size of an Area Three interview room, with a currency-exchange-type security window into the dispatch room. Thinnes noticed a three-minute discrepancy between the time on the twenty-four-hour wall clock and the digital display for the remote video camera surveillance screen next to the clock.

"They handle a lot of cash here?" Franchi asked. "Or is this a *really* bad neighborhood?"

Thinnes laughed. "Maybe they're expecting the Terminator."

"Or someone warned them about you."

She smiled when she said it; Thinnes didn't take offense. Before he could answer, a young man in civilian clothes came up to the inside of the window, and said, "May I help you?"

They started with the Burton file. Thinnes went for the photos first. The school picture of Abby Burton before she was attacked could've been Katherine Lake's high school graduation shot. Thinnes showed it to Franchi, who said. "Jesus Christ!"

"Check this out," he told her. He held up one of the pictures of Burton taken in the ER. The pattern of cuts on her face, neck, and breasts was identical to the pattern of damage done to Katherine Lake.

Detective Angie Hogencamp, who'd met them at the door and escorted them upstairs, must have been assigned to baby-sit. She sat at one end of the table they had the files spread out on and read her paper. She was obviously more interested in the food pages than in finding out about their case.

Thinnes read the entire file, passing each report to Franchi as he finished it. According to the primary on the case, Abby Burton had been a high-school junior when she was abducted on her way home from a basketball game. The car she'd been driving was abandoned in a grocery-store parking lot on the opposite side of town. No one had seen who parked it there. Abby herself had been beaten, raped, and cut superficially with something like a razor blade or utility knife. She was dumped naked in front of Waukegan High School early the following Monday morning where she was found nearly frozen to death by the first teacher to arrive.

Waukegan PD had gone all out to find the rapist but without success. Burton became hysterical when she finally regained consciousness. Talking to the police was out of the question. They'd never managed to get a coherent statement from her because the day after she was sent home from the hospital, she'd hanged herself. They never discovered where she'd been between Friday night and Monday morning. It was presumed she'd been dumped from a car, though there were no witnesses. Judging by the interview reports, the police talked to every student and staff member at the school and half of the rest of Waukegan. With no luck. Eventually they'd run out of people to interview. Still, they'd marked the case closed.

"Why is that?" Thinnes asked Hogencamp.

"Check the Franklin case." Hogencamp apparently did have an interest in her city's crimes.

Elaine Franklin came to the attention of the Waukegan police when the plastic surgeon who'd been called in to treat Abby Burton's wounds recognized the same pattern of injuries in a young woman at Condell Hospital in Libertyville. When he found out the police had never been notified of the attack on Franklin, he went to the Libertyville cops, who subsequently notified Waukegan. When they tried to investigate, both departments were told to butt out. Franklin's family claimed she was schizophrenic and had cut herself during a psychotic episode.

The Waukegan cops were as skeptical as Thinnes, reading the report six years later, especially when their follow-up disclosed that the two injured women had a mutual friend, Claire Ingrahm. And Ingrahm's brother, Kevin, was considered "strange" and "creepy" by classmates and acquaintances.

The police had been prevented from interviewing Franklin herself. After discharge from Condell, she was taken to a private mental hospital, Stormhaven, in Libertyville. An injunction issued to her family prohibited anyone from contacting Franklin "until such time as her doctors feel it could be done without exacerbating her condition." A series of notes in the file documented unsuccessful annual attempts by the Lake County attorney to have the injunction lifted—because "Ms. Franklin's condition has not sufficiently improved." The last note was dated August 1, 1994, and had the addition: "9/14/94 suspect deceased."

Thinnes showed Hogencamp the note. "So what was this guy's name? You got a file on him?"

"Kevin Ingrahm—but you didn't get that from me." She handed Thinnes another folder. "You can look, but it won't help you."

"You didn't list the rapes with NCIC. Why's that?"

"We never had any proof Franklin was raped. And Ingrahm was a *really* good suspect. His family had him committed to Stormhaven—by some amazing coincidence—which has facilities for the criminally insane. They refused to say why, but we had our suspicions. We tried getting court orders to do a little more digging. The family blocked it. Just incidentally, a good part of Stormhaven's operation budget comes from a fund endowed by the Ingrahms."

"There you go. He's out and at it again."

"Not a chance. His room at Stormhaven went up in a really hot fire, after which they found a crispy critter. It was ruled death due to smoke inhalation—careless use of smoking materials. Accidental. But he set the fire, so it may have been suicide."

"We sure this guy's really dead?"

"The teeth matched his dental records. Our coroner doesn't make that kind of mistake, but we had a forensic dentist double-check."

"Too bad," Thinnes said. "Our guy's MO is identical to your two cases."

"So, you got a copycat."

"It has to be someone with access to your files."

"Impossible."

"The details are perfect. What are the odds of that? How well do you screen your cops?"

"Can't be."

"Well, how about file clerks or data-entry personnel? Or maybe a janitor—someone with access?"

Hogencamp shook her head. "More likely one of the other inmates at Bedlam. Somebody Ingrahm hung with. You oughta talk to the head shrink over there."

"We will," Franchi said.

Thinnes paged through Ingrahm's file. Notes and a photo-copy of the death certificate confirmed what the Waukegan detective had just told them. He handed the file to Franchi, who must've been reading it over his shoulder because she just handed it back to Hogencamp.

"What was the story on Coral Davis?" Thinnes asked.

"All I know is what's in the file."

Which was damn little. Coral Davis, nineteen, had gone to visit unspecified friends one evening and never returned. Her mother eventually filed a missing persons report, but there'd been no evidence of foul play. So the police hadn't followed through or listed her with NCIC.

"That was Jim Collins's case. He's retired, but he'd probably talk to you about it.

"And you could try talking to Ingrahm's sister if you can get her to let you in the door. We never had any luck. But now that Ingrahm's dead, she might be willing to talk to you."

"To us? Don't you want in on this?"

"Ingrahm's old man had the court records sealed when he had the kid committed, but we had enough on him for a grand jury indictment if he ever got out. As far as we're concerned, our two homicides are closed."

"You do a DNA test on the crispy critter?"

"Naw. Didn't seem worth the trouble."

FIFTY-ONE

The weather was perfect. Seventy-two degrees. Cloudless.

They found retired detective Collins in Kenosha, sitting on an aluminum folding chair at the end of a pier. He had a six-pack cooler under his seat and a fishing rod in his hand. "You got a license to fish here?" he asked when they were close enough for conversation.

Thinnes showed him his star.

"Fishing for sharks," Collins said. He pointed to a couple of empty plastic stacking chairs a few yards away. "Guys belong to those won't be back 'til they finished drinkin' lunch. Take the load off."

Thinnes dragged the chairs over and offered one to Franchi, then sat down. Franchi took off her jacket and turned to face the sun. Her blouse was sleeveless, and her skin was a warm shade of gold. Thinnes found himself spinning his wedding ring around with his left thumb. His face felt warm, and he wondered if it was because of the sun. He looked at Collins, who was staring at Franchi with undisguised admiration. She seemed oblivious. She put her jacket on the back of the chair and swung it around so she was facing the sun when she sat down.

"What can I do for you?" Collins asked, when she was settled.

"You can tell us about Coral Davis, Abby Burton, and Elaine Franklin."

He nodded. "Davis was a high-school dropout who lived with her mother in a trailer park—trailer trash, according to some. She'd run away before, so when she went missing, the mother didn't pay much attention until she'd been gone two weeks. By that time the trail was cold, but Coral was over eighteen, and some of her friends swore the old lady gave her reasons to disappear." Collins shrugged. "She may have been abducted or may have just run off.

"Burton and Franklin were raped—probably by the same guy. Burton's dead; killed herself. Franklin's in an institution. But I guess you wouldn't be here if you didn't know that."

"We're trying to find out more about the creep who did it," Franchi said.

Collins nodded. "Kevin Ingrahm."

"We had a tip Davis might have been another victim," Franchi said.

Thinnes added, "So what's the story?"

"Off the record. He attacked Burton and Franklin for sure. We never got his prints—not that we didn't try. His old man got him the best lawyers money could buy, and we were told we'd be sued personally if we said a word we couldn't prove.

"The family committed him to an institution for the criminally insane—sealed records. We couldn't get permission to question him. That in itself was pretty incriminating. Moot, though. He set a fire in the place. It killed him."

"You sure he's dead?"

Collins shrugged. "Dental records matched the teeth. And there haven't been any more rapes."

FIFTY-TWO

Kevin Ingrahm's sister Claire lived in Chicago, in a condo in the South Loop. Small world. Or weird coincidence. It was seven in the evening by the time they got back to the city and reported in. They were so pumped at the prospect of breaking the case that they got back in the car and went to talk to her.

When Ingrahm opened her door, they weren't particularly surprised that she was an older ringer for the roommates of the victims in their two cases. Thinnes flashed his star, and said, "Ms. Ingrahm? We'd like to ask you a few questions about your brother."

"He's dead." She didn't invite them in.

"We know that. I'm sorry to have to bother you, but we think someone who knew your brother well, maybe one of his friends, has attacked several women. We need help to catch him."

"My brother had no friends."

"Well, then, an acquaintance."

"I'm sorry. I wouldn't know. My brother and I didn't get on well, so I wouldn't know who he knew. Perhaps you should speak with his therapist. If Kevin ever had a friend, it was Dr. Knowles. He treated Kevin at the institution where my father had him confined when his violent tendencies finally became too obvious to ignore." She hesitated, then added, "I wish you luck. I'm sorry I can't help."

As they walked out, Thinnes said, "Let's find out more about Ms. Ingrahm and this Dr. Knowles."

. . .

The first thing next morning, Thinnes called a detective who'd gone private when he retired. He still knew more than any five guys on the job about what was going on in the department, probably in the city as well. He spent a lot of his spare time hanging out in cop bars and the places politicians went for lunch.

"What's Stormhaven?" Thinnes asked.

"A private institution for the criminally insane—poor little rich bastards that like to set fires and strangle puppies."

Dr. Harold Knowles was a Ph.D., not an MD, according to Franchi's research. He had a private practice on Lincoln Avenue in Lincolnwood, in a glass-and-steel building that had been modern decades ago. Now it seemed bland and dated.

The reception area was beige. The carpet and furniture seemed to have been chosen to pacify if not tranquilize. The receptionist told them the doctor was with a client. They told her they'd wait.

Fifteen minutes later, although no client had come out, the receptionist told them they could go in.

Harold Knowles got up from his chair behind the desk and crossed the room to shake hands. "What can I do for you, Detectives?" he said, looking from one to the other.

He was younger than Thinnes expected—in the eighteen-to-thirty-six-year profile range of the man they were looking for—and as bland as his office, which continued the soothing beige motif of the reception area.

"We're investigating a rape and a rape-homicide, Doctor," Thinnes said, "and it came to our attention that you once counseled someone who fit the profile of the guy we're looking for."

"I'm afraid that doctor-patient privilege would preclude—"

Holding his hands up in the universal signal for stop, Thinnes interrupted. "The patient's dead, Doctor."

Knowles looked confused. "To whom are we referring?"

"Kevin Ingrahm."

Knowles's expression told him that the doctor remembered Ingrahm. "As you say, Mr. Ingrahm is dead. So even if I were at liberty to discuss his case, I fail to see how it would help."

"We wouldn't be here if we didn't think it would."

"I'm sorry. Without a court order, or at the very least written permission from his family, I can't help you."

He didn't ask them to leave, but he stood there as if prepared to wait as long as it took for them to decide to go on their own.

Thinnes nodded and turned to leave; Franchi followed suit.

"You can go out this way," Knowles said, pointing toward a door in the wall at right angles to the reception room wall.

As they went through it, Franchi murmured, "We'll be back."

Waiting for the elevator, Thinnes said, "Do we think Dr. Knowles might be our killer?"

Franchi grinned. "You have a suspicious mind."

"Well, Dr. Caleb once told me a lot of these guys go into head-shrinking to work out their own problems. And even if he was okay to start with, shrinks gotta be like cops—spend enough time with wackos, and you'll go a little nuts yourself."

"Not to mention that with Kevin dead, he's the only one we know of who Kevin might have shared his sick fantasies with."

"Let's see what we can find out about Dr. Knowles."

"I'll get on it."

They got a red light at Addison and Western and sat watching a Mercedes SL 500 convertible convert. A hard shell behind the rag top flipped backward; the top retracted and disappeared below where the shell had been; and the shell folded forward over it. Finally, a roll bar moved into place.

"I wouldn't trust my life to that," Thinnes said. "Would you?"

Her face hardened almost unnoticeably. She said, "Oh, I don't know," then added in a grudging tone, "Probably not."

"Why'd you become a cop, Franchi?"

"Genetics." He waited for her to explain. "Most of the men in my family are in law enforcement." After a long pause, she said, "My dad used to ask me that. He hated that I was on the job. He used to say, 'With your looks, you could be anything.' He never got it that I don't want to do anything with my looks. That's what whores do. I wanted to earn what I got.

"What about you? Why'd you become a cop?"

"Just luck, I guess."

She gave him a look.

"I got drafted. Since the only practical experience I'd had working was in construction, they naturally sent me to MP school."

Franchi laughed. "Natural talent."

"Why the sudden change of heart, Franchi?" He didn't explain the question. He had a strong hunch she'd understand he meant living up to the spirit as well as the letter of the agreement they'd come to after visiting Dr. Caleb.

"Your wife. She's crazy about you. A class act like her wouldn't be nuts about a loser."

FIFTY-THREE

Since they were venturing out of their league, Thinnes and Franchi stopped in at Dr. Caleb's office to ask what to expect from their visit to Stormhaven. It was nearly noon and the receptionist was gone. Caleb was sitting in her place, in shirtsleeves, reading the *Tribune*. He greeted them with no obvious curiosity and, when they asked to have a word with him, invited them into his inner office.

When he and Franchi were seated on the doctor's couch, he asked Caleb, "What kind of place is Stormhaven, a lockup for rich crazies?"

"Not really."

Thinnes raised his eyebrows and waited.

"It provides care for psychotic individuals and those who may be a danger to themselves or others."

Franchi said, "You mean like John DuPont?"

"More of their patients are likely to be suicidal than homicidal."

"What do you mean by psychotic?"

"Disconnected from reality. Some would be street people if they didn't have wealthy families. Others would be incarcerated for violent crimes."

"Are we likely to get anything from them?" Thinnes asked.

"It can't hurt to ask, but I doubt they'll tell you anything without the family's permission. Even with it, they might not feel free to talk."

"We can only hope, Doctor."

Stormhaven turned out to be a converted estate surrounded by eight-foot wrought-iron fences. The buildings were dark red brick, the roofs slate, the landscaping very expensive. The receptionist looked like an import from a downtown law office. The reception area looked like an ad for a plant-maintenance company—all the chairs and couches were surrounded by exotic plants, including orchids. It was nice they had something to look at because they had to wait nearly half an hour to meet with the head shrink.

The director of Stormhaven was Dr. Otto Klein. In a 1900s suit, he would have looked the part of one of Sigmund Freud's circle. In an Armani, he looked uncomfortable.

"You certainly don't expect me to divulge privileged information," he said when they'd laid the problem out for him.

Thinnes said, "If another woman is killed because we didn't get this guy in time, your refusal to help us could be cause for a hell of a lawsuit."

He shook his head.

Franchi said, "We're not the press, you know."

"Relax, Franchi," Thinnes told her. "We'll get a court order."

FIFTY-FOUR

Caleb responded to Thinnes's request for help by rearranging his afternoon schedule. He drove to Belmont and Western.

He went in the police entrance on the north side of the building. No one challenged him as walked past the desk and up the stairs. He didn't see Thinnes or Franchi, so he waved hello to the man behind the desk and walked to Lieutenant Evanger's office. The door was open; he knocked on the jamb.

Evanger looked up from his paperwork. "Come in, Doctor. Sit down." He waited until Caleb was settled, then said, "Well, without revealing any professional confidences, can you tell me if I'm asking for trouble leaving Thinnes and Franchi alone together, armed?"

Caleb smiled. "I think your cat analogy was apt. Detective Thinnes's territory has been invaded. Detective Franchi is understandably defensive in a strange environment." Evanger nodded. "Did you ever introduce a new cat into a household?"

"No. What's that got to do with—?"

"At first, there's usually a good deal of hissing and growling. And once in a while the fur flies. But if you make it clear that fighting won't be tolerated, the hissing ought to diminish over time. They might even become friends."

"I see."

"I thought you might."

Evanger's phone buzzed. He picked it up, and said, "Evanger," then listened. He said, "Thanks." He put the phone down, and told Caleb, "Speaking of angels . . . My star sluggers are here, looking for you. They'll be in the conference room."

. . .

The conference room was reincarnated as a war room. Caleb was pleased to see the two inhabitants weren't warring with each other. Thinnes and Franchi had the case files with the victims' photos laid out on the table and the cases summarized in a grid on the chalkboard. The words in chalk—beaten, raped, cut, murdered—were brutal enough. Thinnes's terse summary, once they were all seated, and the evidence photographs, were nauseating. But Caleb had seen worse in Vietnam. And being emotionally perturbed impaired thought. He forced himself to look at everything objectively.

"From what we could find out," Thinnes said, "the guy who raped Burton and Franklin, and probably killed Coral Davis— By the way," he said to Franchi, "did you tell Evanger we got a positive ID?" She nodded. "Our Jane Doe *is* Coral Davis.

"Waukegan detectives put together a pretty airtight case that a Kevin Ingrahm was responsible. He's dead now. He was from a well-off family that apparently didn't abuse him physically. At least the autopsy didn't show any evidence of head trauma or brain lesions. So how does someone get like that?"

Caleb shrugged. "If we knew for sure, we might be able to prevent it.

"In theory, it's much easier for humans to learn things than to unlearn them. Behaviors acquired with the reinforcement of sexual gratification become particularly entrenched. Aversive conditioning, which might tend to extinguish the behavior, isn't likely to occur because the individual is careful to avoid situations in which it might occur."

"Jargon, Doc."

"Put simply, once he's developed a ritual that turns him on, he repeats it. If he knows others disapprove, he practices in secret so he won't be discovered and criticized or punished. His behavior is therefore rewarding to him with no attendant cost—no punishment, no negative consequences. He continues to repeat and elaborate it.

238

"Incidentally, such individuals often use pornography because other people's unacceptable fantasies give legitimacy to their own basest impulses. It's been demonstrated that shared fantasy is more likely to be acted out. And sharing lets the fantasy escape from the privacy of the individual's mind into the reality of a community of sorts."

"What can you tell us that might help us catch this monster?" Franchi said.

Caleb gave her an ironic smile. "A monster is anybody whose motives we don't understand, or whose behavior we don't approve."

"So make us understand."

"Every villain is the hero of his own myth. And myth is what we're working with here. The myth is what he uses to give his sad, lonely life meaning and purpose.

"No one's born a serial killer. Or a rapist, for that matter. The behavior is learned over time. But it starts with an emptiness. Perhaps with loneliness or an inability to communicate.

"The void is filled with fantasy. The fantasy may never be indulged outside the subject's mind. Or he may—purely by chance—find himself alone with someone who brings his fantasy to life. She may provoke him by acting in a way that's disappointing. He may act out, grab, grope.

"If she screams or slaps him or, worse, laughs, and he tries to silence her with threats or actual violence, he may kill her by accident.

"Killing and whatever accompanied it may frighten him, but in retrospect, it excites him, too. And if he gets away with it, the fear fades as he replays the event in memory. The recollection becomes a fantasy that he relives to fill the emptiness within. He expands on it in his mind, improves it, perfects it.

"But a fantasy's a poor substitute for reality, and eventually the memory fades. Consciously or unconsciously, he goes out to replay the event with a new victim, to renew the dream. This time, he prepares. He lets the victim choose him in the sense that she must be a certain type, but *he* picks the time and place.

Sooner or later he kills on purpose. He develops a ritual, a sacrament, if you will, a little immorality play he rehearses until he's got it perfect.

"But each reenactment is imperfect. And eventually the replay loses its gloss. He has to keep repeating the deed in fact to keep his fantasy alive and vivid."

"Yeah, but how do we find him?" Franchi said. "Kevin Ingrahm's dead, but whoever attacked our four victims is following the same sick script."

"Hogencamp had it worked out," Thinnes said. "Some other psycho from Stormhaven is a copycat. Can these fantasies be contagious, Doctor?"

"The MO can be copied, certainly, but the ritual is entirely unique because it meets the needs of a specific individual. I suppose, in theory, if someone's need was to precisely copy Ingrahm's work, and if he knew the details— What did you find out about his friends or associates?"

"Nothing. His sister is his only living relative—said he had no friends. Everybody else is claiming privilege."

"I'd talk to the sister. Ask her about growing up with him. My guess is he set fires and tortured animals, maybe abused her. She could also tell us if he was psychologically abused. Then I'd tackle his therapist. Ask him if Kevin had contact with anyone especially suggestible or prone to violence."

"How would you like to come with us?"

Caleb nodded. "I have tomorrow morning free."

"We'll pick you up."

After Caleb left, Thinnes could tell Franchi was pissed about something. He said, "What's bugging you?"

"Judging by the places he frequents—alleys mostly—and the time of day he works, this asshole is a big giant rat. If we just set a trap with the right bait, we'll get the sucker.

"And Dr. Caleb gives me the creeps."

"He's good. That's why we consult him."

FIFTY-FIVE

The police had put the fear of God into Terry Deacon, or the fear of something. He called to ask for a special appointment, and when he came in he had all the symptoms of a man under stress. Caleb asked about it.

Deacon told him about being taken to the police station to answer questions about a stolen cell phone. "At least, that's what they said it was about. I think it was really about those rapes. They sent a detective around yesterday—made me show him my arms. He said he was looking for track marks, but I think he was looking for scratches. You know, sometimes rape victims scratch their attackers. Thank God I didn't have any scratches."

"But if you're innocent, what have you got to worry about?"

"They gotta pin it on somebody."

"How often do you masturbate?"

"What? Oh. You mean jerk off. I don't have to answer that."

"True. You also don't have to get anything but receipts out of our meetings. It's your money."

Deacon finally said, "Almost every day."

"What do you think about?"

"You mean while I'm—?"

Caleb nodded. Deacon shrugged as if it were too trivial to discuss. Caleb waited.

"About being with a really good-looking, really hot piece—who'll do anything I ask. For nothin'. Like being with a really high-class hooker who doesn't ask for money."

There was more, less socially acceptable content. Caleb waited, then said, "Go on."

Deacon hesitated, finally said, "Anything I tell you doesn't leave this room?"

"That's correct."

"Well. Then. She fights me. Only it's too late for me to stop. And besides, she really wants me. She just can't give it up too easy. She's really not that kind of girl—easy. Or maybe she's even a virgin.

"So I do her. And when it's over she has tears of gratitude in her eyes." He seemed uncomfortable in spite of his "so, there" tone.

"Is something bothering you?"

"You're messing with my head. I never used to think about this stuff. Now I can't think of anything else."

"What stuff?"

"Rape victims." Caleb waited. "In high school, I had all the chicks I could handle. I was on the football team, and we used to party heavy on the weekends. Cheerleaders, too—titty-tossers, we called 'em. We even had groupies. We'd get wasted, and usually we'd get lucky."

"Did you have to get wasted to get lucky?"

Deacon squirmed on the couch and shrugged.

"Do you think you have to get drunk to interact with a woman?"

"No."

"How do you get along with women when you're sober?"

"Okay, I guess."

"Did you ever have a close friend who was a woman?" He'd asked the question before, but the first time, he hadn't had enough familiarity with Deacon to recognize his idiosyncratic signs of lying or concealment of emotion. Now, as he repeated the question, he recognized fear hidden behind Deacon's smile.

"Did you ever have a close friend who was a woman?"

"No." He seemed distracted, as if he were thinking of something else. Suddenly he blurted out, "I don't know what made me do it! I wanted her, and I got mad—I know it wasn't right— but it was like the devil made me do it. I just couldn't— Once I started, I couldn't think of her as a person with feelings. I just had to.

"Afterwards, in the can, when I thought about what I'd done, it made me puke.

"I never told anybody this before.

"Why did I do it? You're a shrink. You're supposed to be able to tell me. Why?"

"The first time you experienced rape—when your father raped your mother—you were excited. You may have had an erection, possibly even an orgasm. It's not hard under such circumstances for the pleasure of the sexual release to be associated with the act."

For a long time, Deacon sat perfectly still, staring straight ahead. Then he said, "Yeah, so?"

"Rape is really about power. Even lower animals crave power. Humans who don't have it tend to identify with those who do. When your father raped your mother, you identified with him, not her. You experienced his power over others vicariously."

"Why couldn't I think about what I was doing to her?"

"Because you would have had to feel what she was feeling. You'd have had to reexperience the fear and feelings of powerlessness you felt as a child."

"I gotta think about this." The expression on his face was truculent, but tears poured down his cheeks.

Caleb let the silence be. If Deacon were to rehabilitate himself, they would have to talk, eventually, about anger management, the possibility of making amends, of salvation, forgiveness, and the importance of staying sober in order to control his impulses.

"I knew better. I knew if I had too much to drink, I might do something crazy. It's just sometimes, I can't stop."

Insight had its limitations. It didn't necessarily give one the energy or initiative to solve one's problems. And introspection without subsequent action was just mental masturbation.

"Have you considered joining AA?"

"Yeah."

There was a long silence.

"Well?"

"I'm still thinking about it."

FIFTY-SIX

The first thing Friday morning, Franchi volunteered to do the background check on Claire Ingrahm that they'd need to conduct a thorough interview. Thinnes noticed she still smelled good—no cigarette smoke. He didn't get it. If she'd given up smoking, why wasn't she crawling the walls?

The information she came back with wasn't unexpected—no wants or warrants, no bad debts or bankruptcies, no outstanding parking tickets. What was surprising was that she'd recently received her Ph.D. in psychology, in May in fact.

They shared the information with Caleb when they picked him up on Michigan Avenue in front of his office.

His response was, "Are you absolutely sure Kevin Ingrahm is dead?"

"Reasonably. Why?"

"If he were alive, and assuming the cases in Waukegan were his work, the four recent attacks could be seen as a response to his sister's success."

"You mean we're chasing a fucking ghost?"

"Or a copycat who idolized him."

"Let's see what his sister can tell us."

"We appreciate your agreeing to speak with us, Ms. Ingrahm," Thinnes said. "Doctor."

"Claire, please. I'm sorry I was so abrupt last time. I'd had an awful day. How can I help?"

"As we told you, we need to know about your brother—anything, no matter how irrelevant it may seem."

"What was he like?" Caleb asked.

"I've spent a great deal of time studying psychopathology since he was committed. I've come to forgive him because I think I understand him. He was completely indulged as a child, but his needs were never met. He never had any real boundaries or limits. Can you imagine how terrifying that is for a child?"

Neither Thinnes nor Franchi said anything.

Caleb nodded.

"He was a needy child—starved for affection. With me, my parents were warm and loving, but they kept my brother at a distance. They didn't want him to be a sissy. As a result, he was horribly jealous. And he was very intelligent. I'm sure his IQ was in the genius range—way too smart to confuse indulgence with affection. But he was so needy he drove people away.

"And I resented him—the attention he got as the son they'd wanted so desperately. I didn't understand why they weren't satisfied with just me. So I was horrible to him. Until he turned twelve. Then he discovered that he could get to me through my things. He started with my dolls—mutilating them, then my pets. My parents refused to listen to me. By then they'd figured out the jealousy thing, though not the rest. And by that time, he'd learned to be the perfect son.

"In his late teens, Kevin was very charming. Like Ted Bundy. He'd figured out what people—my parents especially—wanted to hear, and that's what he'd tell them."

"When my best friend disappeared, he made remarks about her and constantly reminded me she was gone.

"We found it hard to believe he could be such a monster . . . But my father caught him with Elaine Franklin. And he'd kept souvenirs.

"My father was horrified, but once he was convinced that Kevin was guilty, he took immediate steps to prevent further attacks. He had Kevin confined and evaluated by several independent psychiatrists. When they all said Kevin was crazy, father had him committed. It's moot now."

"That so?"

"It's believed he set the fire he died in because his therapist left to study in England."

"What can you tell us about Dr. Knowles?"

"He seemed competent and empathetic. He sent flowers and a touching letter of condolence when he heard about Kevin. I think he blamed himself. But he couldn't have stayed at Storm-haven forever. I'll call and ask him to cooperate with your investigation. In fact, if you can wait a few minutes, I'll put my request in writing."

She gave them a sad smile. "I've finally gotten to the point where I can accept the fact that nothing I might have done could make up for what my parents failed to do."

FIFTY-SEVEN

They dropped Caleb off at his office—he had patients to see—then went to interview Dr. Knowles. They brought along the letter Claire Ingrahm had written for them, and Thinnes brought his briefcase containing the Monica Nesbit file.

Franchi had done the research, so Thinnes decided to let her do the interview. She started by asking the doctor to roll up his sleeves. "Take my word for it, Doctor," she told him when he protested, "it will simplify things if you humor me."

Knowles blinked, then shrugged and bared his arms. No dog-bite wounds. No half-healed scratches. Franchi gave Thinnes a look he interpreted as I hope you're right about the dog bite. She said, "Thank you, Dr. Knowles. Now would you please tell us what you know about Kevin Ingrahm?"

Knowles nodded. "I first met him when he was committed to Stormhaven, where I worked as a counselor. I had only a master's degree then, but I'd worked summers at Elgin and the psych ward at Cermak, so I was assigned to work with Kevin and several others who were considered dangerous.

"He wasn't a threat to men, so I included him in a therapy group and counseled him individually twice a week."

"Is that usual?" Franchi asked.

"He'd have been lucky to see someone twice a month in some places, but Stormhaven is private. His family was paying well for his care. He lived in luxury until his death."

"Go on."

"I had no illusions about Kevin. When he first arrived, his

father instructed the private investigator who'd put together the rape and battery case against Kevin to show it to me. I also got to see the crime-scene photos and ME's report. The first victim, Abby Burton, didn't die from the attack. She killed herself. The statute of limitations would have run out on that offense if Kevin Ingrahm hadn't died. The other victim was brain-damaged and, ironically, resides at Stormhaven at the Ingrahm family's expense. Ingrahm Senior set up a trust for her long-term care. Kevin never admitted his crimes to me. When I confronted him with the facts, he said he was framed. He told me he cooperated with involuntary commitment to avoid taking his chances in the criminal justice system. He was very intelligent and, once he was institutionalized, he had lots of time to educate himself. I loaned him my books at first, but I came to realize he was using them to become an expert on profiling and police methods. And that if he ever got out, he'd be almost impossible to stop. I have no doubt that he did the things he was accused of."

"Which brings us to the point of our visit, Doctor," Franchi said. "Someone's taken up where Ingrahm left off. He had no friends at school, so we think it must have been someone he met at Stormhaven."

"That's possible but highly unlikely. He was very much a loner. He spent most of his time in his room, reading and watching television."

"You weren't with him twenty-four hours a day."

"True, but he was never allowed out of his room without an escort. Staff had to sign him in and out."

"You said he was in one of your therapy groups. What about them?"

"There were four others, all voluntary commitments, none violent."

"We'd still like to talk to them."

"I'm sorry. I have permission to talk to you about Kevin. That's as far as I can go. If I thought any of the others were dangerous, I'd be required to say something, but that's not the case. It's a matter of doctor-patient privilege you understand."

Franchi looked as if she were starting to get hot, so Thinnes decided it was time to jump in. "We understand about privilege. We just don't agree with you about whether one of your other patients may be dangerous." He added, "You got to see the evidence photos in the Burton case, Doctor?"

"I did."

Thinnes opened his briefcase and took out the Nesbit file. He removed two of the photos—Nesbit before and after the attack—and handed them to Knowles. "See anything familiar?"

Knowles looked. And paled. "It's not possible! Kevin's dead."

Thinnes had seen the pictures of Abby Burton. He'd brought the Nesbit file as a persuader. The injuries Monica Nesbit sustained were nearly identical to Abby Burton's, as Knowles could obviously see.

As he stared at the pictures, Knowles swallowed several times and started to breathe more rapidly. Suddenly he pitched forward. He would have landed face first on his beige carpet if Franchi's reflexes had been slower.

She caught the psychologist midfall and lowered him gently to the rug.

A moment later, Knowles opened his eye. "I'm sorry," he muttered. "I wish I could help you. I really wish I could help."

FIFTY-EIGHT

It was 6 P.M. by the time they got back to Area Three. They called Caleb to ask him to confer, and he offered to pop for dinner. They met at Bennigan's because it was close to Caleb's office and the only place they could all agree on. Their conversation would probably have cleared the place if they hadn't requested seating as far away from the other patrons as possible.

"So what can we say for sure about this guy?" Thinnes asked.

"He's right-handed," Franchi said.

"He had extensive contact with Kevin Ingrahm," Caleb added. "He's got Ingrahm's ritual down to the most minute detail."

"That doesn't help us catch him," Thinnes observed.

"In general, rapists are indistinguishable from the general population," Caleb said. "It's my feeling *this* individual has a job—at least part-time, probably with weekends off."

"He's missed a couple weeks," Thinnes said. "Since Nesbit."

"Maybe he didn't," Franchi said. "If he attacked someone who successfully fought him off, but didn't call the cops, it might explain Grube. Say she was an exception to the alphabet connection because he couldn't score the weekend before. Women in the area are getting really paranoid, and there are men who'd have his balls if they could catch him. Maybe he erred on the side of caution, then got— What do you call it, Doc, when a serial killer gets so hot to trot he can't control himself?"

"Decompensation."

"There's another possibility," Thinnes said. Franchi's idea had given him one of his own. "Maybe he killed someone that weekend, and we haven't found the body yet. These guys don't change their signatures, but the successful ones sometimes change their MOs."

"Maybe the dog bite put him out of commission for a while."

"From that little dog?"

"The guy's a coward, what can I say?"

"As long as we're running long shots in the derby—"

"What?"

"Something Ryan said about Jack the Ripper slinking off in the fog. Maybe she hit the mark. What do you think, Doctor?"

"Low pressure exacerbates depression, so it's possible it affects other mental states. Let's get a weather report and see."

"I'm on it." Franchi pulled a laptop computer out of her bag. She set it on the table and began typing commands into it.

"We gotta talk to somebody who was in on those therapy sessions," Thinnes said.

"Good luck," Caleb told him. "A therapist could lose his license, not to mention incur a lawsuit, by breaking privilege."

"I'll talk to Columbo about getting a subpoena."

"I'm not a lawyer," Franchi said, "but it's my understanding that acts performed in front of other witnesses aren't privileged. How about interviewing former Stormhaven employees? They hire big guys to keep these nutcases from killing each other. And they probably don't pay them much. I'll bet one of them will talk. And they're probably not covered by the privilege thing."

"You may be right," Caleb said. "Usually, the nonprofessionals are required to sign a nondisclosure agreement on pain of termination. But if someone were already terminated . . ."

The former orderly was six-three, maybe 290 pounds, an ex-con. He was PO'd with the deal he'd gotten from Stormhaven, which he referred to as a "lockup for rich crazy bastards." He said he was willing to talk. Even though it was nearly 11 P.M., he came in to the Area. They took him in to the conference room so all four of them could fit. The case files had been cleared away, and the diagram faced the wall.

"I was supposed to sign a confidentiality agreement to work there," their witness told them, "but they forgot. And I sure as hell wasn't going to remind 'em."

Caleb said, "What can you tell us about a patient named Kevin Ingrahm?"

"I remember that guy. He was a piece of work—gave me the creeps. He was always humming that Who song—'Blue Eyes.'

"They used to have me sit in on the group therapy sessions—to maintain order they said, but I think it was really to protect the Doc from Crazy Kev. Everybody was scared of him."

"How secure is Stormhaven? Any of the inmates ever get out of their rooms unescorted?"

The ex-orderly laughed. "It was a joke. That was one reason Crazy Kevin was so scary. He could let himself out at night. Even caught him coming out of the director's office once."

"What did you do about it?"

The man shrugged. "Told him if I caught him again, I'd dislocate his shoulder."

"What about the others in his group? Do you remember their names?"

"They mostly went by first names. I think there was a John, Tom, and Wally. Couldn't tell you their last names. Don't remember much about 'em, either, 'cept only Crazy Kev was considered dangerous. The others were a bunch a wusses."

"Were you there when Kevin died?" Caleb asked.

"Naw."

"You quit or get fired?" Thinnes said.

"Yeah. They told me I needed anger-management training. I told *them* take their anger management and shove it."

They asked for the names of other Stormhaven employees who might know who Crazy Kevin hung with, then thanked him for coming in.

After he left, Thinnes said, "This Who song, 'Blue Eyes.' We got the lyrics?"

He started to write "get lyrics" on his "to do" list.

Franchi stood up. "I'll get them."

"Now?"

"Off the Internet. It'll take five minutes."

Thinnes nodded. "Have a cigarette while you're at it. You're making me nervous."

She said, "Yeah, boss," but she didn't seem sarcastic.

While she was gone, Thinnes called Ingrahm's sister. He apologized for calling so late, then asked about Kevin's musical preferences.

"He was a big Who fan," she told Thinnes. " 'Behind Blue Eyes' was his favorite. He called it his theme song. He played it over and over until I wanted to break the record over his head. He even painted the lyrics on his walls. My father thought it was sick. After Kevin was committed, he had the room repainted."

"You got any pictures of Kevin?"

"Only a few from when he was very young. When he fell from grace, my father disowned him and destroyed every picture in the house."

"How about in his high-school yearbook?"

"I don't have one, but there're probably copies at the high school."

Thinnes said, "Thanks," and hung up. "One more thing to follow up on tomorrow."

Franchi came back in ten minutes with a sheaf of papers. "I wish I had the paper concession for this place." She handed one sheet to each of them and put one in front of her own place. The rest of the pile she put in the middle of the table. "Background on The Who, in case we need it."

Thinnes said, "Thanks."

"I remember this song now," Caleb said. "When I was in Vietnam, there was a guy who sang it until we were all ready to throttle him. One of the lines is 'Keep me warm, but beware your coat.' "

"The fan who posted this could've gotten it wrong. Is it important?"

"It might be."

"The singer describes himself as hated, a liar, vengeful and without conscience. But also sad, lonely, woeful, and in pain. He asks to be protected from his own impulses, but warns his protector to avoid becoming a victim. Very borderline."

"What does that make the guy who wrote the song?"

"Talented. Apart from the words, the music is alternately aggressive and hauntingly sad. It's brilliant. It really gets under your skin."

"And a psycho?" Thinnes asked.

"No more than describing the mind of a murderer made Dostoyevsky one. Artists often sublimate their destructive impulses."

"Sublimate?" Franchi asked.

"Never mind that now, Franchi," Thinnes said.

"The way my crazy buddy sang the song was more in keeping with the pleading/threatening nature of the rest of the song."

"Crazy?" Franchi said. "That a technical term, Doc?"

"Absolutely."

"I don't think you need a Ph.D. to see why Ingrahm might have chosen this for his theme," Thinnes said.

"Ingrahm or anyone else with overwhelming dependency/control issues."

"But Ingrahm's dead—" Franchi said. "What are the chances he's not really dead?"

"I'd say excellent," Caleb said. "No matter how good the forensic dentist was."

"Okay," Franchi said. "Say he's alive. How do we prove it? And where do we find him?"

"And if he didn't die, who did they bury?"

"Where do we start?" Thinnes shook his head. "I don't think a similar MO to a dead guy is going to work for probable cause."

. . .

It was after midnight when Thinnes stopped in front of Caleb's Gold Coast condo. Caleb opened the door but didn't get out right away. "Something's still bothering you about working with Detective Franchi."

"She's got a bad attitude."

Caleb raised one eyebrow.

"And I'm superstitious. I told you my last three partners ended their careers before their time."

Caleb waited.

"If she wasn't such a bitch— I've never cheated on Rhonda. I don't want to—"

The apparent non sequitur was the point. Caleb managed to suppress his smile. "I see. You're afraid of spending too much time with a woman you find attractive."

Thinnes squirmed, then shrugged. "You always see too damned much." After a pause, he said, "What do I do?"

"I try not to tell people what to do."

"In my place what would *you* do?"

Caleb was aware that Thinnes knew he was gay. He smiled. "In your place, I wouldn't have any difficulties working with Detective Franchi."

Thinnes laughed.

"Seriously," Caleb said. "Many of the problems we anticipate never materialize. How do you get on with Detective Ryan?"

Thinnes shrugged. "Fine."

"What's the difference?"

"Ryan's just one of the guys."

"You don't find her attractive?"

"Yeah, but—I just don't think of her that way."

"Why?"

Thinnes shrugged.

Caleb said, "You'll work it out."

FIFTY-NINE

Thinnes had to fight the sandman on the drive home. He knew that there was something he was missing, but he was too tired to work it out. Tomorrow. After a few hours' sleep.

The porch light was on when he got home. Skinner was on the porch, sitting cat-wise, feet tucked under. He stood when Thinnes got to the door and looked expectantly at the knob.

"Glad to see you, too," Thinnes told him.

The cat rubbed against Thinnes's ankle. When he opened the door, Skinner headed for the kitchen.

Toby wasn't waiting, which meant Rob wasn't home. Rhonda had taken the dog upstairs for company.

When he got up to the room, Toby greeted him joyfully. He patted the dog and gave him the hand sign for sit-stay.

Light spilling through the doorway from the hall let him see his sleeping wife. For a while, he just stood watching her, listening to her breathe.

He was undressing when his cell phone rang. He stepped into the hall, so the noise wouldn't wake Rhonda, and checked the caller ID. Franchi. He turned the phone on, and said, "What's up?"

"Thinnes?" She was somewhere with loud music and noisy people. "I'm at McGee's. I think I got a line on our killer."

The news brought him awake like a hit of speed. "Tell me."

"My cousin, Leo, never called when he got back from vacation, so I stopped on my way home to ask him about it. He never got the message. The idiot bartender lost my number. Anyway, he remembered Monica Nesbit."

The background noise increased, drowning Franchi out. He thought he heard, "Hold on a second. I'm going outside. I can't hear a thing."

A minute later, her voice came back without accompaniment. "Leo remembered what night Nesbit was here because it was just before he went out of town. She was with someone. He didn't get a good look, but the guy didn't stand out—our invisible man, I think. He's coming in tomorrow to talk to us about it." Leo presumably.

There was a long pause while an El train screeched by over Franchi's head. McGee's was practically under the tracks.

"Anyway," Franchi continued, "I was just about to leave when my cell rang. The caller asked if I was Oriana. He must've been here and heard me talking to Leo. Or maybe he intercepted the message I left for him."

"Oriana?"

"It's a nickname. When I was a kid, I loved Oreos, so Leo called me Oriana.

"So I asked who wants to know? He said a friend of a friend gave him my number, and if my last name started with a 'P' it would be the luckiest night of his life. I figured it had to be him, so I asked his name and told him my name's Peña. He said his name is Peter. Peter Townshend."

"And?"

"Pete Townshend is The Who member that wrote 'Behind Blue Eyes.' He asked if he could buy me a drink sometime, tonight if I was out."

"Christ!"

"Yeah. I'm supposed to meet him here before last call. That's in twenty minutes."

"Where're you parked?"

"On Webster, east of the El."

"Go back inside and wait for backup."

"If you send the cavalry, they'll scare him off."

"Better than have him pick you off. Go inside and wait. That's an order. I'll see if I can get a tac team over there."

. . .

He took Peterson to Lincoln. He didn't stop for any red lights, just slowed a little. Having a beat car catch him speeding would be great—he could get an escort. None did.

Nine minutes after he left his house, he parked on Sheffield, next to the church.

The tac cops were sitting across Webster, where they could see McGee's front door. Thinnes walked over. He recognized them—Jay Noir and Jaime Azul. Good. They were cool heads.

"They told us to wait for you and keep a low profile," Azul said. "This the Ripper case?"

"Yeah," Thinnes said. "My partner's in there."

"He got backup?"

"*She.* Us."

"You nuts?"

"She is."

"What do you want us to do?"

"I'm going in. Anybody suspicious comes out, stop 'em."

The noisy crowd had cleared out. There were only five people in the bar, including the bartender, none of them Franchi. As Thinnes approached, the bartender gave him a "what'll it be?" look.

"You Leo?" The bartender nodded. Thinnes held up his star. "Where's Oriana?"

Leo looked around and seemed surprised. "Must be in the can." He pointed. As Thinnes turned to go find it, Leo said, "She'll be right back. She asked me to keep an eye on her drink."

Thinnes stopped and looked. There was a bottle of O'Doul's on the bar. He nodded and continued toward the back. There was no answer when he knocked on the ladies' room door. He pushed it open. "Anybody in here?"

There was no answer. There was no one in the room.

In the back of the bar, the emergency exit door was propped

open. The alarm promised by a warning sign next to the door hadn't gone off. Thinnes went outside.

A caged bulb over the door cast a dingy light halfway across the alley, which dead-ended to the left at the businesses facing Sheffield and disappeared, to the right, under the El tracks. The cumulative glow of the city's orange streetlights seemed to decrease the density of the darkness, but didn't let him see into it. On either side of the door, he could make out Dumpsters and empty boxes, stacked pallets and assorted trash. No Franchi.

He had no radio to call his backup.

"Franchi?"

No answer. No way to tell if she was conscious, playing hide-and-seek with a killer, or unconscious in the trunk of a car. "Franchi!"

He thought he heard a rustling, maybe a breeze riffling tree leaves invisible in the dark. Or clothing brushing through a tight space.

He turned on his cell phone and tapped out all but the last digit of Franchi's number, put a finger over that, got out his .38. Then he pushed the last number.

He heard her phone ring to his right, then to his left. There was the sound of something plastic cracking against the El trestle, then two sets of footsteps, one running toward him, one toward the darkness farther under the tracks.

He lunged forward and found himself staring into the barrel of a semiautomatic.

"Don't shoot!" Then, "Dammit! He's getting away!"

His own gun was still pointing skyward. He could feel the chill that comes when adrenaline replaces the blood in your face and brain.

"Jesus, Franchi!"

She recovered first and lowered her weapon. "I wasn't gonna shoot you, Thinnes."

He took a deep breath and let his gun hand drop to his side. His voice seemed to have gone AWOL.

Franchi grinned, and added, "Too much paperwork."

. . .

In the conference room the next morning, Thinnes and Franchi recapped the latest developments for Evanger and the rest of the detectives still assigned to the Ripper cases—Ryan, Swann, Ferris, and Viernes.

"How does he select his victims?" Swann asked.

"Probably by sight," Franchi told him. "Every woman he's attacked has either lived or worked in Lincoln Park, or gone into one of the local bars."

"This guy blends in," Thinnes said. "Maybe he passes her on the street, maybe he sits next to her on the bus or at the Gin Mill. In Nesbit's case, we think she met him for a date."

"What happened last night?"

"The offender got my phone number—I don't know how for sure. He called me and asked for Oriana—a family nickname. After I arranged to meet him at McGee's, I waited. There were seven people in the bar—Leo, the bartender, the five we interviewed last night, and one other guy who left before the fun started."

"What about him?" Ryan said.

"We weren't able to identify him, but he's not the one—too short, wrong eye color—his were brown—and he was left-handed. I *did* notice that.

"Anyway, I go to the ladies' room. When I come out of the stall, the outer door is open a smidge, and there's a blue-eyed peeper looking in. I say, 'Freeze! Police!' He slams the door. By the time I get it open, he's out the back door. So I follow him."

"You leave the door propped," Thinnes asked, "or did he?"

"I did. In case I lost him, I wanted to get back in without having to stumble around to the front door in the dark.

"But there's no sign of him in the alley, so I take out my cell to call for backup. That's when he tackles me—puts one hand over my mouth and grabs my phone with the other. I figure it's better to let him have my phone than my gun, so I let him have it in the ribs with my elbow. He lets go, and I head for the dark end of the alley because he's between me and the door. At that point, Thinnes comes out and the asshole takes off under the El tracks, right in my direction. I hide. Thinnes calls me."

"Why didn't you answer?" Thinnes had asked her that last night, but she hadn't answered.

Today she did. "I couldn't see where he went, and I was betting he didn't know where I was. I didn't want to give him my position and risk a hostage situation or worse. By the way, Thinnes, calling my cell was inspired."

"More like dumb luck. What if you'd still had it?"

"I could've clued you in."

"Yeah, yeah, yeah," Ferris said. "Just tell us what happened next."

"We called for backup and spent two hours chasing our tails trying to find him."

"All right," Evanger said, "let's get back to work. Incidentally, I want you to lose the term 'Ripper.' If the press gets hold of it, someone's going to spend the rest of his career writing parking tickets."

SIXTY

They still haven't caught the rapist who killed that woman last month." The woman's affect seemed flatter than usual, congruent with her depressing choice of topics.

In spite of the seasonal weather, she wore a long-sleeved suit with slacks. It was navy linen and made her makeup-free face look anemic. As always, she sat straight in her chair with her legs pressed together, her elbows clamped against her sides.

"He's not the man who raped you."

"I know. I've seen the statistics. He's probably too young. And the women he raped will have to go through hell to get him locked up.

"I've studied the subject. He won't stop until he's caught or killed. You know that. Sex offenders are incorrigible."

Caleb thought about Terry Deacon. He seemed genuinely repentant, but Caleb wouldn't bet money that he'd follow through on his resolution to reform. "It's not possible to know that."

Her smile never got to her eyes. "I have a gun," she said. "I used my mother's address in the suburbs to get a FOI card. Then I just walked into a gun store and bought a gun."

"Do you ever think about killing yourself?"

She seemed to find the question amusing. "Not for fifteen years. I'm really more of an anger-out sort of girl.

"I know it's against the law to have a gun in the city, but I'll take my chances with a jury if I ever have to use it. I keep it hidden in my apartment. And if anyone ever breaks in, I'll kill him, then call the cops. It'll be one less rapist in the world."

SIXTY-ONE

The squad room was crowded when Thinnes came in the next morning. All the Violent Crimes dicks were there—Swann, Viernes, Ryan, Ferris, and Franchi—three others from Property Crimes and two tactical cops.

"What's up?" he asked Ryan.

She was wearing jeans and a T-shirt that said: I USED UP ALL MY SICK DAYS, NOW I'M CALLING IN DEAD. "Something bad went down last night. I thought you guys knew."

Thinnes shook his head and looked at Franchi, who seemed tired or hungover. She was wearing a pantsuit like the ones Ryan usually wore. He wondered if she'd be wearing jeans tomorrow, too. She shrugged.

Ryan said, "Evanger told us all to sit tight until he's done talking with the deputy chief, then he'll brief us. You really oughta try'n be on time for work, Thinnes."

Ferris was half-hiding behind a *Sun-Times*. He put it down, and said, "You know what happens to cops who become perps?"

"Perps?" Ryan said. "This isn't *New Yawk*. We don't call offenders perps here."

"Franchi?" Ferris said.

"What?"

I should have warned her, Thinnes thought.

"They go in tight ends and come out wide receivers."

Franchi just stared at him, no change of expression.

"You don't get it, do you?" Ferris said.

Thinnes could see the muscles of her jaw tightening. "She gets it, Ferris."

"I thought she wanted to be one of the guys. How come she's not laughing?"

" 'Cause it's not funny. It wouldn't be funny unless the cop was you."

Ryan looked past Thinnes, at Franchi. "You want coffee?"

Franchi shook her head.

Ryan picked up her coffee mug and wandered toward the coffeepot, grabbing Ferris's *Sun-Times* as she passed him. Before he could grab it back, she tossed it to Viernes, on the other side of one of the desk-cubicle dividers. Viernes turned and passed it to someone behind him. Ferris said, "Dammit!" and went chasing the paper. Ryan continued her quest for caffeine.

At that moment, Evanger walked into the room with Rossi and the district commander. Everyone but Ferris shut up.

Ferris said, "What's up, boss?"

"We got another woman missing."

Thinnes said, "Oh, shit!"

"Ophelia Palmer. She's a nurse at Grant Hospital—works nights. She was supposed to get off at midnight but she had something she had to finish up, so she told her boyfriend to pick her up at one. When he got there, she was gone."

"She fit our profile?"

"Five-seven, one hundred and fifteen pounds, black hair, brown eyes. Twenty-five years old."

"Last seen?"

"By the security guard at the door. At 12:47 a car pulled up. She told the guard, 'That's my boyfriend.' She said, 'Good night,' and went outside and disappeared."

SIXTY-TWO

They held the neighborhood meeting at the Eighteenth District because Grant Hospital was in the Eighteenth and, so far, so were most of the crime scenes.

The room was full; the atmosphere ugly. Even if he hadn't interviewed Ophelia Palmer's boyfriend, Thinnes could've picked him out. He was pacing the side of the room, front to back. None of his anger had been blunted by police assurances or the actions he, himself, had taken to find Palmer—handing out flyers with her picture, stopping passersby in front of the hospital, talking to the press and anyone else who'd listen. A lot of them were here tonight, to give him moral support and register their outrage.

It wasn't a press conference—nothing to report—but there was full press coverage.

The district commander started off by summarizing what was being done and appealing to the public for information. An official from the hospital got up and announced a five-thousand-dollar reward. The head of hospital security reported that escort service for employees was being expanded—they'd all be accompanied to their cars or public transportation by a guard—whether they requested it or not. A representative from DePaul University upped the reward to $10,000. Evanger added that an anonymous donor was raising that to $15,000. Thinnes knew that was McGee's management, who took a dim view of anyone stalking their customers. The Neighborhood Relations officer got up and repeated the advice to women for protecting themselves that had been broadcast in the media since the attack on Katherine Lake.

Then there was a Q and A. Questions from neighborhood residents were mostly anxious or hostile. Those from the press seemed intended to embarrass the cops. Evanger and the DC fielded them with their usual finesse.

As the primary on the case, Thinnes was on the firing line, too, though he was able to answer most things with "I can't comment on that without compromising the investigation." Then a young woman who reminded him of Franchi asked why *he* was qualified to work rape cases.

"Fourteen years in Detective Division, mostly in Violent Crimes."

"But why aren't there any women working this case?"

As far away as she was, he could see Franchi's smile.

Mentally, he counted to ten. "There are two women on the squad, both very much involved in this investigation."

Before the back and forth could escalate, Evanger jumped in and said Thinnes was in charge because he had the highest clearance rate in the Area.

While Evanger fielded other questions, Thinnes studied the audience. Katherine Lake's roommate and several friends were there. Monica Nesbit's father, Father Cannon, Mrs. Henderson, and her neighbor, Walter Lennox, as well as Officer Neil O'Rourke. Franchi was in the back, but most of the squad had elected to watch highlights on the six o'clock news.

Thinnes was brought back to business when an angry man demanded to know why all the registered sex offenders hadn't been rounded up. He had a handful of photocopies—information he claimed he'd gotten off the Internet. "Why are these guys still at large?"

Evanger disarmed him somewhat by pointing out that the detectives had interviewed hundreds of people since Monica Nesbit died, dozens since Palmer disappeared. He told the speaker to talk to Detective Thinnes if he had evidence against any of the individuals he was concerned with.

The guy immediately trotted up to the front with his papers, putting copies into the half dozen hands that reached out as he passed. One of those belonged to Ophelia Palmer's boyfriend, who stopped his pacing to read the sheet. That could be trouble.

Thinnes looked over the copy handed to him. Names and addresses of convicted sex offenders. The CPD site didn't give addresses, but if you had a name and were good at research . . . Whoever put the list together was good enough. It was in alphabetical order, starting with Deacon, Terence. Eames, Dennis, was just below that. Every name was familiar. Most had been contacted three or four times since Katherine Lake's attack. He turned to Evanger and quietly said so, then folded the paper and put it in his pocket. Evanger announced that the detectives had determined there was no evidence to indicate involvement by anyone on the list.

Thinnes didn't think Palmer's boyfriend was listening. He paced toward the back of the room, then kept going. Right out the door. Since he couldn't leave before the meeting ended, Thinnes looked around for someone he could send after him. Franchi had disappeared.

The meeting adjourned five minutes later, but Thinnes was detained another fifteen answering questions. When he finally got out to the desk, there was no sign of the boyfriend, though the duty sergeant remembered him. "Really hot about something— a man on a mission."

Franchi was outside, staring at an unlit cigarette the way a drunk stares at an unopened bottle. She'd come in her own car so she could go home after the meeting, but Thinnes said, "Franchi, you with me?"

She shoved the cigarette in her purse. "Yeah, what's up?"

"Call for backup!" Thinnes nearly threw Franchi through the windshield braking. He jammed the gearshift into park before the car stopped in front of the apartment on Southport. He had the keys out of the ignition and was racing toward the crowd on the sidewalk before she could even say, "Dammit!"

He had to push the bystanders aside. "Police! Let me through."

The guy on top was clearly out of control, sitting on the other man, holding him down with one hand while he bashed his face in with the other, accompanying each blow with a question: "Where is she, you asshole? Where? Where *is* she?"

Stepping up behind him, Thinnes grabbed his wrist as he pulled back for another blow. The man tried to strike again. Still holding the wrist, Thinnes grabbed his collar and pulled him backward, then twisted his hitting arm behind his back and forced him facedown onto the sidewalk.

"Stop it!" he yelled. "Stop resisting!"

Ophelia Palmer's boyfriend screamed, "Fuck you!"

Thinnes understood perfectly. Rape wasn't about passion, but about power and rage and the humiliation of the victim. And to have your woman raped was a worse violation than being raped yourself, a double dose of shame—your lover defiled, you powerless to stop it. It wasn't just husbands and boyfriends that rape stirred up. He'd seen cops and paramedics, even hospital staff get mad enough to kill. There oughta be something like "homicidal incitement" you could charge the bastards with, on top of the rape.

But he pulled out his handcuffs and applied them. Keeping a knee on the man's back, he looked around.

Franchi was talking on her cell phone. ". . . We need backup and the paramedics."

Thinnes wiped off the blood he'd picked up from his captive on the man's shirt, and shouted at the spectators to get back. He knew they'd all scatter when the sector cars arrived, and they started asking for names.

Franchi shouted, "Get back," with enough menace to make an impression. At least four of the five people still on the scene moved out of range of her fists.

She turned to the beating victim and probed his neck with two fingers. He wasn't breathing, and it didn't seem worth it to bother with CPR—his face was mangled. She said, "This guy's dead, Thinnes." She patted his pockets, pulled out a wallet and read the ID. "Terry Deacon." She looked at Thinnes. "You knew this was happening! How did you know?"

Thinnes pulled the sex offender list out of his pocket and handed it to her. "First name on the list."

He pulled his captive to his feet and told him, "You have the right to remain silent. You understand?"

Ophelia Palmer's boyfriend seemed in shock. He kept his eyes on his handiwork as Thinnes continued.

"You have a right to an attorney and to have an attorney present during questioning. Are you listening?"

The boyfriend glanced at Thinnes, then back at the corpse.

"If you give up your right to silence, anything you say can and will be held against you." He shook the man. "Did you get that?"

"Yeah."

He lowered his voice so only the prisoner could hear. "Repeat after me: 'I want a lawyer.' "

SIXTY-THREE

It was eleven o'clock by the time they'd finished all the paper-work and turned the prisoner over to the lockup. "We gotta find his girlfriend," Thinnes told Franchi, "before he bonds out and works his way down the rest of the list."

He'd spent only fifteen minutes talking Columbo into charging manslaughter rather than murder. Then he'd called Rhonda and told her he wouldn't be home anytime soon.

Dr. Knowles lived in Skokie in a house that advertised the success of his bland practice. When he opened the door and saw who it was, he held up both hands, and said, "No more pictures!"

"A man's been murdered, Doctor. And another woman's missing. She may be dead by Monday."

Thinnes could see conflict on his face. Finally, he stepped back, and said, "Come in."

They followed him to a room that was surprisingly colorful, in contrast to his office, with a large-screen TV, bright abstract art, and a red Oriental rug. There were also lots of family pictures.

Knowles offered them seats, then said, "How can I help you?"

"We need to know everything you do about Kevin Ingrahm and anyone he may have known or influenced."

"I told you everything about Kevin. I can't—"

"Talk about your other patients. Yeah, we know. But you

blew your chance to claim privilege when you brought a body-guard to your group meet. He wasn't a patient, and he's not a doctor."

"He signed a confidentiality agreement."

"As a matter of fact, he didn't, and he told us that besides Kevin, your group consisted of John, Tom, and Wally. We need their last names and their addresses."

"John and Tom are still at Stormhaven, so neither of them could be the one you're looking for. Walt wasn't violent. It couldn't be him."

Out of the blue Franchi asked, "Was Kevin Ingrahm affected by bad weather or low pressure?"

"He used to get frantic on gloomy days—pace like a caged wolf. Why?"

"Just wondering. What about his friend, nonviolent Walt?"

"No."

While Knowles was occupied answering Franchi, Thinnes looked at the photos—Knowles with an attractive woman, presumably his wife; with his kids; with groups of people from Stormhaven—Thinnes recognized the architecture. One was a picture of Knowles with his arms around the shoulders of two young men, one quite familiar to Thinnes. He picked up the picture and handed it to Knowles. "This Walter?" He could tell from the psychologist's startled look it was.

"How did you know?"

"I've interviewed him. He's our killer."

"Who?" Franchi demanded.

"Walter Lennox." He handed her the picture.

"You told me he was a leftie, Thinnes!"

"The guy sitting next to you at McGee's—left-handed, right?"

Franchi took a closer look at the picture of the trio. "That's him!"

Thinnes looked at Knowles. "So Walter took up where Kevin Ingrahm left off."

"Impossible! Walter was never violent."

Thinnes handed him the picture. "Which one is Lennox?"

Knowles pointed to the young man Thinnes had never met. "That's Walter."

Thinnes pointed to the person *he* knew as Walter Lennox. "Who's this?"

"That's Kevin, of course."

"Of course."

"But Kevin's dead!"

"Someone's buried in his grave," Thinnes said. "You talked to Walter lately?"

"Not since I left Stormhaven. He sent me a letter when I was in England. He said he was moving to Alaska."

"How convenient. Was that before or after Kevin *died*?"

Knowles paled, and Thinnes was afraid he'd faint again. "But they identified Kevin's body. Dental records . . ."

"Stormhaven's records, right?"

"I don't know. I suppose—"

"Right. We checked with the Lake County coroner. Stormhaven supplied the records. And Kevin had the run of the place, according to our informant. So switching his records with Walter's couldn't be too hard."

"Oh, my God!"

SIXTY-FOUR

Back in the car, Thinnes said, "Call in. Have them send somebody to watch Ingrahm's place—front and back. It's better if he doesn't know we're on to him, but the most important thing is we don't lose him. And tell them to get Felony Review started on an arrest warrant for Kevin Ingrahm, aka Walter Lennox, and a search warrant for his house, garage, and any storage buildings or containers on the property."

"Why don't we just go pick him up and get the search warrant later."

"Because all we can really prove is the attacks on you and Grube. If he's not holding Palmer in his apartment—and he's nuttier than we thought if he is—we could spook him. If he finds out we're on to him before we get him in custody, he'll destroy any evidence. We might never find Palmer."

She shook her head, but took out her cell phone. As she dialed, it occurred to him that he was giving her orders just like he used to do with Oster.

When they stopped for the next red light he pulled out his own phone and punched in Caleb's number. As the light changed, he heard a sleepy, "Hello."

"Sorry to wake you, Doctor."

"S'all right. I'm awake now."

"We think we've ID'd the Lincoln Park rapist. We're putting together a search warrant application. We'd like your input."

He heard Caleb yawn. "Be there in half an hour."

"What've you got for me?" Columbo asked. He and Thinnes and Franchi were crammed together in the tiny Felony Review office. Columbo looked as if he'd been on duty for a week.

"A positive ID on our suspect by his former shrink that proves he's assumed another man's identity."

"Got proof it wasn't by mutual agreement?"

"We think the other man was murdered. You get us the records we need, we'll prove it."

"What've you got linking him to the Lincoln Park rapes?"

"A victim profile and MO identical to two rapes the Waukegan police are sure he did up there eight years ago."

"He was convicted?"

"Never charged. Before he could be arrested, he was committed to an institution for the criminally insane."

"Do we have the records?"

"Sealed."

"So you've basically got nothing on those because the statute of limitations has run out. What *have* you got?"

"He grabbed the nurse," Franchi said.

"And he grabbed Franchi. We can put him at the scene."

Columbo turned to Franchi. "But can you swear you saw him clearly?"

"No. But he'll have a dog bite on his arm and a bruise on his ribs or stomach where I hit him."

"That's a start. Okay. Say you pick him up for attempted kidnapping. If he's got the bite marks and bruise, you arrest him for that. You *do not* search his place without a proper warrant."

"Why not?" Franchi said.

"You have no probable cause, *yet*, to search for the kind of evidence we're going to need to nail him for the rapes or for Nesbit. If you jump the gun, he'll walk."

"What about exigent circumstances. We know he's got Palmer."

"You've got no proof of that. Cop logic isn't going to sway a judge. So just do it my way, will you?"

"Yeah," Thinnes said. "What do we do?"

"Pick him up. Ask him to give up blood sample—"

"And a hair sample," Franchi said. "The lab found two human hairs on my shirt that weren't from me or Thinnes."

Columbo said, "Whatever. If he won't cooperate, we get a court order, and with luck, we can charge him with the two attacks. That along with the MO and victim similarities will get us a warrant to search for Palmer and enough evidence to put him away."

He glanced at the door and nodded as Caleb walked in. "You go pick him up. We'll put together an application for the search warrant. And as soon as we're ready, I know a judge who has two daughters." He turned to Caleb.

"Morning, Doc. You ready to go to work?"

Thinnes and Franchi had brought all the pictures Dr. Knowles had of Kevin Ingrahm. In most of the group pictures, Ingrahm seemed to be an enthusiastic participant, but there was one in which he looked ready to kill Dr. Knowles—apparently he hadn't noticed the photographer. "I don't know if this would prove anything in court," Caleb said, "but in psychiatry this is very telling."

The single portrait of Kevin was probably a good likeness, displaying his arrogance and hinting at his cunning. The focus was very sharp; Caleb was able to read some of the titles in a bookshelf behind him in the picture. *The Talented Mr. Ripley* stood out, as did *The Silence of the Lambs*. Caleb showed them to Columbo. "This is the sort of collateral evidence they should look for."

"What else? I got plenty of experience with your run-of-the-mill gangbangers and domestic murderers, even financially motivated hits, but this guy is special."

"Erotica, of course."

"Yeah, I got that."

"Educational materials."

"Like *How to Commit the Perfect Murder*?"

276

"Or police or detective magazines, articles for women on how to fight off a rapist, home-security manuals . . ."

"What else?"

"Materials indicative of introspection on his part—psychology books, or articles on the genesis of mental disorders, things of that nature."

"This is going to be a hell of a long warrant."

Caleb shrugged.

"Anything else?"

"Evidence of intelligence gathering."

"Got that already. Goes to how he targeted his victims. Obviously he didn't just wander around in the fog and grab the first brunette that came along."

"They're ready, Thinnes." Franchi put her cell phone in her jacket pocket and brought her gun out. She let it hang down at her side, almost out of sight, her trigger finger pointing down the barrel. "Let's do it." She stepped back against the house, between the door and the front window, where she wouldn't be seen.

Thinnes keyed the handheld and told his hidden backup they were going in. He pushed the doorbell. He could hear it buzz inside the apartment. He leaned on it. After a long thirty seconds, a voice from his radio said, "Upstairs light on."

He bounced his thumb on the bell. Another long moment, then a muffled voice said, "Knock it off, dammit!"

The door flew open. The brown-eyed man who filled the opening said, "Do you have any idea what time—?" He was wearing a brown terry-cloth robe over his pajama pants, holding it closed in front with his right hand, trailing the belt along the floor. His eyelids drooped. His face was puffy with sleep.

Thinnes held his star in front of his face, and said, "I sure do." For a fraction of a second, he wondered if he'd made a huge mistake. This putz couldn't be the predator they'd been hunting for a month.

Then Kevin Ingrahm backed into his living room, and

Thinnes glimpsed a change in his expression, a flash that passed so quickly it left him wondering what he'd really seen. He crowded in after Ingrahm, glancing around the room for clues to Palmer's whereabouts. He said, "Put your hands out to the side."

Ingrahm's face sagged with surprise. "Wha—?"

"NOW!"

Ingrahm jerked—just a fraction of a second too late to be a genuine startle response—and stretched his arms out, letting the robe fall open, baring his chest. Showing off a beaut of a bruise. "What's this about?" His voice was whiny, carefully rehearsed, no doubt.

Thinnes smiled. "Turn around and turn your palms toward me."

Ingrahm turned slowly, craning his neck as he did, to keep Thinnes in view. Then his eyes widened and he quickly turned his face away.

Thinnes became aware of Franchi standing behind him. "You're under arrest," he told Ingrahm. He slipped his cuffs out of their case and snapped the first on Ingrahm's right hand.

Franchi moved to the side, keeping a clear view—and clear sight line—of their prisoner.

Thinnes gripped the middle fingers of Ingrahm's right hand and swung the hand around behind his back. He brought Ingrahm's free hand back and snugged the other cuff around his wrist. "You're under arrest," he repeated. "You have the right to remain silent—" He turned Ingrahm around.

"What did I do? At least tell me what I did."

"You know what you did. We'll get to the formal charges. First, you have the right to an attorney—"

"This is crazy!"

Thinnes ignored him. He finished reciting Miranda, then pushed Ingrahm's right sleeve up his arm. Above the elbow was a jagged, scabbed-over cut and a healing puncture wound. Bingo! He caught Franchi's eye, and she smiled.

"Tell me what you're looking for," Ingrahm pleaded. "Maybe I can help you."

"Yeah, right." Thinnes noticed how Ingrahm's eyes kept straying toward Franchi.

"Can I at least get dressed?"

That might get them some plain-view evidence. Thinnes nodded. "Where're your clothes?"

Ingrahm half turned toward the back of the house. "In my room." He extended his cuffed hands as far as he could in the detective's direction. "Please?"

Thinnes stepped close and put a hand on his shoulder. "In a minute. Let's go."

There was nothing suspicious in sight on the way to Ingrahm's room. Only a lack of personality made the room seem unusual. The bed looked slept in. Clothes were draped over a straight-backed chair next to it. There was a dresser with a wall mirror above it and a laundry hamper to one side. Thinnes unlocked the cuffs, and said, "Don't try to bolt. Detective Franchi's waiting in the hall to finish what she started the other night."

Ingrahm blushed, or maybe flushed, with anger—his expression wasn't clear. He started toward the dresser.

"Hold it."

"I need underpants."

"I'll get 'em. Which drawer?"

"Top."

Thinnes opened it and took out a pair of briefs, then closed it. He felt like a kid on Easter morning having to wait for his parents' permission to hunt for the candy.

He handed the pants to Ingrahm, who turned his back to drop his pajamas and pull on his briefs. Thinnes handed him his shirt and slacks after carefully checking each for weapons. There was a Swiss Army knife and a bunch of keys in the pants pockets. He put the knife on the dresser and the keys in his own pocket. "Socks?" he said.

"In the second drawer."

Thinnes took out a pair and closed the drawer. Ingrahm started to sit on the edge of the bed to pull on the socks. Thinnes said, "Sit on the chair."

"What? Why?"

"Because I said so." Ingrahm shrugged and complied. Thinnes said, "Shoes?"

"Under the bed."

"Stand up and turn around."

Ingrahm did. Thinnes put the handcuffs back on, then opened the door. As promised, Franchi was waiting outside.

"Keep an eye on Kevin, will you, while I get his shoes?"

She nodded.

"What's your first name?" Ingrahm asked her.

"You know."

"Franchi? Is that your married name?"

"What's it to you?"

Thinnes thought this time the blush was a blush.

He looked under the bed for booby traps but found only brown loafers. After checking them for contraband, he dropped them next to Ingrahm's feet. When the prisoner had stepped into them, he said, "Let's go."

Out on the porch, after locking the front door, Thinnes told Franchi to put Ingrahm in the car. He walked over to the unmarked squad now parked in next to a fire hydrant. The plainclothes cop in the front seat nodded at him. Thinnes returned the gesture, and said, "I know how badly you guys want to find Palmer, but if you go in there because you heard a woman scream, you'd better have independent civilian corroboration."

SIXTY-FIVE

When they got back to the Area, they put Ingrahm in the interview room and asked the sergeant to keep an eye on him.

Fifteen minutes later Evanger, Columbo, and Caleb watched him through the two-way mirror while Thinnes and Franchi filled them in on the arrest. "We have enough for a search warrant yet?" he asked Columbo.

"I believe so."

"Good. He was practically begging us to search his place without one. I want to do it before we question him. This guy's as slick as black ice. We need all the ammunition we can get."

"What about a court order for a blood test?" Franchi asked.

"I'd rather wait on that," Columbo said, "unless the judge says we need it for the warrant. He hasn't asked for a lawyer yet, but that will definitely change when we ask for blood."

"What else do we need in the meantime?" Evanger asked.

"Could you call Claire Ingrahm," Thinnes said, "and find out the name of her family dentist—see if she'd be willing to come in and make a formal ID?"

"Surely."

"Columbo, could you subpoena the dental records and whatever else Stormhaven has on him. Also Lennox's dental records."

Columbo nodded.

"Lieutenant, maybe you could send Ryan or Swann to check with Lennox's employer—see if he called in sick any of the days our victims went missing. And what about getting Waukegan's records?"

Columbo said, "I'll see what I can do."

· · ·

By 9:30 A.M. they were back at Ingrahm's house, along with Caleb and Columbo. The crime-scene van was parked out front when they got there, as were two squadrols to cart off the evidence. Bendix got out of the van when he spotted them and walked to the porch with two techs trailing. Thinnes let them all in with Ingrahm's keys and they did a quick sweep—attic to basement. As he'd expected, there was no sign of Palmer.

"Where do we start?" Bendix asked.

The basement was empty except for the furnace and hot-water heater, and a washer and dryer, so Thinnes said, "The attic."

Thinnes, Franchi, Caleb, and Columbo waited by the stairs while the evidence crew took photos and dusted for prints. When they were finished, and they'd looked carefully for fluids and bloodstains, they went downstairs, and the detective team moved in.

Bookshelves reached to the sloping ceiling on either side. The gable-end walls had tall windows in them with an empty blanket chest under one, and a writing desk and chair below the other. The desk top was bare. The desk drawer contained pens and paper but no written material. A reclining chair and a floor lamp stood on a rug in the center of the room. Donning gloves, Thinnes and Franchi moved the furniture off and rolled up the rug. There were no trapdoors or bloodstains on the wood floor underneath.

The bookshelves were instructive, organized into nonfiction and fiction sections. The former seemed to be books on criminology, psychology, and security, and lots of true crime, and the latter, hard-boiled detective stories and thrillers.

Among the books, Caleb spotted *The List of Adrian Messenger* by Philip MacDonald, the story of a man who murders a list of distant relatives so he'll be the sole surviving heir. He pulled the book off the shelf and paged through it. A half sheet of paper fell out, a list of names with addresses. The printing was so small it might have been made on a typewriter. Lines had been drawn through the names: Abby Burton, Coral Davis, Elaine Franklin.

Caleb said, "Detective Thinnes . . ."

Thinnes went back downstairs and called in the cops from the squadrol. "We're gonna need all the books collected from the third floor. Make sure they've been photographed and try to keep them in order in case they have to reconstruct the scene for a jury."

"How many are there?" one of the cops asked.

"No idea, but I hope you brought a lot of boxes."

"I told you this was gonna be work," the copper told his partner.

In the bathroom, Thinnes found a contact-lens storage case, and soaking and cleaning solutions for lenses. He handed the case to one of the techs to log in.

He went into the living room and looked around. The furniture looked like vintage Salvation Army store stuff. The CD rack was a built-in-shop-class model. The television—with rabbit ears, stereo, and VCR were different brands and ages, with videotapes stacked on all three. There was also a bookshelf stacked with videos. Titles that jumped out were *Men in Black, Psycho, The Blues Brothers, Animal House*, and *Friday the 13th*, about a hundred commercial tapes in all. Behind the rows of videos were rows of home-recorded tapes.

"Take the videotapes," Thinnes told the evidence tech.

"All of them?"

"Yep."

"But everybody's got these."

"If they are what they say." He let him think about that.

The tech wasn't slow. "Jesus!"

Bendix—who never actually collected evidence, just supervised—came into the room, and said, "Thinnes, look at this."

He handed him a see-through evidence bag with a capsule and a one-inch square of paper with the words 2XLD50KCN GUARANTEED RELIEF. "Found it taped to the underside of his underwear drawer, where he could reach it when he went for his jocks."

"What is it?"

"Got me. Looks like one of those time-release cold capsules with baking soda instead of cold medicine."

Thinnes called for Caleb and handed him the bag. "What do you make of this?"

"According to the paper, a lethal dose of potassium cyanide."

"Nice thing to keep in your sock drawer," Bendix said.

"Does that mean we have to keep him on suicide watch?" Franchi said.

"My guess is he wasn't planning on being captured."

Thinnes said, "Keep an eye out for more of these."

Bendix nodded. "Or maybe he's just a practical joker. I'll have the lab confirm the label."

"Hey," one of the techs said, "there's a car in the garage."

They all trooped out to look. The car under a very dusty cover was a classic Mustang. It didn't look as if it had been moved in years. They let the tech photograph it, then lifted the tarp. It had no plates or stickers. None of Ingrahm's keys fit the lock. They raised the hood and tried to hot-wire the engine, but the battery was dead.

"Better check it out anyway," Thinnes told them. "Find out who owns it and have Columbo gets us a warrant."

"Thinnes, where're you going?" Franchi asked.

"They started to recanvass?"

"Yeah, sure. We haven't found Palmer yet."

"I'm going next door to talk to Mrs. Henderson."

She came to the door so quickly, Thinnes knew she must have been watching the free show next door. "Who's there?" she demanded.

"Detective Thinnes."

The door flew open. "Please come in." When he did, she said, "Is Walter in trouble?"

"I'm afraid so."

"He hasn't gone postal and shot someone, has he?"

"What makes you say that?"

"It's always the quiet ones who do it. And afterward the neighbors all say, 'He was such a quiet man.' "

Thinnes had to smile. "What do *you* say?"

"Walter is very nice. I think he's just lonely. And maybe a little sad."

Thinnes recalled the lyrics to The Who song—Kevin Ingrahm's theme.

"Walter borrows your car sometimes, doesn't he?"

"Yes. He's a very careful driver, so I let him use it. He also drives me places when I need to go out."

"Would you mind if we searched your car?"

"I suppose not. What has Walter done?"

"I'd rather not say until we can prove it."

SIXTY-SIX

When they got back to the Area, Ingrahm was sitting in the interview room with his head in his hands. The sergeant reported that he'd been fed and taken to the john. He hadn't asked for a lawyer.

"He won't right away," Thinnes said. "First he's gonna want to see if he can work out what kind of case we have against him. If he's sees it's really good, we might have some leverage."

"I doubt it," Caleb told him. "Judging by his library, he's pretty savvy. I doubt if you'll ever coerce him into confessing."

"What have we got to lose?"

"Thinnes is very good," Columbo said. "Trust him."

No pressure there.

"You're gonna be the bad cop again, Franchi." Before she could get mad, Thinnes added, "He's never gonna believe a woman would be sympathetic. And he's too smart to think you'd come on to him at this point, especially after you nearly broke his ribs."

She made a face—probably didn't care for the exaggeration— but she didn't protest the assignment.

"When we get in there, I want you to just take notes and look pissed. But on the way in, say something to me about this whole interview being a waste of time because he's never gonna explain himself—and say 'explain,' not confess. Make it clear you don't think we need to hear his side to make a case—we got enough on him and don't want to know if there's any extenuating circumstances."

She grinned. "Got it."

"Ready?" She nodded. "Let's do it."

They put on their little charade as they walked into the interview room. The prisoner watched them bicker. Thinnes ended
the show by telling Franchi to just sit down and take notes. He
took the chair, turned it around, and straddled it, leaning forward on its back. She stood at right angles. He pretended to
forget she was there.

"We found your list, Kevin," he told the prisoner.

"I'm not Kevin. I'm Walter."

"If you say so."

"What list?"

Thinnes took it out of his pocket. It was sealed in a clear
plastic sleeve—protected but legible.

"Walter" stared at it for several seconds, then said, "I never
saw that before. I don't even know what it is."

"That's funny. We found it in your house."

"Where?"

"In one of the books in your library."

"They're not my books. They came with the house."

"Whose are they, your landlord's?"

He shrugged.

"Who *is* your landlord?"

"I don't know. I think the house belongs to a trust."

"Who do you pay your rent to?"

"A real-estate company."

"You ever read any of the books?"

"No."

"Funny. We found your fingerprints on them." It was a lie—
they hadn't checked yet—but a safe one.

"I may have looked at one or two. But I didn't read them—
too creepy."

"Why is that?"

"Did you notice what they're about?"

"Yes, I did. That your landlord's Mustang in the garage?"

"No. It belongs to a guy down the street."

"What's it doing in your garage?"

"He pays me fifty bucks a month to store it."

"You got a key?"

"No. He won't let anyone drive it. Anyway, it doesn't have plates or a sticker."

"This guy have a name?"

"Joe."

"Joe what?"

"I don't know. He lives on the other side of Mrs. Henderson. Second floor."

"What can you tell me about this?" Thinnes held a slip of paper in front of him that had 2XLD5OKCN printed on it.

"Nothing." Thinnes waited. "Looks like a password. I never saw it before."

"How did you get that bruise on your chest?"

"Somebody hit me on the El."

"Somebody?"

"I didn't see who."

"You file a complaint with the CTA? Or a police report?"

"It didn't seem worth the bother since I didn't see who did it."

"What happened to your elbow?"

"I cut myself on a nail."

"You go to the hospital?"

"Yeah. Ah . . . well . . . I went to the emergency room, but then I decided it wasn't so bad, so I went home and bandaged it myself."

"That's not from a nail," Franchi said. She was ignoring his orders, but he let her run with it. They were running out of time. Palmer was running out of time. "That's a dog bite! You got that when you tried to kidnap that nurse!"

"No! You think I— That wasn't me! I'd never! I couldn't!" He looked genuinely distressed.

"Sure it was you," Franchi said. "Just like it was you who grabbed me at McGee's."

"No! I never touched you!"

"So you admit you were there!"

He didn't answer.

"What were you doing there?" Thinnes asked.

He turned sideways, facing away from Franchi, so he was looking at Thinnes at an angle. "Just having a beer."

Thinnes reached out and grabbed his knee and swung him back around. "And what else?"

"Just looking. As soon as she left—" He glanced toward Franchi. "I went home."

"You used to be in Stormhaven, didn't you, Kevin?"

"Stop calling me Kevin. Kevin's dead."

"Were you in Stormhaven?"

"Yes."

"Why?"

"My mother was afraid I'd kill myself."

"When did you get out?"

"Just before Kevin died."

"What do you know about that?"

"Nothing."

"You were in his therapy group, weren't you?"

"That wasn't my idea. He gave me the creeps."

"You like The Who?"

"They're okay."

"What's your favorite song?"

"'Pinball Wizard.'"

Thinnes pulled the lens case out of another pocket. "Would you mind taking out your contacts?"

"Yes, I would. I can't see anything without them."

Suddenly, the door opened and Ryan put her head in. "Thinnes."

He said, "Hang tight a sec," and went toward the door.

"Wait!"

Thinnes stopped. The prisoner pointed at Franchi. "Don't leave me in here alone with her. Please!"

"You afraid of a woman who can fight back?" Franchi said.

Walter didn't answer her. He just stared at Thinnes.

Thinnes shrugged and looked at her. "We don't want any brutality beefs." He hitched his thumb toward the door. Franchi shrugged and went out.

Dr. Caleb was standing in front of the two-way mirror, watching "Walter." Ryan, Evanger, and Viernes were, too. Columbo was leaning against the wall next to them.

"Thinnes," Ryan said, "there's a Claire Ingrahm on her way up with some dental records you wanted. Any relation to this guy?" She hitched her thumb toward the mirror.

"His sister unless we got the wrong guy." He turned to Viernes, and said, "You wanna get this guy a drink or something?"

"Sure."

The whole group turned to watch Claire Ingrahm enter the squad room. To those who hadn't met her, she must have been a shock, a ringer for Joy Abbot. She spotted Thinnes or Franchi and came over to greet them. Thinnes thanked her for coming.

She handed him a manila envelope. "These are from our family dentist—Kevin's chart and X rays. I hope they help."

"I'm sure they will," Thinnes said. He stepped sideways, so she could see into the interview room, and pointed. "Do you recognize him?"

She looked. Her expression didn't change. "No. Should I?"

Thinnes felt like he'd just been hit by a bus.

"Are you sure?" Columbo asked.

"Of course."

"Where are the photos they got from Dr. Knowles?" Caleb asked.

Columbo said, "In the office. I'll get 'em."

While he was gone, Caleb asked Claire. "Did you ever visit your brother at Stormhaven?"

"No, I'm ashamed to say. I was so horrified by what he'd done I never wanted to see or hear from him again."

Columbo came back with the pictures. He was out of breath, as if he'd run all the way.

Thinnes grabbed them and shuffled through, pulling out the one of the trio—"Kevin Ingrahm" with his arms around Dr.

Knowles and "Walter Lennox." He handed it to Claire.

"It's Kevin!"

"Which one?"

She pointed.

Franchi said, "Oh, my God!"

SIXTY-SEVEN

Thirty minutes later, they met two Skokie detectives a block from Knowles's house. Thinnes parked three spaces away from their unmarked Skokie car. He and Franchi got out and got into Skokie's back seat. After introductions, one of the dicks said, "How dangerous is this guy?"

"He's killed three people that we know of, raped at least seven women."

"He a threat to us?"

Franchi said, "Even a rat's dangerous when it's cornered."

"You got somebody on the back?" Thinnes said.

"You betcha. It was all we could do to keep all our patrol officers from responding."

Thinnes understood. Suburban cops didn't see a lot of major action. A rapist–serial killer would be a welcome change from belligerent drunks and domestic violence.

"What are we waiting for?" Skokie asked.

"We just take Ingrahm," Thinnes said. "No search until Columbo gets here with the warrants. This guy's smart and slippery. We don't want him—"

"What about exigent circumstances?"

Franchi smiled.

"We even sure he's home?" Thinnes asked.

"One of our SWAT team spotted a figure going past a window earlier. Neighbors say he lives alone."

Thinnes's cell phone rang. When he turned it on, Columbo's voice said, "The judge signed the warrants. I'll bring 'em. Go!"

Thinnes turned off the phone, and said, "Have someone pull a car in front of the garage. We don't need him going out as we're coming in."

With Franchi on his heels and the Skokie detectives trailing, he went to the front door. A SWAT team member materialized with the battering ram. He had POLICE stenciled on the back of his assault vest.

Thinnes knocked, called out, "Police! Open up!" then stepped aside.

The SWAT guy applied the ram to the door. The jamb splintered. The door flew open and rebounded against something inside. Thinnes shoved it wide and went through in time to see the real Kevin Ingrahm disappear through a doorway on the other side of his living room. With Franchi on his heels, and the Skokie detectives behind her, Thinnes crossed the intervening space in four steps. He paused to peer cautiously around the doorjamb, and stepped into an empty hallway. He heard a door close softly. He took two steps to the next door and kicked it open.

The room beyond the door was an office. Ingrahm was on the far side, leaning over his desk to take something from the center drawer. He put a hand to his face.

No time to explain! Thinnes dived across the room and whacked him—open-handed—in the center of his back. He sprawled onto the desk with a huge, induced cough. The object he'd put in his mouth skittered over the desk top and dropped to the floor on the other side.

The Skokie dick said, "What the hell?"

Thinnes said, "Nice try," to Ingrahm as he pushed his upper body down on the desk top. The expression that contorted his face was impossible to decipher in profile, Thinnes could guess at it. "Franchi," he said, "cuff him."

She holstered her weapon and quickly moved to do it.

"Put your gloves on and pick that up." Thinnes pointed to the object beyond the desk. He jerked Ingrahm to his feet and searched him. Thoroughly. He found keys in his pocket that he transferred to his own.

Franchi came over and held up the capsule she'd recovered. "How'd you know?"

"What *is* that?" the Skokie detective demanded.

Thinnes answered him first. "Cyanide."

"Christ!"

"Caleb warned us," Thinnes told Franchi. He turned to the junior Skokie detective who was standing behind his partner looking at a loss for something to do. "How 'bout you take this guy out to the car and watch him 'til we're done? Careful. He may have another suicide pill that I missed."

The junior dick looked at his partner, who nodded. "Yeah, sure." He didn't seem enthusiastic.

"Detective Thinnes?" Columbo had arrived. His voice sounded far away. Thinnes located him in the hallway. "I've got the warrants."

"Good timing," Thinnes told him.

The Skokie cops had finished sweeping the house. "No sign of the woman," one of them reported. He was a big, husky officer, young and fit.

"You look in the trunk of his car?"

"Jesus, no!"

Thinnes threw him the keys. He went away but was back in a couple of minutes. "Not there." He held the keys toward Thinnes.

"Why don't you go see if you can match those to the locks they go with?" The cop nodded. "Don't sweat it if some don't match up," Thinnes told him. "Some are probably from his office."

Thinnes went back into the room. Franchi, Columbo, and the Skokie dick were standing in the middle, looking around. "We got the evidence team on the way," Skokie told him. "And there's an ambulance standing by—in case we found the woman." He walked over and started pawing through the desk drawer, screwing up the scene. At least he was wearing gloves. And Franchi had given Columbo a pair.

The beat cop came back and returned the keys to Thinnes.

"These three don't match anything," he said, holding up two that looked like commercial building issue and a very odd key with an extra long, thick shaft.

While Thinnes stared at the key, trying to figure out what it could open, Franchi prowled the room like a cat in search of mice. She picked up the wastebasket and pawed through it. "Look at this." "This" was the remains of a shredded matchbook from McGee's with writing on it. She put the shreds on the desk top and pieced them together. On the back of the reconstructed cover was the word ORIANA and her cell-phone number—written in her own hand. "That answers one question," she said.

She stepped in front of Ingrahm's computer, on the sideboard next to the desk, and turned it on. Thinnes heard the usual start-up noises, then, "Damn! It needs a password."

Without stopping to think why, he said, "Try 2XLD5oKCN." He heard her tap the keys, then, "That's it. We're in."

Thinnes kept looking at the odd key. Ingrahm was a control freak. He wouldn't want his victim too far away, where someone else might find her. He'd want her close. Unless he'd dumped her already, she must be here. Someplace.

And they'd had everything else in this case but hidden rooms and secret passages. He turned to the copper, and said, "What's the layout of this place?"

"Three bedrooms upstairs—one's a master with a bathroom, another bathroom and a linen closet; living room, this room, kitchen, laundry, mudroom, and garage on this level; half basement—empty—below."

A half basement. In a house like this.

Franchi said, "You gotta see this, Thinnes! He's got victims targeted all the way to Yvonne Zimmerman! Must've been collecting names since he got out of Stormhaven."

"Anything about where he hides them?"

"Not yet."

"Then leave it for now." He turned to the cop. "Show us the basement."

They followed the officer out. The Skokie dick hesitated, apparently torn between the computer and the search, then he fell in behind Franchi and Columbo.

The basement was empty as reported, but much smaller than the footprint of the house. It was lit by a dim, naked bulb in the center and a window at the end near the stairs. It seemed cleaner than an unused space would warrant. All the better to hide footprints . . .

Thinnes turned to the cop. "You got your flashlight?"

The man took a mini-Maglite from his duty belt and handed it over. Thinnes went to the far, dark end of the room and flashed it on the wall, which was made of poured concrete. Seams showed in the wall from the concrete forms. There was a little hole in the center, about the height of a doorknob. It looked like an accidental void, the kind often found in concrete walls, but Thinnes walked over and shoved the odd key in. It went halfway and stuck. He pulled it out and turned it over, and it went in to the hilt. When he turned the key, a door-sized section of the wall receded six inches in and slid sideways, revealing a hidden room.

Thinnes shone the light in. In the center of the bare concrete floor was the naked body of a woman. Her knees and wrists and ankles were wrapped in cloth, protecting them from damage by the ropes binding her. There was a black cloth over her head.

Thinnes said, "Ophelia?"

She gave a little whimper.

Twelve hours later, he felt like he'd gone twenty rounds with the Tar-Baby. Ingrahm didn't lawyer up, but he answered most of their questions with "I don't know," or "Why do you ask?" or "I have no idea what you're talking about." He never even admitted to being Kevin Ingrahm. When Columbo asked to have a turn, Thinnes was happy to let him.

The ongoing interrogation was the entertainment of the day. Dr. Caleb had been observing since Thinnes started. Others wandered over to the mirror window, watched for a while, then walked away. Three times while Columbo was giving it his best shot, Evanger walked past and sent those not directly involved in the case about their business. As soon as he went back in his office, they drifted back.

After Columbo gave up, Franchi went in.

"Is Peña your maiden name?" Ingrahm asked her.

"No. It's a name I made up just for you," she said.

"Come closer," he told her. "Or get out." When she did neither, he ignored her completely. After twenty minutes, she gave up and went back to watching from outside.

Ryan, Ferris, and Viernes joined them and Caleb. Columbo came back from a break with coffee. He looked like a stiff drink would do him more good.

Thinnes turned to Caleb. "What do you think, Doctor?"

"I doubt he's going to tell you anything."

"Ah, duh!" Ferris said.

"I think this is a waste of time," Columbo said. "With all the stuff in his computer and the trophies we recovered, we got enough for an indictment. And we'll get more when we interview his neighbors and the clients he's been seeing."

"How does this wacko impersonate a shrink for three years?" Viernes asked.

"He had five years at Stormhaven to study psychology and observe psychologists at work," Caleb said.

Ryan turned to him. "I thought these bastards never stop once they start. What was this guy doing between the time he got out of Stormhaven and when he raped Highlander?"

"Good question. Perhaps he was successfully resisting his urges. Or it may be that it just took him that long to identify victims who fit his exacting standards. We'll have to ask him."

"We should just give it up and book him," Columbo said.

Caleb turned to face him. "Mind if I have a try first?"

SIXTY-EIGHT

The interview room was stark for a reason—no distractions. There was the bench Kevin Ingrahm was sitting on, the chair for Caleb, and the two-way mirror. Caleb pulled the chair to a conversational distance from the prisoner and sat down.

"Your sister paints a rather bleak picture of you, Mr. Ingrahm."

"No one knows me better."

"Does she?"

"Sure she does. Just ask her."

Caleb shook his head. "Her testimony is suspect."

"How could that be? She's a model citizen—never been arrested. Or institutionalized."

"But she's not unbiased."

"Did she tell you I used to damage her things?"

"Did you?"

"Yes. I suppose that's safe to admit. I'm sure the statute of limitations has expired on that."

"No doubt."

"What else did she say about me?"

"Nothing of consequence."

"*Really!*"

"I got the impression she doesn't know you at all."

"Didn't she say I was a monster?"

"She said you were unfeeling."

"And you think she's right on?"

"Why would I think that?"

Kevin laughed.

"She said you told her your theme song is 'Behind Blue Eyes.' That would hardly be the case if you were unfeeling." Caleb paused to let that make an impression.

The man's body language subtly reinforced the impression Caleb had that he was making headway.

Kevin leaned into Caleb's personal space to finger the sleeve of his suit coat. "This is a pretty expensive suit for a cop. You on the take?"

"I'm not a police officer."

"No? A State's Attorney?"

"I'm a consultant."

"What kind of consultant?"

"A special consultant."

"Special? What does that mean?"

"I only get called in on really difficult cases."

Kevin laughed and sat back on the bench. "You're jacking me around. Or are the cops getting a kickback? This is a simple case of unlawful detention, nothing more—when you cut through all the crap. And when my lawyer gets done negotiating with her lawyer, *that* might even go away."

Caleb wasn't going to disabuse him of the idea. "Is that what they told you?"

"That's what I told them. Then they went away."

"That's why you're still in custody?"

"They can hold me up to seventy-two hours. They're hoping I'll lose my nerve and confess."

"Will you?"

Kevin laughed. "I've nothing to confess."

"They don't need a confession."

"Oh, yeah? Then why have they got *you* here?"

"I asked them to let me do an interview."

"And they just let you because you're the big consultant?"

"No, they let me because they know I can empathize with you. To them you're just another violent rapist. But you and I both know that you have depths beyond imagining."

Kevin smiled.

"And you're the depth-finder?"

Caleb didn't respond.

"Do you have any idea how it feels to be in absolute control?"

Caleb didn't, of course, except intellectually. But he knew the subtle difference between cognition and affect would be apparent if he gave it words. And if he lied, and said, "I know," Kevin would know. Someone as skilled at lying would recognize the clumsy effort of an amateur. Someone as skilled as Kevin at manipulating others' perceptions must surely read others as skillfully as a polymath reads figures. So he kept his expression as neutral as possible, except his eyes. He let his eyes say, "Yes, I know."

Kevin read the miscue as intended. "You know!" But then his natural cynicism—what would be instinct in another sort of predator—kicked in, and he said, "*How* do you know?"

Caleb ignored the question. "I understand you had a difficult father."

The implied answer seemed to galvanize Kevin. Why not? As far as he knew, he'd psyched out the shrink. Winning had become his drug of choice, and he was winning. As far as he knew.

As a child, Caleb had never questioned that he was the beloved, the alpha offspring, the golden child. He had never doubted his superiority to his siblings or resented them. Far from it. He had been their protector, mentor, cherished older brother. At least until puberty.

He said, "Tell me about your father."

"Too boring. I'd rather hear about yours."

"A cliché," Caleb said. Not, why do you ask? Kevin surely knew all the tricks shrinks played. None of them would work on him. Nothing he expected or could anticipate would pry new information loose from him. Only surprise had a chance.

Caleb said, "What is it about brown-eyed brunettes that attracts you?"

A single blink was the only evidence of Kevin's surprise.

"My first crush was a brunette, a brown-eyed innocent. She killed herself. But they'll have told you that."

Caleb nodded. They'd also told him Kevin had driven her to it. "Sure it was a crush and not simple covetousness?"

Kevin laughed. "That, too."

"What did you do about it?"

Kevin smiled. "I'd love to discuss it with you in the privilege of a therapy session. Not here. Sorry."

"Are you pleading the Fifth?"

"Not yet." Caleb waited. "The cops are so slow they couldn't find a rotting corpse right under their noses, let alone— Never mind. The point is, they tag-team you, keep you going 'til you're too exhausted to think. When one gets tired, he sends for reinforcements. If he's out of his league, he sends in a designated hitter—like you. I'd love to play with you, Doctor, but you're on the opposition team. And I'm getting winded. So I'm going to ask for *my* pinch hitter." He turned to look at the mirror wall, and said, very slowly and clearly, "I want a lawyer."

Columbo was seated across the conference table from Ingrahm and his attorney, a member of the best criminal defense firm in the city. Thinnes stood against the wall with Franchi, behind Columbo. Dr. Caleb had gone home to shower and change his clothes.

"We'll take the death penalty out of the equation," Columbo said, "if he gives us a full confession."

The lawyer whispered something in Ingrahm's ear. Ingrahm shook his head. "Sorry, impossible."

"I'm sorry, gentlemen," the lawyer said. He nodded his head toward Franchi. "And miss."

"What would it take?" Columbo asked.

"My freedom," Ingrahm said.

Columbo looked at the attorney. "You're pleading insanity, right?"

. . .

Much later, Caleb rejoined Columbo, Evanger, and the detectives outside the interview room.

"He won't talk to anyone else, Doctor," Columbo said. "So if anyone's going to get a confession out of him, you're it."

Evanger said, "How does a guy like this, from a good family, with every opportunity in life, turn out to be such a fuck?"

"Absolute selfishness is a survival requirement for infants," Caleb told him. "Proper socialization usually convinces them to abandon it in favor of more acceptable alternatives. But if a child's needs aren't met, or if he receives improper socialization, the selfishness becomes a lifelong habit. It's as if there's a critical period in human development for the acquisition of empathy that's analogous to the acquisition of language. A child who doesn't receive the right input during that crucial time loses the ability to develop the attribute—empathy or language."

"Yeah. Well, see if you can get him to talk about how and why he set Lennox up. And how he targeted his victims. Even without a full confession, that ought to give us enough to put a needle in him."

There were moments of clarity. Like in Vietnam when he'd broken through a crimson mist of rage knowing that only he could stop the sniper who'd blown away his comrades. An awful dread accompanied such moments. He'd taken aim knowing it would change his life but feeling compelled to raise the bloody rifle. At that moment he'd known taking a life was wrong but that he wouldn't miss . . .

He shook off the memory.

"What is it, Doctor?" Franchi said.

"An observation. Humans come programmed to communicate. Even when our programming fails or is overwritten by abuse, neglect, or trauma, vestiges remain. They may take the form of the need to keep a diary, or record 'progress' on videotape. Most of that is self-communication—so the experience can be relived later. But part of the urge to keep a record is the hope

302

that someone will find the work and be impressed."

"Which is relevant how?" Columbo asked.

"Kevin needs to brag about what he did. He needs our recognition."

"Does *he* know that?"

Caleb smiled. "We'll see."

In the interview room, Kevin was facing the mirror. He knew, undoubtedly, that the police were watching, and he could observe his own performance. Or he could watch Caleb and assess it by Caleb's reactions. If he tried to do both, he'd be distracted. And this game would go to the most focused.

Caleb went in. He sat with his back to the cops. He said, "Why did you dismiss your lawyer?"

"Why not?" Kevin smiled. "He can't help me. And he spoils the game."

"They said that you would talk to me."

"I said I'd *only* talk to you. I didn't say I'd tell you anything."

Caleb nodded as if that were fair enough. "When you used to mutilate your sister's doll—"

Kevin smiled. "I plead the Fifth."

"What were you feeling?"

He could see Kevin looking back inside his mind, the pleasure of it lighting up his smile.

"Delightful."

"Do you remember the first time?"

"That I damaged her dolls?"

"That you felt delightful about it."

"I was five. It was an accident. I was playing with her doll because it was hers, and I broke it—purely by chance. But she was so outraged it was wonderful."

"And you were in control."

"*No one knows what it's like.*"

Caleb recognized the line he was quoting, from The Who. "Why don't you explain?" he said, softly.

"Do you remember your first?"

"Everyone does. That was Abby Burton, wasn't it? What was special about her?"

Kevin's face softened, and he seemed to be remembering. Then suspicion, then a sly amusement crossed his face. "Oh, you're very good. So seductive. So empathetic. You're trying to suck me in."

"That would imply naïvete on your part. But no one could accuse you of that."

Kevin laughed. "But why should I tell *anyone* anything?"

Caleb waited to see if he would answer the question himself, but Kevin was waiting for Caleb's response.

"Because they only know the crude outline," Caleb said. "They've made a case. They'll present facts and physical evidence in court, and motives that may not be accurate but will be convincing to a jury. The only way for the real story to be told is if you tell it."

"They'd never understand."

"I would."

"But you won't be on the jury," he said so softly only Caleb could hear. He raised his voice to a normal tone and added, "I wouldn't know where to begin."

"At the beginning. When did you first get the idea?"

"Of being someone else?"

Caleb shrugged and nodded. A start in the middle was still a beginning.

"All my life I wanted to be someone else."

"Why Harold Knowles?"

"He was there. He was getting out. He came to say good-bye—I don't know why. I don't think he even liked me. He felt guilty—he was getting out. I was staying.

"And he was so unlike me it was a challenge."

"How did you kill him?"

"Oh, he died of smoke inhalation. I'm sure they told you that."

"They didn't tell me how he came to inhale smoke."

"Why do you care?"

"Whether his death was inadvertent or intentional?"

Kevin smiled. "I've read Inbau and Reid. You don't have to bother with euphemisms. But why do you care if my story's truly told? As you said . . ." He waved his hand at the two-way mirror. "They don't need the details."

"But *I* want to know."

"Why?"

"You fascinate me."

Kevin seemed to find this disconcerting, and he feigned annoyance. "Come on, Doctor. Don't try to pretend you're a groupie."

Caleb pushed his advantage. "Call me a connoisseur."

Kevin smiled. "More like a *voyeur*. A secret sharer. *Who knows what evil lurks?* . . . All right I'll tell you." He glanced at the mirror. "Being Harold had its compensations."

"Limits?"

Kevin's eyes widened briefly, then conflicting emotions contorted his face. Comforting to be understood. Terrifying to have your secrets known.

Kevin smiled. "I was young when I started, and easily impressed. I read something—*The ABC Murders*, I think—and decided Abby would be the first in a brilliant crime series."

"Why Abby?"

"She was my sister's friend. And she wouldn't give me the time of day."

"What did you do to her?"

"The details are unpleasant." His smile belied the words, but Caleb didn't press. They *were* unpleasant to normal people.

Kevin looked very deliberately at the mirror, and said, "Oh, and I killed Coral Davis, too." He looked at Caleb, and said, "That was an accident. I don't know my own strength sometimes. And Elaine Franklin—what can I say? I drive women crazy." He looked at the mirror again, and mouthed "Oriana," and stared at his own reflection as if struck by Franchi's beauty through the glass.

"Why the long hiatus after Franklin?" Caleb said.

"I was unavoidably detained."

"For the last three years?"

"It's like smoking—you know? You try to quit, but you get stressed and you slip back into it."

"Your sister's Ph.D. didn't have anything to do with it?"

A micro expression, a nanosecond of pure hatred flashed across Kevin's face, telling Caleb his barb had hit the mark. "Are you getting tired?" he asked. "We could postpone this until you're feeling up to it."

"Are *you* getting tired?"

"Not at all. How did you find your targets?"

Kevin laughed out loud. "You mean my victims? I have no guilt. No empathy. I'm a classic predatory psychopath. I know they're not going to let me go. Ever. So if you can keep me entertained, I'll tell you everything."

No, Caleb thought. If I can keep you bragging.

"Going out of sequence—trying to grab the nurse instead of waiting for Ophelia—was the only mistake I see you making. A rather large mistake, wasn't it?"

"Was it?"

"Risky."

"Compared to playing the role of shrink for three years?"

"Good point."

"The nurse was to set Walter up. I was at Grant Hospital, observing Ophelia, the night he came in for treatment. He'd fallen on a nail and cut himself. When they told him he'd have to have a tetanus shot, he fled without giving them his name. He has a phobia about needles. You can check his record.

"I knew the visiting nurse kept a regular schedule and so did the dog walker. And I knew Walter's blood type. It wasn't hard to arrange. I made a deposit at a blood bank and made a simultaneous withdrawal when they weren't looking. Then it was just a matter of putting on the charade."

"How did your library get in Walter's house?"

Kevin laughed again. "My house. I used to live there—I'm

surprised Mrs. Henderson didn't mention me. I knew eventually things would get complicated, so when I moved to Skokie, I left my library. I thought perhaps I'd have to give the police someone to suspect. It was pure serendipity that Walter saw the FOR RENT sign and applied."

"How did you manage to rent to him without being recognized?"

"Through a Realtor. I gave him some bullshit story about wanting to help out an old friend without making him feel obligated. Walter's been a model tenant, by the way . . ."

Much later, when Caleb was standing outside the interview room with Thinnes and Franchi, watching Kevin initial each page of the confession he was signing for Columbo, Caleb felt a great sadness.

"I had a kitten once," he told them. "I taught her not to bite so she wouldn't hurt me when I played with her. One day she caught a mouse. She didn't kill it because I'd taught her not to bite. She just tossed it around like a cat toy until its screeching brought me to the rescue."

"What's your point, Doctor?" Thinnes said.

"Kevin's not insane by any legal standard, but he's no more capable of empathy for his victims than my cat was. It's sad. Such a waste."

"Save your sympathy, Doc," Franchi said. "That one's just pure evil."

Caleb looked at her. "You're forgetting. *Lucifer* was the most beautiful archangel. And the most beloved."

SIXTY-NINE

The sun was up by the time Kevin had finished his confession. Caleb was exhausted, and he felt unclean. He recognized the sensation. He'd felt just so, with this intensity, only twice before in his life—both times when circumstances had forced him to take a life. There was some connection between those events and his wresting a confession from a serial killer. Perhaps it had something to do with the fact that Kevin Ingrahm would almost surely die. Illinois was a death penalty state; Kevin a poster boy for execution. In that sense, his death would be on Caleb's head.

For now he was just staggeringly tired. He wanted to spend a week in the shower. To wash the filth away. To wash away the guilt.

There was a message on his answering machine, but he decided to retrieve it later, when he'd showered and changed.

The message was from the patient with the gun: "Sorry, I won't be able to make my next appointment, Doctor. Something's come up."

It was a great leap of intuition from that simple statement to the certainty that she would try to kill the rapist, but intuition is usually just logic with a few steps omitted.

The woman wasn't suicidal. She'd said herself that she was more the anger-out type. And now she had someone on whom to focus rage.

He knew that she would be very good. She would know her

gun as well as any cop did. And she'd have practiced with it.

He went to the phone and punched in Thinnes's cell phone number. He got the standard message: "The cell-phone customer you've dialed is out . . ."

Okay in an emergency—

"Nine-one-one . . ."

Caleb got to Belmont and Western in ten minutes. A crowd had gathered. He drove around to the police entrance and double-parked, though not in the fire lane.

The cop by the door recognized him and let him in. "Just in time, Doc. They're bringing 'im down now."

Caleb looked around for the shooter.

The police had dressed Kevin for his television debut in a safety vest, and his hands were cuffed together in front, chained to his waist. He seemed to be enjoying his entrance.

It wasn't slow motion like the movies. She was moving toward Kevin at a deliberate pace. It was Caleb who was slowed by the horror of what he could see coming. He pointed and yelled, "That woman has a gun!"

But he might have been speaking Latin for all the good it did. People looked his way as "gun" penetrated. Their faces expressed the anxiety the word elicited. Not listening to his words, the police closed in on *him*, deafened by *the* word.

In the instant before the cops tackled him, Caleb saw the newsmen turn their cameras his way, catch what he was saying, then turn back to catch the denouement.

The woman brought her gun up and angled the barrel above the protective vest.

There was a flare of muzzle fire. A—

CRACK!

The concussion slammed the eardrums, reverberating off the tile floor and masonry walls, echoing among the screams and shouts.

Kevin dropped as if his legs had been jerked from beneath

him. In the second before he disappeared behind a wall of cops, Caleb saw a pool of red form where one blue eye had been.

The shooter was slammed floorward as Thinnes broke through the spectators to tackle her. More quickly than Caleb could describe it, Thinnes had her hands cuffed and was urging Franchi to search her.

Kevin lay heaped where he had fallen. Caleb's experience in Vietnam told him the prognosis was hopeless; the bullet had macerated Kevin's bizarre brain. Lieutenant Evanger bent over him briefly, then announced his condition with a brief, grim shake of his head.

The rest of the police brass, whose triumphant media circus was suddenly a disaster scene, shouted orders. All the while, the cameras rolled—a spectacular coup for the nightly news.

Before the detectives hustled her off, Caleb looked long at the shooter. Thinnes and Franchi had her on her feet, and she was staring at her handiwork, her expression resonating between triumph and horror. She looked up and caught Caleb's eye but gave no sign of recognition. He thought she seemed regretful.

Then the detectives hurried her away.